THE
HOLY GRAIL
OF BABYLON

RANDY C. DOCKENS

Carpenter's Son Publishing

The Holy Grail of Babylon

©2022 by Randy C. Dockens

Published by Carpenter's Son Publishing, Franklin, Tennessee

Published in association with Larry Carpenter of Christian Book Services, LLC
www.christianbookservices.com

Edited by Robert Irvin

Cover and Interior Layout Design by Suzanne Lawing

Printed in the United States of America

978-1-952025-67-9

ABOUT THIS BOOK

The story of the Tower of Babel is one of history, mystery, and debate. The premise of this book is based upon a literal view of Genesis 11:4, which states, " . . . a tower that reaches to the heavens . . . " I therefore have created a place called Adversaria where the Adversary can speed up technology to work toward his aim to make a superhuman who can impress and lead the world into a kingdom of his own design.

This will present a rather science fiction twist to the story. Yet I feel it doesn't detract from the biblical narrative because, in the end, it shows that God's prophecy and God's commands always come true. In addition, they are never thwarted by either the efforts of mankind or the efforts of the Adversary. One can always rest in the truth of Scripture.

CONTENTS

CHAPTER 1

THE TOWER

Raphael's eyes went wide. His gaze went up and up as his head went back. He turned to Mikael. "Well, it's definitely impressive—by anyone's standards."

Mikael nodded. In many ways mankind had made so many advances. The ability to build such a magnificent structure like this massive, towering ziggurat was a clear example.

"Well, I see Yahweh's spies are here."

Mikael turned when he heard the words spoken behind him. Before them stood Lucifer with a seemingly smug smile on his face. He found Lucifer could be quite irritating just by being in his presence. And to think this was the one every other angel looked up to in the early days prior to his Creator making this world.

Mikael gave a forced grin. "Just checking up on you." He glanced back at the tower. "What are you up to this time?"

"Me?" Lucifer placed his hand on his chest with a look of shock. "I'm simply giving everyone what they want." He looked from one angel to the other. "And what's wrong with that?"

"Nothing is ever that simple with you, Lucifer," Raphael said. "You don't do anything for others without it benefiting you."

Lucifer's eyes widened. "And what's wrong with that? A win-win scenario is always a good thing, isn't it?"

"It always comes down to motives. You know that, Lucifer," Mikael added. "Your track record for pure motives, to say it politely, is nonexistent, you have to admit. Your motives are selfish and only harm humans."

"Oh, I don't have to admit anything." Lucifer suddenly pursed his lips and gave a slight squint. "And I certainly don't have to justify myself to the likes of you." Lucifer then produced a smile and held his arms out wide. "But I'll share my *creation* with both of you." His tone then turned condescending. "After all, you have to go back and report *something*, right?" He shook his head slightly. "I can't let you go back with nothing to report. What kind of a host would I be then?" He gave a chuckle, leaning in slightly, but still had a tinge of sarcasm in his voice. "Don't want the Ancient of Days to think I was inhospitable to his two . . . reporters." He produced a broad smile. "So, come. Come see my creation."

Lucifer placed one hand on Mikael's shoulder and his other on Raphael's. The next thing Mikael knew they were in a room with several other humans. Being next to a window, Mikael could see they were high in the tower itself. Besides the people, the only thing in the room with them was what looked like some type of sculpture on a high pedestal. The piece was beautiful, composed almost entirely of various colored and various sized crystals arranged roughly in the shape of a large square, and this formed a three-dimensional cube structure with two sides open so one could see through it.

"Well, your artwork is beautiful," Mikael said, looking at Lucifer. "But what is its purpose?"

Lucifer smiled. "All in good time. All in good time."

Mikael noticed the people in the room were guards of some type. Two men stood on either side of the structure, spear in one hand with one end pointed at the ceiling and the other end on the floor. Their torsos were bare except for wide necklace-type decorations around their necks which seemed to be composed of beaded material contrasting with their dark bronze complexion. Two similar guards stood at the door of the room just inside the hallway. Each wore loincloths, but they were ornate in design. These men were evidently not ordinary guards.

"You must think highly of your sculpture to have so many guards protecting it," Raphael said, looking from the guards to Lucifer.

Lucifer gave a forced smile. "Well, once you understand its importance you will understand why."

"Importance?" Mikael asked. "What do you mean?"

"Today," Lucifer said, "we are embarking on a journey that will be heralded by all in the days to come as the triumphant pinnacle of humankind. And since you are here, you will be able to witness it."

Mikael glanced at Raphael, who shook his head. Evidently, Raphael didn't understand Lucifer's cryptic message any more than he did.

Mikael looked back at Lucifer. "*What* are you talking about?"

Before Lucifer had time to answer, the sculpture began to glow. The crystals refracted the light being produced and formed a kaleidoscope of color on the room's walls.

The guards in the hallway looked in, their eyes growing wide.

One of the guards next to the structure pointed at one of the guards near the doorway. "Go tell the queen he has returned."

The man nodded and trotted quickly down the hallway. Mikael could hear the *pat pat pat* of his bare feet growing fainter the farther away the man ran. The other three guards genuflected while facing the structure. Evidently, they expected someone to appear.

Lucifer turned to Mikael and smiled. "This is the beginning of a journey to bring me and my chosen greatness beyond mere greatness. My chosen will go beyond the heavens and bring heaven to earth."

Mikael sucked in a breath. "You can't be serious! What are you saying?" He didn't know what Lucifer had done, or was doing, but this did not sound good at all. Lucifer was talking as if he was God the Creator himself.

"And what do you think you are achieving?" Raphael asked.

A smile slowly came across Lucifer's face.

"Something wonderful," he proclaimed.

CHAPTER 2

THE HOLY GRAIL

"**W**hat is this?"

Dr. Andrew Latham, apparently irritated, threw a graded test on the desk. In bold red it had the number 67 circled at the top.

Zane Archer looked up from his writing and into the eyes of a man whose gaze all but shot daggers into him. He sighed on the inside. He knew it had been a bad idea to allow Dr. Latham's son in his class. Latham's glasses hung low on his nose. Zane thought it almost comical because, from this angle, the man's bifocals caused his bottom eyelashes to appear larger than those at the top of his eyes. He repressed the urge to smile, but he also told himself he was not going to give in— no matter what. It didn't matter that this was the dean of his department. He had graded fairly.

In as deadpan a fashion as he could muster, Zane replied, "It's a test paper, Andrew."

11

The daggers practically flew out of the man's eyes as he pushed the glasses back onto his nose. "Don't get smart with me, *Doctor* Archer. Of course it's a test paper." Andrew folded his arms in a huff. "The question is: why does it have a 67 at the top of it?"

Zane opened his mouth to reply, but Andrew held up his hands. "And if you say, because that's where the grade goes, I may just do something unbecoming of a dean."

Zane sat back, picked up a mechanical pencil and held it using the fingers of both hands. He felt he needed something to handle to prevent him from doing something *he* would do unbecoming of a professor.

"Look, *Doctor* Latham, if you want to be formal. What do you want me to say? That's the grade Evan deserved."

Andrew Latham's face turned a shade of red, causing the short white hair around his temples to stand out more. Zane sat, remained quiet, and let him fume. He had nothing to be sorry about.

"That's all you have to say?"

Zane leaned forward and gave a slight shrug. "There's nothing more *to* say."

Andrew took quick breaths as though he was about to explode. "You told me your class was an easy A. Evan only needs one more elective to graduate. You know he must spend time on his pastoral internship. This . . . this . . . " He pointed at the exam. "This is *not* what you promised."

Zane sat more upright. "What *I* promised? I didn't promise anything!"

"You said it was a slam dunk—an easy A."

"Well, yeah, if one does the requested assignments."

Andrew cocked his head like he was daring Zane to defend that statement.

"Look, I'm not requiring a lot from this class. I'm astute enough to know biblical archaeology is not as interesting to pastoral majors as how to produce a riveting sermon in five easy steps. But assignments have to at least be done."

Andrew put his finger on the exam and tapped it repeatedly. "But Evan *did* do the assignment. Look, it's twice as long as those from most other students."

Zane sighed. "Length doesn't—" He stopped and cocked his head. "How do you know how long his report is compared to the other students?"

"Edith collected them for me."

Zane bit his bottom lip. He and his administrative assistant would have a good discussion about procedure tomorrow.

Andrew threw another exam on Zane's desk. "You gave Ximen Peterson here a 97. It's half as long as Evan's and . . . " Andrew paused, crossing his arms again. "It looks like you're giving preferential treatment."

"*What?*" Zane's eyes widened. He felt like he had just been slapped with a gauntlet.

"Is it because he's not a pastoral major—or that he's your girlfriend's nephew?"

Zane narrowed his eyes. "That's low, Andrew. I will not be forced to defend how I grade my exams." He took a deep breath to calm himself before he did something rash. "Besides, many of the students did better than Evan. Even those who are pastoral majors. Take Kevin, for instance, Evan's sidekick. He did considerably better as well if I recall. I'm *sure* you noticed that, seeing Edith let you see all the exams?" He cocked his head with a forced smile. "So, no. No preferential treatment."

"Well, you may not want to defend your grading, but I think you have to—to me."

"Look, there's only one reason Evan got a low grade."

Andrew gave him a hard stare.

"He didn't do the assignment."

"But—"

"Yes, he wrote a paper—and a long paper. But he went off on a tirade as to why the assignment didn't make any sense to him. He never addressed the point of the assignment."

"You're saying everyone but Evan had better ideas?"

Zane shook his head. "No. I hated most of the ideas presented. But they at least attempted to address the question of the assignment. Your son refused to do that."

"Well, he said your question was unbiblical." Andrew shook his index finger at Zane. "I warned you when you started that you had to not get too radical. This is a conservative school."

"Oh, for crying out loud, Andrew! I'm the most conservative professor in your whole department. So don't go throwing blame where it doesn't exist." He sat back again and looked at Andrew for a few seconds. "Do you even know what the assignment was?"

"No. But I know my son."

"No, Andrew. No, I don't think you do."

"What are you talking about?"

"Your son says he's conservative, but he's closed-minded—not conservative. There's a difference."

"He knows his Bible back and forth."

"Oh, of that I have no doubt. But he can't debate or support a topic because he knows nothing outside the Bible. Knowing the content of the Bible is very important as that's the basis of truth. But to defend his beliefs he needs to know what others think and why. If he's not willing to listen to others, he'll wind up just turning them off, not convincing them of the real truth. They won't see him as caring about them. Believe it or not, I'm trying to get our students to think, and then to use Scripture to back up their beliefs."

"So, what was the assignment?"

Zane turned the exam to the second page and pointed.

Andrew shook his head and rolled his eyes. "I'm on board with Evan. This is all crock."

Zane sighed. "It's an exercise of thinking outside the box, Andrew. This one really has nothing to do with Scripture. It's an exercise to get them to think. That's it. *Think*. I didn't imagine anyone would blow this one. Should have been an easy A. But your son had to go ballistic and tell me all the things wrong with it even considering that the Holy Grail could be anything but the chalice Christ drank from."

Andrew scrunched his brow. "Why would anyone think otherwise?"

Zane looked at Andrew dumbfounded. *I guess the apple doesn't fall too far from the tree,* he thought. "Because, Andrew . . . " Zane tried not to sound condescending, but was pretty sure he failed. "Scholars over the centuries have thought that it could be something different. Being thought to be Christ's chalice is only one of the more recent myths—"

"Myths?"

"Yes, Andrew, myths. The Holy Grail being the chalice Christ drank from is just as much myth as any of the other stories."

"You're . . . you're demeaning Christianity!"

"And you're iconizing Christianity!" Zane stopped and took a deep breath. "Please. Let's not get into that argument again."

"Really, Zane. It's one thing to think the Holy Grail has reference to something outside Christianity, but to teach the students that is . . . is almost blasphemy."

"Are you sure you didn't write Evan's paper for him?"

Andrew stood straighter. "Well, it's better than what that Peterson kid wrote. He went on and on about time travel, spaceships . . . "

"Wormholes."

Andrew stopped midsentence, a confused look on his face. Zane almost laughed.

"What?" Andrew sounded quite annoyed at being interrupted.

"Ximen talked about wormholes, not time travel and spaceships."

Andrew rolled his eyes. "Whatever. Who could understand it anyway? He then tried to tie that back to Genesis." He picked up the paper with the 97 and shook it. "Preposterous! But you gave him a 97. A 97!"

"An easy A, remember?"

Andrew slammed the report on Zane's desk. "Except for those who actually speak sense."

"Look, Andrew. I told you. I was looking for them to think outside the box. I didn't care where it went. I just wanted them to think. Evan didn't." He tapped the paper with a 97. "Ximen Peterson did." And to be sure Andrew knew he wasn't singling out Evan, Zane added, "Kevin did."

Andrew shook his head, walked to the door, and turned. "Next time . . . "

"Next time tell Evan to do the assignment. It will then be an easy A."

Andrew stormed out of the room.

Over the next hour, Zane tried to get back to grading his other papers, but his mind just wasn't in it. He thought he'd do it later when he could truly focus on what the students wrote. Some of the papers needed his clear focus. These students needed to learn how to express their thoughts. That was his aim. Not to make them like archaeology, although that would be a nice bonus, but to help them learn how to put an argument together and back it up.

Zane paused and sat back in his chair. He wished Andrew could see they were both on the same side.

He had taught other places, but usually not archaeology. His passion was biblical archaeology, so when a friend of his mentioned that Dr. Andrew Latham, extremely well respected within the field of ancient literature, was setting up an archaeology study program at a new theological seminary he desired to make world-renowned, Zane thought it would be a great way to teach and do research in the field he loved. He had hoped for a win-win scenario, but that was yet to be realized. Andrew's idea of archaeological study was vastly different from his own. Somehow, literature extending outside the biblical text was okay, but not archaeology that may not support the biblical text.

Zane thought he had been clear in his interview: he believed the Bible and believed that archaeological discoveries would eventually uphold the biblical text. Yet he had also stated he wanted to help students realize that not everyone believed that, and to help them see all sides of an argument. Evidently, Andrew heard what he wanted to hear in that interview.

Zane smiled. His coming to Idaho wasn't so bad, though. He had met Dr. Alexandria Hadad, head of Middle Eastern Studies. She said he could call her Alex. *A good first step,* he thought. He found her smart, articulate, charismatic, and beautiful. Her mother was Iraqi, her father Egyptian. This yielded her a beautiful, tanned appearance, dark wavy hair which just touched her shoulders, and dark sultry eyes that seemed to twinkle as she talked.

Zane's smile broadened. And she loved sushi.

Sushi! Zane looked at his watch. It was getting close to six. He was to meet her at the downtown sushi restaurant at six-thirty. He did quick mental calculations. If he went home first, he would be late, and he didn't want that mark against him. Their relationship was too young for such a mistake. He gathered all his papers, put them in his leather satchel, and headed to the men's room. He washed his face and brushed his teeth. He always kept a few grooming products with him since, it seemed, he was always rushing somewhere.

He stared at himself in the mirror. *I know what I see in her, but what does she see in me?* He too had dark, neatly trimmed hair, but it was definitely not as dark as Alex's. His eyes, on the other hand, were much lighter. Some had told him they looked smoky. He shrugged. *Maybe.* They were blue but also had a grayish tint to them. At any rate, whatever Alex saw in him, he was glad—and definitely wanted it to continue. Being late would not help with that goal.

He looked at his watch again, rushed out of the restroom, and down the hall.

CHAPTER 3

SUMERIAN GRAIL

Zane stepped out of his yellow Corvette convertible. Everyone told him having such a car in Idaho was a waste of money. Yet on days like today, he was glad he had it. The day was perfect: the skies clear, the air fresh, the temperature ideal for a change.

He stepped out of his prized possession, pressed the button for the top to raise, and hurried toward the restaurant. Alex, always punctual, was likely already inside.

As he walked briskly toward the restaurant, Zane noticed the surroundings. He had no idea why Andrew Latham had chosen the outskirts of Sandpoint, Idaho to build his seminary, but he had to admit this area was a good choice. Being on the waterfront provided a great view of Lake Pend Oreille and of Schweitzer Mountain in the near distance. Getting to places via plane proved a big pain as there were no large airports in close driving distance. Sandpoint sat in the northern part of Idaho's panhandle, seemingly away from everything except nature's beauty. Other than this one drawback, living here was really quite nice. This was one of the more picturesque places he had lived.

Sure enough, as Zane entered, Alex was already sitting in the lobby and reading something on her phone. As he came close, she looked up and smiled.

"Been waiting long?"

She shook her head and stood, putting her phone away. "Just arrived a couple of minutes ago. I took the scenic route."

"And that would be?" Zane asked. "Every route up here seems scenic to me."

Alex gave a light laugh. "True."

He adored her laugh and hoped he could get her to chuckle often this evening. Her laugh had a light but sincere quality to it—one you had to join whether you wanted to or not.

Zane gave the maître d' his reservation information and they were seated immediately at a table with a lakeside view. Once the sun set, the lighting along the lake would provide a perfect ambience. The maître d' provided menus and announced their waiter would be by shortly.

Zane had seen Alex briefly that morning, so he realized she had come from work as well. He would never have known otherwise. As always, she looked elegant, even radiant. The chocolate and eggplant colors in her blouse, forming a geometric design, complemented her skin tone perfectly. Her earrings would occasionally catch the light just so to provide a purplish twinkle which seemed to complement her blouse as well as her vibrant personality. He wasn't sure if his sports coat was up to the designer standards she seemed to possess, but it didn't seem to bother her. Yet another unassuming quality in her he found attractive.

She continued the conversation they had started as they sat. "And to think I almost turned Dr. Latham down and would have missed all the beauty surrounding this place."

Zane smiled. "Until winter hits."

Alex gave her charming laugh again and leaned in slightly. "I'm planning—no, plotting—how to be in the Middle East by that time."

Zane's eyes widened. "Oh? Do tell."

The waiter arrived and they each ordered a glass of wine and an upscale bento box; it had more trimmings with their sushi than he had seen before.

After the waiter left, Zane looked back at Alex. "And your brilliant plan is?"

She shook her head, her earrings twinkling. "Not really a formalized plan, but I'm trying to get Dr. Latham to let me go to several places in the Middle East to get students and graduate students to apply here."

"And you think it will take the entire winter to do that?"

Alex developed a sincere look. "Oh, absolutely."

They stared at each other for a few seconds and then both burst into laughter.

"That was almost convincing," Zane said, picking up his water glass and giving her a toast.

She gave a wary smile. "Well, I might have something for you as well."

Zane cocked his head. "I'm listening."

Their meal arrived along with their wine. Zane picked up his wine glass and held it up. "Here's to warm winters."

Alex laughed and clinked her glass against his. "Warm winters, indeed."

"So, fill me in. What's your second brilliant plan—the one involving me?"

"Ever heard of the Sumerian Grail?"

Zane had just picked up his second bite of sushi but froze. The piece of fish fell from his chopsticks into his small bowl of teriyaki sauce. He jumped, but the splash wasn't large enough to cause an issue.

Alex laughed again. "I guess you have."

"Of course. It ties into my theory about the Holy Grail."

Alex took her own bite of sushi. "I thought it might. Ximen showed me what he wrote for your class." She giggled. "I told him he would likely flunk. But I hear you gave him a 97."

Zane scrunched his eyebrows. "How do you know that? I haven't returned the exams."

"I heard . . . well, I think everyone heard, your . . . " She did air quotes. "Discussion with Dr. Latham."

Zane cringed. "That loud, huh?"

"Thin walls, I think."

He could tell she was trying to make him feel better. He shook his head. "Sorry about that."

Alex gave a small shrug as if to say she didn't think it was a big deal. "I'm curious, though."

"About?"

"Why you gave Ximen a solid A."

Zane tilted his head back and forth. "I gave a lot of students an A. This was supposed to be an icebreaker, something easy for them to do." He chuckled. "I guess I was wrong on that point." He looked back at her. "But Ximen's point, though a little out there, was well argued."

"A *little* out there?" She laughed again. "It was *literally* out there."

"He's not by himself, though."

"Oh? There are well-renowned archaeologists who believe that?"

"Absolutely. One very prominent."

"Who?" Alex exhibited an intensely curious look.

Zane smiled. "Me."

Alex didn't move a muscle for several seconds. A smile slowly crept across her face. "No, seriously."

"Seriously."

Her eyes widened. "Does . . . Dr. Latham know that?"

Zane gave a scowl like he had eaten a lemon. "Heavens no. He can barely get over the fact that I don't believe the Holy Grail is the chalice Christ used."

"Well, that does seem to be the popular theory."

"Only because of the fiction books and movies that have been produced."

Alex raised her eyebrows.

Zane gave a sigh. "Look. I'm as conservative as the next guy."

Alex just looked at him.

"I am. Being conservative doesn't mean you stick your head in the sand."

Alex took another sip of wine and then leaned forward. "You have a theory?"

Zane cocked his head with a slight shrug.

"Tell me," she said.

"Really?"

"Absolutely. No matter how crazy it may seem to us rational people."

Zane gave her a smirk. "Okay, Dr. Latham's clone."

Alex giggled. "Sorry. I couldn't resist." She waved her hands toward herself. "But tell me. I really want to know."

"Well, as you know, there are a lot of myths surrounding the Holy Grail as the chalice Christ used at the Last Supper: King Arthur, Knights Templar, Joseph of Arimathea, and others who either used the chalice or hid it because of its power to sustain life or even create life. But other cultures have similar beliefs to something like the Holy Grail. Some have talked about the chalice of Solomon, made of a pure emerald, which supposedly had alchemist powers. There is Persia's Cup of Jamshid, made of pure turquoise, which many touted to have the power to reveal the future and turn mortals into immortals. Some tell of the Nartmongue, a chalice passed from Persian knight to Persian knight for centuries, even before the story of Arthur and his knights.

"In China and Mongolia are tales of the Chalice of Buddha. Then in China there is the tale of the Royal Cauldron which supposedly gave long life to many Chinese emperors." Zane leaned in farther. "And I think all of these are tied to the Sumerian Grail."

Alex's eyes went wide. "And why is that?"

"This particular chalice is believed to have been owned by the original Sumerian king, Dur, who had captured it from Chaldean serpent worshippers. He and his grandson, King Udu of Kish, turned the serpent worship into a sun cult worship."

"And you think all are tied to the Sumerian Grail?"

Zane nodded. "Yes, because that is where the languages were divided. As each language left in their grouping, they took the worship with them, and their history developed uniquely with each culture adapting the story as needed."

"Ah. That explains Ximen's Genesis connection."

"Precisely." A few seconds of silence followed.

"Forgive me," Zane said, ending the silence. "This is sort of off topic. I can understand your nephew's first name being Ximen, as you also are of Iraqi descent. But where does Peterson come from?"

Alex laughed. "My sister, Ava, married an American, Roger Peterson. He's a physician and works in Boise."

Zane smiled. "I knew there was some logical explanation. I guess Ximen gets his interests from you rather than your sister."

"Perhaps, but Ava, though not formally trained, has a lot of Middle Eastern cultural knowledge. My uncle, who told me about the Sumerian Grail, goes on many digs throughout the Middle East." She chuckled. "They send me information, and then I validate their reports and finds to give the information legitimacy in academic circles."

"Your own little information mafia."

Alex produced a broad grin. "Something like that, I guess." She pointed at Zane. "But what about you?"

"Oh, I have to do my own digging for information and clues."

"Oh, stop. I'm talking about your family. Any siblings?"

Zane shook his head. "No, I was an only child. I know the spelling of my name is an Americanized version of the common Arabic forms. My father died when I was very young." He cocked his head. "I think he may have had some Middle Eastern roots as well." He shrugged. "But mom didn't talk about him much. She basically raised me, but she died just a few years ago."

"Sorry to hear that."

Zane shrugged. "My circumstances do give me free reign to go wherever the action is, so to speak." He finished the last two bites from his bento box, pushed it aside, and leaned in. "So tell me more about the Sumerian Grail."

"Well, you should start working on Dr. Latham for yourself. According to my uncle, there is a dig that has already started. It will take some finagling on his part to get you invited on the expedition, but he feels he can get you in by early December. I can tell him to go ahead and get started on that, but you have five months to get Dr. Latham's approval to go."

"Won't he think we're conspiring just so we can be together?"

Alex displayed her serious look again. "Dr. Archer, I'm very hurt at your insinuation. This is of vital academic importance, one that requires expertise from different, but related, disciplines. A mere coincidence, I assure you."

Zane had to smile at that. "Oh, forgive me. I most definitely see your point."

Both chuckled and toasted again with their now almost empty wine glasses.

Alex displayed a strange expression: a look of curiosity but also one of concern at the same time.

"Anything wrong, Alex?"

"I'm not sure. There's a guy sitting at a table in the far corner that, it seems to me, keeps staring at us."

"Strange you say that. My spidey senses had been activated a while back."

"Well, it's all very unnerving. Can we just go?"

Zane waved for the waiter, received the check, paid, and escorted Alex out. As he waited with Alex for the valet to bring her car around, he got an unsettled feeling. At first he simply tried to ignore it, but the more he did, the stronger the feeling became.

"Alex, why don't I drive you home?" Zane asked. "I don't know who that was observing us or why he was doing so. I'd rest better if I knew for sure you arrived home safely."

The valet hopped out of Alex's car and held the door open for her.

Alex gave a dismissive hand gesture. "I'm sure it's nothing. I'll be all right."

"Alex. Please. Let me."

"Excuse me," the valet said. "If the question is can you keep your car here overnight, the answer is yes. We have a small lot we use for that. It's gated." He shrugged. "We haven't as yet had any trouble with cars left there."

"See?" Zane said. "Problem solved. I can drop you off tomorrow to pick it up."

Alex seemed to be in thought for a few seconds. "Oh, all right. I think you're overreacting, but I'll concede." She gave a smirk. "I think you just want me to ride in your Corvette to try and impress me."

At that, the valet gave Zane a wink, hopped back in Alex's car, and pulled away from where they were standing.

Zane laughed. "That obvious, huh?" He guided her in the direction where he had parked. "But seriously—"

Zane's words were cut off by a huge explosion. They both ducked while feeling the heat of the blast. The air compression the fiery eruption created caused Alex to lose her balance. Zane grabbed her just before she hit the ground and pulled her back to her feet.

"Are you okay?"

"I . . . I think so. What *was* that?"

They both looked back and stood, transfixed in horror.

Alex pointed with one hand, the other over her mouth. "My car! That was my car!"

CHAPTER 4

KIDNAPPED

Zane looked at his watch: three-thirty in the morning. He sat on a bench in the police precinct waiting for officers to finish with Alex. He wasn't sure why they took longer with her. Probably because it was her car that exploded. He just hoped her ethnicity didn't become a factor. Yet why was she targeted? The incident had to be tied to the guy at the restaurant.

Finishing his third cup of horrible coffee, he looked up and saw Alex approach. She looked haggard. *Poor girl.* She deserved far better than this. Once Alex saw him, she shuffled over and sat next to him.

"Zane, you didn't have to wait for me. I could have gotten a cab. You need your rest just as much as I do."

"Wouldn't dream of abandoning my ticket to a warm winter."

Alex gave a short chuckle but then put her palm over half her face and shook her head. "None of this makes any sense." She looked back at him. Her eyes were wet, but no tears came. "What's going on? Why would anyone want me dead?"

"It must be tied to that creep who was watching us. You never saw him before?"

She shook her head. "No. Never." She paused and then asked, "Did you tell the police about him?"

Zane shook his head. "I left that up to you."

"I didn't say anything either."

Zane grabbed her arm. "Alex, why? Don't you want this guy caught?"

Alex suddenly got a stern look. "I don't know if he's connected or not. The police are already suspicious of me, I think. Why is an Iraqi living in Idaho?"

"Because you're a brilliant scientist with skills and knowledge that makes you the perfect candidate for an academic position offered here."

Alex gave a brief smile. "I didn't want to add any fuel to their suspicions. Mentioning him would only lead them in a direction that would not be helpful."

"So what do you plan to do?"

"For now? Go home and get some rest. You should do the same."

"Okay. I'll drive you."

At that moment an officer, likely in his thirties, looking muscular and yet somehow familiar, came over. He tipped his hat slightly.

"Ma'am, I'm Officer Bradley. The captain feels someone should watch your house for a couple of days." He gave a brief smile. "I have the shift tonight and can drive you home. I'll be outside your home all night, so hopefully that will allow you to get some needed rest." He gestured toward the door. "Shall we?"

Alex nodded and stood. "Officer Bradley, this is a fellow colleague, Dr. Zane Archer."

The officer gave Zane a nod. "Yes, I was the one who questioned him earlier. Don't worry, Dr. Archer. I'll be sure she's safe for the remainder of the night."

Zane touched Alex's arm. "Have a good night. I'll see you tomorrow."

Alex walked with the officer out of the precinct.

Zane sat for a few more seconds to allow his last cup of coffee to do its thing and give him enough energy for the drive home. He noticed another officer approach. He thought it uncanny how alike this officer looked compared to the last one.

The officer nodded and smiled. "Dr. Archer, I'm looking for Dr. Hadad. I know she was sitting here a minute ago. I'm Officer Bradley. The captain asked me to escort her home."

"What? But you . . . " Zane pointed toward the door and then looked back at the officer. "You just left with her." He felt himself getting a buzz, but this energy wasn't from the coffee. A surge of adrenaline was shooting through him.

The officer squinted. "*Who* left with her?"

"*You* did!" Zane shook his head. "Or someone who looked amazingly like you. What's going on?"

"That's what I want to know." Bradley turned and shouted at someone. "Miller! Miller, pull up the security feed! We've got an imposter among us."

Zane felt confused. The nightmare wasn't over after all. While Bradley did whatever he was doing, Zane ran for the door Alex and the other . . . imposter . . . had walked through. Once he was outside, he looked around. A car was turning the corner and entering the highway. *Could that be them?*

Zane ran as fast as he could to his car. He jumped in and took off, tires squealing. He didn't slow as he turned onto the highway. His turn cut a car off and he heard a horn blare. He didn't care. He had to find Alex.

He drew up behind a car. Its color looked similar to what he had seen, but the bumper displayed Wyoming plates, so this car likely wasn't the one. He sped around the car and took a quick look at the driver. A teenager gave him a nasty look. Zane plowed past this driver and headed for the next car. This one, white in color, wasn't the one containing Alex either. He sped around this one as well, not even considering he was approaching a curve. Suddenly, lights almost blinded him as an oncoming vehicle came into view. He heard the horn of a semi. Rather than slowing, Zane sped up and zoomed around the car just before the semi got to his position. Sweat was now bleeding through his shirt. Alex's life likely stood in the balance; chances had to be taken.

The next car ahead looked familiar. The sedan's body, dark in color, looked like the one he had seen, but was it them? The light from an oncoming car showed two silhouettes. That seemed to verify it was them. Zane decided to pass them and see who was in the driver's seat. When he went to drive around them, though, the car sped up. Zane did the same and the car responded in kind once more. *Definitely them.*

Zane thought hard about what to do. If he kept this up, his efforts could put Alex's life in even more danger by forcing the driver to do something reckless. Zane pulled back into the right lane and continued to follow them. He fumbled for his phone, found it, and dialed the precinct he had just left.

"Sandpoint Police Department. How may I be of service?"

"I need to speak with Officer Bradley. This is an emergency."

"Please tell me—"

"Look." Zane's voice turned forceful. "I don't mean to be rude, but I'm behind the car of the imposter who just kidnapped Dr. Alexandria Hadad." Then, with even more deter-mination, he repeated, "I *need* to talk to Officer Bradley."

"Just a moment."

In a short time Bradley was on the line, but Zane felt the time took way too long for something so important. "Officer Bradley. Is this Dr. Archer?"

"Yes. I'm on Highway 2 West just past Wrencoe. The imposter officer has Dr. Hadad in an unmarked car."

"You shouldn't be doing that, Dr. Archer."

"You already know this?"

"No, but . . . "

"Just jot this down and do your job." He heard Bradley sigh. As long as this officer took the information and acted on it, he didn't care what Bradley thought of him. "It's a dark Honda Accord. I can't quite tell the color. I think it's dark navy, but I'm not completely sure as it's dark out here."

"What's the license plate?"

"Idaho plates. 7B-LU-991."

"Got it. Now let us take over from here."

"I'll follow in case they turn off somewhere."

"We'll find them. I don't want to have to find two people instead of just one."

"Just do your job!" Zane knew this was probably too force-ful, but he didn't care. "When I see another police car, I'll let them take over."

"Dr. Archer!"

Zane disconnected. He wasn't going to let this officer tell him what he needed to do. Alex's life was on the line.

Zane continued to follow, and the Honda continued on Highway 2 without pulling off. Zane saw a sign for Thama, and the Honda suddenly slammed on its brakes. This caught him off guard and he slammed on his. An elk appeared in front of him. *Where did that come from?* Zane turned sharply to avoid hitting the animal as there appeared to be another in front of it. He quickly turned again, but this caused his car to spin out of control and land facing the other way in a small ditch. Zane looked back and saw the other car still on the highway, now easing its way between the slow-moving elk. Once cleared, the car sped off again.

Zane tried to continue his pursuit, but his tires only spun without gaining any traction. Hitting the steering wheel in frustration, he looked out his window and saw an elk standing there eyeing him with a quizzical look.

"Yeah, it's all your fault, buddy. You hear me?" In frustration he pointed at the window. "*Your* fault."

The elk continued to stare for few seconds and then sauntered away.

Zane sighed, sat back in his seat, and shook his head. He prayed Bradley and any other officers would reach Alex in time. He reluctantly picked up his phone and dialed for roadside assistance.

CHAPTER 5

DANGER REALIZED

Zane woke with a start. *What was that?* He heard the sound again. Someone was at the front door. He sat up and tried to focus on his bedside clock: *11:34.* He heard the knock again. This time more forcefully. After pulling on some sweatpants, he donned a T-shirt as he headed downstairs. The next knock was even more forceful.

"Okay, okay," he shouted. "I'm coming."

He reached the door and opened it; an officer had his hand raised to knock again. Once his brain registered the man as Officer Bradley, the recognition gave him the adrenaline jolt he needed to focus.

Zane spit out the words. "Did you find her?"

"She's asking for you," Bradley said. "May I take you to her? I, uh, heard you had an elk incident."

"Something like that," Zane replied with a forced smile. He looked down at what he had on. "Give me just a few minutes to get ready." Zane turned, then turned back. "No offense, but can you wait in the car? You're probably the good officer, but . . ." Zane shrugged. "I won't take long."

Bradley nodded. "I understand. No offense taken."

Bradley closed the door behind him, and Zane locked it. He hurried upstairs and changed into some jeans and a better pullover. After putting on some loafers, he combed his hair, ignored his shadow of a beard, and headed downstairs.

Zane glanced at his many paintings, sculptures, and vases from some of his finds over the years. He couldn't afford for a counterfeit Officer Bradley to see his valuables.

After Zane climbed into Bradley's cruiser and he started off, the officer was quiet on the way. Zane felt this was not a good sign.

"Can you tell me what happened? Is Alex all right?"

"She's physically fine, Dr. Archer. A little shaken up. But that's pretty understandable."

Zane nodded, not knowing what else to say, but breathed a huge sigh of relief on the inside.

Bradley glanced at Zane periodically as he drove. "I think both of you are good people, but there's something you're not telling me. I need to know what's going on, Dr. Archer. Someone's car doesn't just explode, and the owner of that same car get kidnapped, without something going on."

Zane shook his head. "I don't know what's going on."

"Dr. Archer?"

"No, really. I'm just as confused as you are."

Zane could see Bradley turning a slight shade of red. Evidently he was getting upset.

"Look, the only thing I didn't tell you last night was that some guy kept staring at us while we were in the restaurant."

"What guy?"

Zane gave an exaggerated shrug. "I don't know. He may have been Middle Eastern. He was bald on top with short pepper-colored hair around the sides and back of his head. Looked to be in his late fifties, I guess."

"And you had never seen him before?"

Zane shook his head. "No. Never."

"And no idea how he was connected to the kidnapper?"

Zane shook his head again. After a pause, he added, "Were they connected?"

"You tell me."

"I. Don't. Know." Zane gave a long sigh. "Look, I wish I did. But I don't."

Zane realized Bradley had pulled up to a house in a residential neighborhood. "Why are we stopping here?"

"I let Dr. Hadad rest a while. I thought we'd finish our conversation here at her house."

Zane's eyes widened. He thought that unusual, but where they had the conversation mattered little to him. He was surprised the officer had left Alex alone while he was being retrieved. He wondered about this—until he met a female police officer inside the house.

Zane noticed many modern abstract artworks in the living room. Not what he had expected. The female officer directed them to the back of the house. Here the room looked more like a study area that contained all sorts of Middle Eastern artifacts: pictures, vases, sculptures, wall hangings. Zane smiled. This was what he had expected.

Alex had been sitting on a sofa and stood the moment she saw him. "Zane, are you all right? I heard you had an accident."

Zane smiled. "I'm fine. I'm more worried about you."

Alex gave him a warm smile. "Fine now."

Officer Bradley motioned for them to sit. Zane sat next to Alex, and both looked the officer's way with expectation.

"Dr. Archer, your story matches what Dr. Hadad here has told us. I just wish you both had been as truthful when we first questioned you."

Zane started to say something, but Bradley held up his palm. "No matter why now. I just trust you both will be cooperative going forward."

Zane nodded and noticed Alex doing the same.

"What information did you get out of the kidnapper?" Zane asked.

Alex grabbed his arm and gave Zane a frightened look.

"What's wrong? Did he hurt you?"

She shook her head. "No. He's dead."

"What?" Zane looked from her to Officer Bradley. "What happened?"

"We were spotted by local police," Alex said. "Just past Diamond Lake. During the pursuit, the car spun and hit a guardrail."

Zane grabbed her hand. "Were you hurt?"

Alex shook her head. "Not really. Just this little skin burn on my forehead from the airbag."

"And the guy?"

"He was all right as well."

Zane scrunched his brow. "So, if he was all right, what happened?"

Zane felt Alex's hand start to tremble. His eyes shot to hers. "Did something bad happen?" he asked in a hushed voice.

"When . . . when . . . "

Bradley completed Alex's sentence. "When the man was being cuffed, a sniper took him out."

Zane's eyes widened. "*What?* Why?"

"That, Dr. Archer, is what I was hoping one of you could tell me."

Zane started to get irritated once more. "And why do you think we know anything?" His words came out in a more irritating tone than he wanted. "And why not ask the sniper? Surely, you caught him."

Bradley shook his head. "Got away, I'm afraid."

Zane leaned back with a sigh. After a second, he repeated his question. "And why do you think we know anything about any of this?"

Bradley leaned forward. "Because typically people don't go around blowing up vehicles at random or kidnapping random people."

Zane sat back and nodded. "True." Officer Bradley had a point. Something had to be going on. He looked at Alex. "Any ideas?"

Her eyes widened as she shook her head. "No." She glanced from Zane to Officer Bradley. "Really. I have no idea."

Bradley gave a loud sigh. "Well, it has to be something." He glanced around at the walls. "Maybe their actions have something to do with some of your artifacts. Any of them worth anything?"

Alex followed Bradley's gaze. "Well, yeah, but not enough to kill for. Besides, if they wanted something here, why not just steal it rather than try to kill me or kidnap me?"

This time, Bradley sat back and nodded. He shook his head. "It has to be something." He pointed between the two of them. "Not to pry, but what did the two of you talk about at the restaurant? Maybe the guy there overheard you say something that got him—them—worried."

Zane looked at Alex and she at him. Both gave blank stares to one another.

After a few seconds, Zane looked at Bradley and shrugged. "Alex talked about going to the Middle East in the winter to encourage students there to attend the seminary here."

"Yes," Alex said. "And I told Zane about the possibility of going on a dig."

Zane looked at Bradley and nodded. "That about sums it up. More or less."

"A dig for what?" Bradley asked.

"Just an ancient artifact," Zane said.

Bradley twirled his hand in a circular fashion, clearly a bit annoyed. "And is this artifact valuable?"

Zane's eyes widened. "Oh, absolutely. Priceless in fact."

"If true," Alex interjected.

Bradley looked from one to the other. "Mind filling in the newbie here? What is it? And why is such an artifact priceless?"

"Oh," Zane said. "The Sumerian Grail. Something touted to bestow immortality."

Bradley's eyebrows raised.

"Or so the rumor goes," Alex replied. She shrugged and looked at Zane. "Likely just rumors, though. Right?"

He cocked his head. "Well, there are some who might think otherwise."

Bradley stared at them, eyes wide. "And you thought this information not important enough to tell me the first time?"

"Well," Zane replied. "It does sound kind of important when you say it out loud."

"Wait, though," Alex said. "It's not like we have the artifact or know anything about its location. Not yet, anyway." She shook her head. "That can't be the reason someone tried to kill me—to silence me before I know anything. If that's the case, then it's very poor planning on their part."

"Whoever 'they' are," Zane said.

Alex nodded her agreement.

"And who told you about this Sumerian Grail?" Bradley asked.

"My uncle."

Bradley gave Alex a stare. "Your uncle. And that didn't seem important?"

"Well, not at the time." Her tone was a bit defensive.

Bradley shook his head and wrote a bit more in his note-book. "Maybe someone wanted to send a message to your uncle."

Alex sat up straighter. "I . . . I never thought about that." Zane felt her grab his hand. "You think my uncle's in danger?"

Bradley stopped writing and looked up. "That's what we have to find out."

He turned to the female officer who had entered the room. "Officer Kinnick here will stay with you for a couple of days until we get this sorted out."

Kinnick gave Alex a brief smile and slight nod.

"But I have classes to teach," Alex said.

Bradley cocked his head. "Dr. Hadad, it would be much better to lay low for a couple of weeks."

Seeing her start to object, Zane placed his hand on her arm. "Don't worry. I'll teach those for you."

She looked at him. "You think you can? For two weeks?"

"Well, not as well as you, of course. But I've taught those subjects before. It's been a while, but I think I can give the students a run for their money."

Bradley stood. "Good. Settled then." He turned to Kinnick. "Report in every two hours."

She nodded. "Roger that."

Bradley turned to Zane. "Mr. Archer, can I drop you off somewhere?"

"The mechanic over on Ella Avenue, if not too much trouble."

Bradley shook his head. "That's pretty much just around the corner from the precinct. No problem."

Zane gave Alex a hug and a kiss on her cheek. "I'll check in with you later."

She nodded and forced a smile. "Evidently I'll be here." She walked them to her front door. "I'll text you my access code. All my notes are online."

Zane nodded, followed Bradley to his car, gave a final wave as he got in, and they were off. He could see now that withholding information had not been wise even though doing so had seemed the right thing at the time.

Yet would sharing that information have changed anything? He wasn't sure. The whole scheme seemed so elaborate. He had a bad feeling in the pit of his stomach that more was to come.

CHAPTER 6

MULTIPLE BRADLEYS

The following two weeks were largely uneventful. Alex's classes went fine, although the students seemed a little weirded out in the beginning. Zane was able to put them at ease by the end of the first week. The second week went much better. He could tell, though, they would be grateful to get Professor Hadad back as soon as possible.

Dr. Latham was a different story. He kept giving Zane a cold shoulder, at least until the next essay was returned to the students. Evan did a better job, so Zane rewarded him, although he couldn't quite convince himself to give Evan an A on the paper—much of the text still complained about the validity of the subject matter. Zane felt an 88 was as generous as he could be. Both Evan and Latham seemed satisfied.

That Friday, feeling all crises were, at least temporarily, averted, Zane stopped and picked up sushi for three and headed to Alex's. This was the last night of Alex's confinement, so he wanted to celebrate. Including Officer Kinnick would hopefully allow everyone to part on good terms.

When Zane arrived, Officer Kinnick looked ecstatic; she helped set the table. "I haven't had sushi in a long time. Thank you, Dr. Archer, for including me."

Zane laughed. "Wanted to give you a good send-off. I appreciate all you've done for Alex."

Kinnick stopped setting the table and looked at Zane. "I'm not sure I've done anything. I feel like I've taken a two-week crash course on Middle Eastern literature."

"Then this can be your freedom dinner."

Kinnick held up her hand. "Oh, I'm not complaining. Being here actually became kind of fun. Something different for a change."

Alex entered the room and began taking the meals from the carrying bags. "Well, Marcy here has helped me get a lot of my lesson plans together." She looked at Officer Kinnick. "Although the precinct may not appreciate all the work you did for me, I certainly do."

Kinnick laughed. "I may even take some night classes now."

Zane laughed with her. "I guess you've fallen into her charms like all of her other students." He looked at Alex. "They are really looking forward to your return. I was not . . . vibrant enough."

Alex smiled. "They're a great class." She gestured toward the table. "Okay, let's eat. I'm starved."

The meal was vibrant. Alex seemed to have a contagious charm. Each of them talked about some of their exploits in the field. Alex pointed to several of her artifacts on the wall and provided colorful detail as to how she obtained them. Zane tried to match her stories, but they paled in comparison. Marcy contributed to the conversation with some of her police stories, which were just as riveting as anything the two of them came up with.

The meal came to a leisurely end, and just as Marcy stood to help clear the table . . . a cannister of some sort came crashing through the window; the sound of the breaking glass startled them. Marcy pulled her gun within a second, but smoke from the cannister filled the room quickly, causing Marcy to drop her gun just before she fell to the floor unconscious.

Zane tried to crawl to where the gun fell. He got close, but whatever the smoke contained made him dizzy, and he had a hard time focusing on what he was trying to do. His hand almost reached the gun, but his fingers fell short by just a few centimeters when he was overcome. As he lay there, he saw Alex's body scooped up by someone wearing some type of mask. Evidently a gas mask of some kind, but it looked minimalistic from what he would have expected. Just as he was on the verge of losing consciousness, he felt his body lifted as well. His last thought before losing consciousness: *Where are they taking us?*

* * * * *

Zane woke slowly as if coming out of a deep sleep. It seemed as though he was in slow motion; everything appeared distorted. This went on for several seconds, but reality started to settle into his mind. *Kidnapped.*

That thought gave him an adrenaline jolt, and he sat up quickly. But that made him slightly dizzy, and he had to reach to steady himself. His hand hit a window. He looked over. A small window. As he attempted to focus on the window, he saw clouds. That confused him at first—until he looked in the opposite direction. He was sitting in some type of jet. The décor looked quite modern and roomy. He noticed Alex slumped in the leather seat on the opposite side, apparently still unconscious. He attempted to stand but was pulled back into his seat. His hands, waist, and legs were restrained. If he moved slowly, they would give and allow movement, but any sudden movement caused the restraints to quickly retract.

Zane looked around but didn't see anyone. In a loud whisper, he tried to wake Alex. "Alex. Alex!"

She stirred a little but didn't wake.

He opened his mouth to call to her again but saw movement from the corner of his field of vision. He turned in that direction, his mouth falling open in disbelief.

"Dr. Archer," the man said. "You look like you've seen a ghost." The man laughed. "Or in this case, a doppelganger."

Zane wondered if he was fully awake. "Officer Bradley?"

The man chuckled and took a seat opposite Zane. "Hardly. Although Officer Bradley does get his good looks from me."

Zane shook his head slightly. "What are you? Twins or something?"

The man just continued to look at Zane with a wry smile, not saying anything.

"Wait." Zane slowly moved his hand to keep the restraint from retracting. "You're the *third* one of you I've seen."

The man nodded approvingly. "Yes, Dr. Archer. I think you're starting to put the pieces together."

Zane furrowed his brow. He wasn't putting anything together.

He heard a gasp and turned to see Alex giving a look of near horror. "But you're . . . you're dead. I saw you get shot. Your face was totally destroyed with the bullet."

The man grinned. "But voila! Here I am." He followed his statement with a chuckle. "No, that wasn't me. He just looked like me."

Alex had a look of utter confusion. "How many of you *are* there?"

"On this planet? Right now?" He grinned again. "Three."

"But you're not like Officer Bradley," Zane said. "There's something different about you compared to him."

The man's eyes widened, and he became excited. "Oh, oh. Like your Dr. Jekyll and Mr. Hyde. Right?" His eyes seemed to twinkle. It seemed odd they would twinkle for something so twisted.

"Maybe," Zane said.

"I think that's a very good analogy." He looked rather smug with his statement.

"And . . . which one are *you*?" Alex asked with trepidation.

"Which one of the two had no moral compass?" He looked between the two of them. "I'm that one."

Alex's expression turned to one of intense worry.

The man laughed. "Oh, that expression is priceless. But don't worry. I can still be fun."

"At whose expense?" Zane blurted.

The man looked at Zane and laughed harder. "Oh, you two are a riot." He waved his hands in the air. "Oh, we're going to have so much fun."

Zane felt this guy was bonkers. He tried to think about what might possibly help their situation. Maybe establishing a personal connection would help.

"And what do *you* call you?" Zane asked.

The man seemed to think for a few seconds. "You can call me Bradley One." He looked at Zane and smiled. "How's that?"

"And Bradley Two?"

Bradley One gave a dismissive wave. "Alas. He is no more."

"And Bradley Three?"

Bradley One became irritated. "Now, he's the one causing all the problems." He gave a pout. "He's the one who shot Bradley Two."

"What do you want with us?" Alex asked.

Bradley One leaned forward. "You're going to just love this." He held up an index finger. "But before story time, how about a little meal. Hungry?"

Zane shook his head. Alex did the same.

Bradley One gave a scowl. "You two aren't fun at all." He stood in a huff. "Well, I'm hungry. So you'll just have to wait for story time."

Bradley One took two steps when a flash of light startled them all. Suddenly, *Officer* Bradley appeared on the plane.

Bradley One pointed at him and yelled, "Cheater!"

In a flash, Officer Bradley raised his pistol and shot Bradley One in the head, causing him to crumple to the plane floor in a heap.

Bradley quickly hurried to Alex and cut her loose from her restraints, then did the same for Zane. He had them stand next to him.

"I only have one more teleport left," the man said. He placed a hand on a shoulder of each of them.

Zane felt himself go weightless and, the next thing he knew, he was standing in a hotel room with both Alex and Bradley.

Zane and Alex looked at each other with disbelief in their eyes. *What just happened?* Each took a step away from Bradley.

Zane held up his hands as if trying to set a perimeter of defense. "Bradley, what's going on? I thought you were a good guy, but I'm not sure. I don't even know what or who you are."

Alex nodded. "No human can do what you just did."

Bradley patted the air as though seeking to calm them down. "I know. I know. Let me explain. Sit, and I'll do my best to tell you everything."

He gestured for both to sit on the sofa near the room's window. Bradley then sat in the desk chair and rolled to where they sat and faced them.

"I have a lot to tell you," he began. "I just hope you have an open mind. What I will say, more than likely, will sound like science fiction. Yet I want you to know that what I tell you is true."

"Why should we listen to you?" Alex asked.

Bradley gave her a stern but sincere look. "Because the fate of the world rests in your hands."

CHAPTER 7

ADVERSARIA

Alex seemed as dubious of Bradley as Zane was of him. If Officer Bradley was a real nutjob, as he sounded, they were likely in as much danger as they had been with Bradley One.

Yet Zane had to consider what they had just experienced. They were literally teleported off the plane into this hotel room. As far as he knew, that level of technology did not yet exist. That meant he should at least hear the guy out.

"You're not really an officer, I take it. Mind if I just call you Bradley? Or what name should we call you?"

The man tilted his head back and forth slightly. "Since I'm in your world, Bradley is fine." He smiled. "My real name would sound odd to those who live here."

"What is your real name?" Alex asked. "Just so we know."

"Ekmenetet."

Zane nodded but gave a quick wide-eyed look at Alex, who produced a slight shrug. He turned back to the man, who was displaying a forced smile. "Bradley it is, then," Zane said.

"There is so much to tell you. I'm not sure where to begin. I fear you will not believe me, although what I have to convey is of vital importance—both for you as well as the future of all of us."

Zane glanced at Alex, who seemed to be as dumbfounded as he was. He turned to Bradley. "You can start with how you got us to this hotel room."

Bradley gave a brief smile. "Hopefully, that will help you believe what I have to tell you."

Zane's eyebrows shot up, but he didn't say anything.

Bradley cleared his throat and continued. "I wasn't sure what understanding you would have about early Mesopotamia. I was pleased to find out you both have professions that will likely help you better understand what I say is true." He bobbed his head back and forth slightly. "Although the information I give will still be hard for you, I'm sure."

"I'm having a hard time already," Alex said.

"Yes, I'm sure," Bradley said. "So let me start by asking what you know about Nimrod?"

"Of the Bible?" Alex asked.

Bradley nodded.

She glanced at Zane and then back to Bradley. "Uh, well, he built a kingdom after the Flood. And he built the tower of Babel."

"Why?"

Alex scrunched her brow. "Why a kingdom or why a tower?"

"Both."

"A kingdom to prevent people from scattering and following God's command to spread across the earth."

"And a tower," Zane interjected, "to reach to the heavens. The Bible isn't really explicit as to why. But some historical records seem to imply his name was a character reference to his rebellion, and that he may have been the touted Gilgamesh of history."

"Good," Bradley said with a nod. "That's good you already understand that. Your Bible states he became 'a mighty hunter before the Lord.' So what does that mean?"

"I've always had trouble with that part," Alex said. "Most writings seem to indicate the passage is talking about his ability to conquer to establish his kingdom. But I've always felt the words were implying something more. I'm just not sure what."

"Yes," Zane added. "There was apparently some spiritual connection with the tower, or ziggurat. Some believe another cult of worship became established."

"There *is* evidence for that," Alex said. "The only difference between the gods of different cultures are the names they are identified by."

"All that is true, but there is more to it," Bradley said.

Zane wondered what Bradley referred to, so he waited quietly for Bradley to continue.

"He was not merely a hunter of men to conquer, but a hunter of men for their favorable genetic qualities."

Zane cocked his head; that statement was something he had not expected. "Uh, I don't think their culture really understood genetics."

"No, but Marduk, or the Adversary, did."

Evidently seeing the confusion on their faces, Bradley held up his hands. "I'm sorry. It's hard to have this make sense. Let me just tell you, and then I can go over what you don't understand."

Both nodded.

Bradley paused in thought for a few seconds, sat up straighter, and continued. "Gilgamesh was a tyrant who did conquer. He established a large kingdom throughout

Mesopotamia. He married Summer-amat, one of the most beautiful women in the land, who some know as Semiramis. Their lust for power knew no bounds. I think this is why Gilgamesh allowed himself to become Marduk for periods of time."

Alex held up her palm. "Sorry for interrupting, but you're saying that Gilgamesh became a god?"

"Sort of. You believe in the Adversary?"

"You mean the devil?" Zane asked.

Bradley nodded with an expectant look.

Both nodded in return. "Yet, he certainly isn't a god," Alex added.

"Depends upon your perspective," Bradley replied. "The Adversary would possess Gilgamesh at times. That's when miraculous things would happen."

"Like?" Zane was having a hard time with this.

"Marduk is the one who instituted the gathering of men and women with certain genetic qualities. He established the portal to send those to the new world."

Zane shot a quick glance at Alex. Her expression of disbelief seemed to match his own.

"Look," Bradley said. "I know this sounds preposterous, but let me finish."

Zane gestured for Bradley to continue. At the same time, he was beginning to think this guy was a total fruit loop.

"In the end times of your world, your Scriptures state the Adversary will raise up a person to lead your world through the chaos that will come. He is preparing for that day even as we speak: a superhuman who will help him gain control of this world and have ultimate power.

"Yet things haven't gone quite as planned. The portal allows one to travel great distances instantaneously but does have a side effect: teleportation tends to render the person sterile. Not initially, mind you, but over time with continuous use.

"Our world has had to institute cloning for procreation. Yet, as you know, that leads to genetic breakdown and, without another infusion of fresh genetic material, even that will not be possible in the long run.

"In order to keep the new cult going, Gilgamesh had to keep returning to Babylon to perform as Marduk to keep his subjects loyal. Only Gilgamesh could travel to the new world. The Adversary was, and is, confined to this world. Once the sterility problem was discovered, Gilgamesh had to return less frequently. As you may recall from your history, Summeramat reported her husband as dead but turned him into a sun god and stated her child was created within her by the rays of the sun. Her son, Tammuz, has been worshipped by many cultures since as the sun god. This cult's main purpose was to find new genetic material to create the ultimate superhuman—which your Scriptures refer to as the Antichrist."

Zane held up his hands to form a T. "Whoa. Time out. That's a lot to process!"

"You keep saying 'your world, your Scriptures,'" Alex said. "Where are you from, if not from earth?"

"I come from Adversaria, the world created by Marduk and Gilgamesh."

"And the Antichrist will come from Adversaria?"

Bradley nodded. "That was the original objective, but as I stated, the plan hasn't gone as Marduk intended. Revisions had to be put in place."

"Revisions?" Zane asked.

"That's why I'm here. You two are key to this revision. Marduk needs your DNA to continue his plan."

Zane opened his mouth to say something, but Alex stepped in. "I thought you said you were already getting genetic material for this 'experiment.'"

"Not just any genetic material can be used."

"You need *ours*?" Zane asked.

"Marduk does. Yes. As you know, no two people are genetically identical."

Both nodded.

"Yet every few millennia, although random, almost identical genetic makeups are produced. You two are those random manifestations."

"What?" Zane felt like he was listening to an episode from the old TV show *The Twilight Zone.*

"And who exactly are we almost identical to?" Alex asked.

"Why, Gilgamesh and Summer-amat, of course."

CHAPTER 8

MORE DETAILS REVEALED

Zane wiped his hand across his mouth. Was Bradley telling the truth, or was he truly off the deep end? His story seemed too remarkable. *Could something like this really be true?* He thought back through all that had happened to them within just a few weeks. Alex was almost killed in her car, she was kidnapped twice, and he was kidnapped along with her the second time. Each time, this Bradley fellow appeared. But . . .

"If what you say is true," Zane said, "and Gilgamesh, or Marduk, or whoever, needs our DNA, then why have the other Bradleys been trying to kill us?"

Bradley sighed. "I know this sounds like fantasy, and it's very complicated when you don't understand the history. Two factions have developed. Both have a similar end goal. Theirs is to overthrow Marduk's plan by substituting the Adversary's choice of a superhuman being with another. Then there is our plan: to prevent the Adversary's choice of a superhuman entirely. The first requires your demise. The second the demise of Adversaria."

Zane rubbed his temples. "All this is giving me a headache." He looked back at Bradley. "I'm really trying to understand what you're saying, but just when I think I'm beginning to, you throw in another twist."

"Bottom line," Alex said. "Get to the bottom line. What do you want from us?"

Bradley gave a smile. "That, my dear, is a rather lengthy story. Why don't we discuss that topic in the morning over breakfast? It's late, and we can all think more clearly then."

Zane looked at his watch as Alex looked at hers. Bradley was right. It *was* getting late: already a little past midnight. Both their eyes grew wide at the same time. Dinner with Officer Kinnick had been many hours ago.

Alex gave a slow nod. "Okay. What do you suggest for sleeping arrangements?"

Bradley pointed to a doorway. "You take the bedroom. Zane and I will sleep out here."

As Alex stood, she gave Zane a smile. "Well, goodnight." She stepped into the bedroom and closed the door.

Bradley found blankets and gave one to Zane, gesturing for him to sleep on the sofa.

"What about you?" Zane asked.

"Oh, it's no problem," Bradley said. "I'm used to sleeping on the floor. It'll be like old times." Bradley put one blanket on the floor, slightly away from the sofa, laid down, and placed the other over himself.

Zane had no idea what Bradley was referring to. Yet he found himself suddenly too tired to care. He retired on the sofa and pulled the blanket over him as exhaustion overcame all other thoughts and emotions. His last thought was his hope that when he woke all of this would be just a nightmare he could laugh at and then forget.

* * * * *

Zane, still woozy and in a light state of sleep, had a feeling someone was standing over him. He slowly opened his eyes but didn't move. He saw a shadow on the wall from the moonlight coming through the window. Turning his head slightly, just enough for his eyes to see the man standing over him, he realized the figure was . . . Bradley. "Bradley, what are—"

Before he could complete his sentence, Bradley put something over his nose and mouth. The substance had a sweet smell and taste—too sweet. He struggled but felt himself starting to lose consciousness. He then recognized Bradley being yanked away from him. Zane gasped for air and felt his strength slowly coming back to him. Glancing at the struggle, his eyes widened. *There are two Bradleys! Again!?*

The struggle looked to be an even fight. That stood to reason. If they were both duplicates of each other, their skills would likely be matched. Zane then saw Bradley's gun where he had been sleeping. He rolled off the couch, picked up the weapon, rolled to his feet, and pointed the piece at the two men. But which one to shoot?

The two men saw him standing with the gun raised. One shouted, "Don't just stand there, shoot him!"

The other said, "Yes, shoot him! You're in danger."

Zane pointed the gun at one and then the other. He couldn't tell which was their Bradley. Maybe if they were standing still, he would be able to see the evil gleam in the other Bradley's eyes, but there was no way he could see that under these circumstances.

One Bradley suddenly turned and got the other in a choke hold, but the other pushed at his arm to prevent him from succeeding. The one with the choke hold said, "Shoot him. I won't be able to hold him much longer."

In a flash, Zane saw Alex leap from her room and quickly move forward to crash a pewter ewer on the head of the man holding the other in the choke hold. The man crumbled to the floor. The other breathed in deeply. "Thank you, Dr. Hadad."

The man then turned to Zane with a smile, then held up his hands. "Dr. Archer, it's me."

Zane kept the gun pointed and whipped his head toward Alex. "How did you know which one to hit?"

Alex shook her head. "I didn't. I figured if I got the wrong one, you could shoot the other one."

Zane gripped both hands tightly around the gun to steady his shaking hand and gave a determined look to the Bradley standing in front of him.

This Bradley patted the air. "It's okay, Dr. Archer. It's me. I'm the one who rescued you from the plane."

"Keep your hands up." Zane walked forward and stared into the man's eyes. He didn't see the evil gleam that he had with the Bradley on the plane, so he lowered his gun.

Bradley then lowered his hands. "Thank you, Dr. Archer."

Alex looked from Bradley to Zane. "Are . . . are you sure?"

Zane nodded.

Alex pointed to the Bradley crumbled on the floor. "What about this one?"

Bradley went to the nearest lamp and ripped the cord from it. Next, he turned the other Bradley on his stomach and tied his hands and legs together. Bradley then propped him against the wall. He took his pillowcase and ripped a long strip from it, tying the cloth around the man's head to form a tight gag over the man's mouth.

Zane sat on the sofa, his legs feeling weak and slightly trembling. "Just how many of you are there?"

Bradley gave a weak smile. "Hard to say."

Zane gave him a stare. "Well, that's just . . . peachy."

Alex stood with arms folded. "You have a lot of explaining to do."

Bradley nodded. "Yes. Let's get cleaned up and head downstairs to breakfast. I'll do my best to explain everything. Like I said, it's complicated. But I'll do my best."

Zane nodded toward their prisoner. "What about him? You're just going to leave him here?"

"For now." Bradley went to the desk on the other side of the room and pulled a syringe and vial from a satchel. He pulled a small amount from the vial into the syringe and walked back to the man propped against the wall.

"What are you doing?" Alex asked.

"Making sure he doesn't go anywhere." As he injected the liquid into the man's arm, he added, "This should keep him out quite a while."

Alex shook her head and went to splash some water on her face in the bedroom's bathroom. Zane looked at the clock next to the sofa: *5:37. Not much sleep*, he thought. Yet there was no way he could get any rest now.

Breakfast was probably a good idea, especially not knowing what would be happening later. How many Bradleys would they have to fight off?

Bradley gestured to the bathroom off of the living area. "There's a sink and shaving supplies, if you wish to use them."

Zane nodded and headed into the half-bath. Washing and shaving his face helped him feel human again. He also did a quick sponge bath; he wanted to get the information from Bradley as quickly as possible before the next Bradley showed up.

After being seated in the downstairs restaurant, ordering, and waiting for their breakfast entrées to arrive, Zane looked around the room. The décor had a rustic look with a touch of elegance. The surrounding windows gave a beautiful view of the lake before them. It was then he realized they were back in Sandpoint.

Zane took a sip of water and gestured to Bradley. "Okay, Bradley. Spill everything."

Bradley took a deep breath and let the air out slowly. "Marduk used Gilgamesh's and Summer-amat's lust for power for his own gain."

Zane started to take another sip of water but stopped and asked, "And by Marduk, you mean . . . "

"The Adversary. Yes. When the Adversary possessed Gilgamesh, he became Marduk. So, over time, the Adversary and Marduk become synonymous to many.

"Marduk has always wanted to rule humans. So did Gilgamesh. Yet because Marduk failed prior to the Flood, he was now making contingency plans. He promised Gilgamesh would be part of his plan and be in on his rule of Earth."

Alex scrunched her brow. "And this 'contingency plan' is the other world you talked about?"

Bradley nodded.

"And this was needed why?" she asked.

Before Bradley could answer, the waiter came by with their entrées. They paused the discussion until the waiter left. As they began eating, Bradley continued.

"Sorry," he said to Alex. "What was your question?"

"The contingency plan. Why?"

"Oh, yes." He gave a brief smile. "How long do you think it would take to make a superhuman?"

Alex shrugged. "I don't know. How super is he supposed to be?"

Bradley took a bite of egg and waved his fork as he spoke. "I saw a program the other night." He laughed. "I remember wondering if the idea came from one of Marduk's followers."

Evidently seeing the bewildered look on their faces, Bradley paused. "Sorry. *Superman* was the show. Think of Superman and how long it would take to breed those traits into someone's descendant."

Zane's eyes widened. He looked at Alex, who gave a similar look. "Oh," Zane said. "About forever, I guess."

Bradley nodded. "Exactly. So, what do you need that you don't have that you must have to achieve your goal?"

"Time," Alex said.

Bradley pointed his butter knife at her and then finished buttering his toast. "Precisely. That's why a time dilation field was created."

Alex's eyes remained wide. "A *what*?"

Bradley took a bite of toast and looked at her as if he didn't understand her confusion.

"A time dilation field. Time in Adversaria is about 100 times faster than here on earth." He shrugged. "How else could they send so many clones here?"

Zane, who felt remarkably tired and thus fidgety, gave him an irritated look. "Well, I don't know . . . *Bradley*. Why don't you tell us how things work on Adversaria."

Bradley's face turned a tinge of red. "Apologies, Dr. Archer. I didn't mean to be condescending." He put his knife and fork down. "A time dilation field was created so that many more generations could be established in order to make the necessary changes to produce a superhuman that Marduk could eventually bring back to earth to wow everyone, someone who everyone would follow."

"But . . . " Zane said with upturned eyebrows.

"But it didn't go as planned. The many travels through the portal caused Gilgamesh to become infertile, so cloning techniques were put into place. The followers of Marduk would find people with advanced features: excellent health, special physical qualities, heightened mental abilities, and the like. Those would be sent to Adversaria so their genetic material could be used to try and overcome the defects that inadvertently got transmitted through the cloning techniques."

"So what do they want with me?" Alex asked. "If it's all about Gilgamesh and his traits."

Bradley's eyes widened. "Oh, no, my dear. It's about both of you. Summer-amat continued with the Marduk cult in Gilgamesh's absence and made the religion a strong force, one to be reckoned with. When the One Who Shall Not Be Named stepped in and made everyone speak different languages, Summer-amat went through the portal. Although the ziggurat became abandoned, Marduk ensured the cult continued within the various cultures which developed around each language. That cult continued to find the best and brightest for his use. At least until the portal became damaged."

Zane pushed his plate away and drank more water. "Don't tell me. The portal became buried by an earthquake."

Bradley smiled. "Something like that. The portal is composed of crystals which are able to store data and power. The earthquake caused some of the crystals to become dislocated from the portal itself."

Zane sat up quickly. "So that's how the Solomon chalice myth became about an emerald—a green-looking crystal—and why the chalice of Christ was noted to be crimson in color: due to another piece of crystal being dislodged from the portal."

Bradley nodded. "More than likely. Each piece would have power, but not ultimate power like the portal itself."

Alex leaned in. "And you think the rest of the portal is still intact?"

"I know it is."

Both Zane and Alex gave him a quizzical look.

Bradley looked from one to the other. "How else would I have gotten here?"

CHAPTER 9

HARD DECISIONS

Bradley stood and motioned for the two of them to follow. "Let's go outside and sit near the pool," he said. He gave Zane a smile. "Your women wear far less than they do where I come from."

Zane laughed. "Trying to turn work into a vacation?"

Bradley chuckled. "Something like that."

Zane noticed Alex roll her eyes, but she followed them outside. Bradley found a table with a covering away from the pool's edge, but still in a spot where he had a decent view of the women entering and leaving the water.

Alex restarted the conversation. "So, Bradley, want to pick up where you left off?"

"Travel between Adversaria and Earth occurred for a little over a millennium. Remember, for Adversaria, that was over one-hundred thousand years. But then, one day, the portal could not establish a link. For the next three Earth millennia no link could be established. Then, just a short Earth-time ago, the link was reestablished. That's when the prophecy was discovered to be true."

"Prophecy?" Alex asked.

"Yes." Bradley cleared his throat and looked hard at both, pointing to them. "You two. Ever since the beginning of Adversaria, there was a prophecy that the two of you would arrive. No one knew when, and no one knew how important you would become in Marduk's vision of a superhuman. You two have become the hope of the salvation of his plan. Until now, there was no hope for infusion of fresh DNA."

"So what now?" Zane asked.

"We find Alex's uncle, recover the portal, and you destroy Adversaria." There it was: Alex's requested "bottom line."

Zane's eyes widened. "Oh, is that all?"

Bradley smiled. "Simple plan. Complex execution."

"Just how complex are we talking?" Zane asked.

"When you use the portal, you will have no memory for a short time. Remembrance will come back, but full memory may take a day or so."

"Well, that's a horrible plan," Alex said, leaning in. "What kind of a plan is that? Who knows what all can happen in . . ." She paused. "Did you mean an earth day or an Adversarian day?"

Bradly grinned. "Adversarian day."

Zane breathed a sigh of relief. "Good. Better for a few hours than for a little over three months if we have to arrive on Adversaria." Zane paused. "Is it a 'we'?" He glanced at Alex and then at Bradley. "Or just a 'me'?"

Bradley gave a slight raise of his eyebrows. "Depends. The creation of the superhuman requires both of you. My plan, on the other hand . . ." He nodded toward Zane. "Only requires you."

Zane gave a slight nod. That meant it was possible to keep Alex out of all of this. Maybe.

Bradley got a stern look. "Whatever you do, both of you must not touch the portal at the same time."

"Because?" Zane could not imagine how much worse this scenario could get.

"Because you will both disappear."

Both his and Alex's eyes grew wide.

Bradley held up his hands. "That's just a precautionary statement. It's not like that's a likely scenario. If you know that, then you won't be tempted to do so."

"Disappear to where, though?" Alex still had a worried look on her face.

Bradley shrugged. "I don't know. Such a thing has occurred only a few times. No one saw the disappearing persons again."

Alex looked at Zane and shook her head.

Zane shrugged. "What choice do we have? It's either play along or defend ourselves from more Bradley clones."

Alex seemed to pause in thought. She turned to Bradley. "And why are your clones trying to kill us, but you are not?"

Zane realized he had not considered that question. It was a good question, and it upset him he had not raised it earlier. "Yeah. What gives?"

"Before the portal went silent, one person was sent through who was a follower of the One Who Shall Not Be Named."

Zane cocked his head, squinting his eyes. "You mean Yahweh?"

Bradley almost went hysterical while waving his hands. "Shh! Shh! He'll hear you. Saying his name is a giveaway to our location."

Zane looked at Alex, who just shrugged. He had never heard of such a thing.

"What are you talking about, Bradley? *Who* is going to hear it?"

"Marduk. He knows I'm here. Saying the Name will alert him to where I am."

Alex shook her head. "Your ways are very strange, Bradley."

"To you, perhaps. But this is how we have functioned for millennia." Bradley seemed almost hurt by Alex's words. "Anyway, this man was a worshipper of the One. Slowly, one by one, others on Adversaria became converted. Even when our belief was deemed unsanctioned, hope continued. My master's enemies had clones made of me to do their bidding."

"Why?" Alex asked.

"I think that way, if they get caught because of their deeds here, I would be blamed as only . . . myself is on record here." He smiled. "I've lived here for almost four of your years so I could first find you, then keep an eye on you. Conveniently, you both took positions at the same school."

Zane put his palms on the table and tapped its surface a few times as he bit his lip. He needed to go back over this in his mind. "Okay. Let me see if I have this straight. There are three groups we're dealing with here. One group wants us alive because they need our DNA somehow to repair whatever has gone wrong in producing a superhuman. A second group wants us dead because they want a different superhuman than the one originally planned. Then there is a third group, and it wants us alive so we can somehow destroy Adversaria."

Bradley nodded. "Pretty much. Although the second group can't produce a superhuman. They are working to produce a perfect human. They have the same goal but a different idea of how to achieve it."

"Okay," Alex said. "So, two groups want to rule Earth with either a superhuman or a perfect human. But why do you want to destroy Adversaria?"

Bradley gave a dumbfounded look. "We don't feel this is part of the holy Scripture from the One."

Alex shook her head. "But neither is any of this."

Bradley leaned his head sideways and gave a slight shrug. "I think it is, though subtly. Scripture calls Nimrod a hunter of men. Yet what history implicates is that he was a hunter of *certain* men."

Zane gestured his way. "Because of their desirable genetic traits."

Bradley nodded. "And Scripture implies the tower reached into the heavens. We believe that is referring to the portal. And the verse saying, 'Nothing they plan to do will be impossible for them,' is likely implying the building of the superhuman. Now that belief in the One has spread to Adversaria, we feel our duty is to complete his command that the people should scatter over the Earth—not be sequestered in space. Therefore, Adversaria must be eliminated—and the balance of the universe restored."

"Okay," Zane said. Although, in truth, he found that last part a bit of a stretch. "Even if that is a true interpretation, how do you expect me to do that?"

"And why haven't you done that already?" Alex asked.

"I have no access," Bradley said.

"And you think I do?" Zane replied, eyes wide.

Bradley gave a small sigh. "I'm not sure you really understand who you are. You will be treated as the transcended Gilgamesh because you look exactly like him. You'll have access to everything."

Zane just stared at Bradley as this statement began to register.

Bradley looked from one of them to the other. "Understand? Zane, you are almost identical in looks to the original Gilgamesh. And you, Alexandria, to Summer-amat."

Zane, still a little taken aback, sighed. "So, how am I supposed to destroy their planet?"

"Farzad has developed a perpetual power source that gives the forcefield and all establishments power."

Zane put his hands to his temples and shook his head. "Bradley, are you trying to destroy my mind on purpose?"

Bradley gave him a blank stare. He uttered a quiet, "What?"

"Farzad? Forcefield?"

Bradley gave a weak smile. "Sorry. The city is on an uninhabitable planet. Farzad is the scientist who developed the perpetual power source and oversees the forcefield it generates. This forcefield protects the city and allows life to be sustained there."

Zane squinted as he tried to understand what Bradley was saying. "So you want me to destroy the forcefield?"

Bradley shook his head. "Not just the forcefield. Everything."

"What does that mean?" Alex asked.

"The perpetual power source uses exotic energy which can be very unstable if disrupted. Farzad has this energy under control, but exotic energy can be made to go critical."

"Creating an explosion?" Alex asked.

"Not exactly. Annihilation occurs without a true explosion." He shrugged. "Existence to nonexistence."

"And what about Zane?" Alex asked. "He just ceases to exist?"

Bradley became quiet for a few seconds. "We're not entirely sure. Since he is not part of that world, I think the universe would go back to a natural state. And he would wind up back here. But . . . "

Both Zane and Alex looked at him with raised eyebrows.

Noticing their stare, Bradley gave a defensive shrug. "This has never been done before, and the physics is quite technical—beyond my understanding. I just don't know for sure, but it makes sense he would not be annihilated, and all would go back to normal."

"And you surmise that . . . how?" Alex asked.

"Because Adversaria is not a natural state of the universe and was not created by the One Who Shall Not Be Named—but by Marduk." He held up his hands. "I know. It's not a lot to go on, but some things are left to faith."

"Or fate," Zane replied.

Bradley gave a small smile. "I choose faith."

Bradley's countenance suddenly tensed.

"What is it?" both Zane and Alex asked almost simultaneously.

"I just saw another of my doppelgangers. We need to go."

CHAPTER 10

FINDING THE PORTAL

After Bradley hailed a taxi, Zane realized the three of them were headed to the airport.

"Bradley, Dr. Latham is going to wonder where we are," Zane said during the ride. "We can't just leave here without any kind of cover story."

"Plus," Alex added, "we have classes to teach. Dr. Latham is not going to allow us to shirk our responsibilities."

Bradley looked at his watch and smiled. "I think enough time has passed. Check your e-mails. I think Dr. Latham has a mission for each of you."

Both gave Bradley an I-don't-believe-you look, but each took out their phones and checked their e-mail. Zane read his and looked at Alex in disbelief. She displayed the same look back at him.

Zane turned to Bradley. "How did you accomplish *that*?"

"You actually got him to request us to go to the Middle East during the middle of a semester?" Alex asked, her eyes still wide.

Bradley smiled. "Well, when he became aware just how valuable the find of the Sumerian Grail would be for the school, he suddenly felt your classes could be taught by someone else."

And I'm sure he also got someone who would give his son a solid A, Zane thought. Thankfully, that was one serious headache now avoided. Yet, just as quickly, he realized he was going from constantly defending his grading to Andrew to now trying to figure out how to not annihilate himself. Not quite a fair trade.

"There's one more thing I should tell you."

Zane looked at Bradley, eyes wide once more. "What now?"

"Be aware when you arrive in Adversaria."

Confused once more, Zane narrowed his eyes. "What do you mean by that?"

"Just remember, the same three groups looking for you here are there as well. So choose your friends well—and be wary of everyone."

Zane nodded. "Good point." But he wasn't aware how he would pull any of this off. Actually, believing what Bradley said as truth—or any part of it, for that matter—proved difficult.

Once the taxi arrived at the airport, Bradley instructed the driver to a private airfield. Zane and Alex looked at each other in amazement.

Alex gave Bradley a stare. "Just who *are* you? You've been here less than four years and have all this clout?"

Bradley gave a smile. "The Marduk cult is still operational; they don't really know my true agenda—yet. That gives me a window of opportunity with their connections."

The taxi stopped at one of the jets on the tarmac. As they boarded, Zane had a déjà vu moment. The interior looked exactly like the jet Bradley had teleported them out of the day before. He was just glad he could now sit without being restrained. Zane felt even better when Alex took a seat next to him.

"Too bad," Zane said, "you can't teleport us to wherever we're going."

Bradley nodded. "Indeed. But, unfortunately, the device only allowed that to happen twice."

"Where exactly *are* we going?" Alex asked.

"To find your uncle."

Alex cocked her head. "But if you arrived through the portal, don't you know where it is?"

"When I came through, no one was around, but I couldn't take the portal with me and escape unnoticed at the same time. Apparently, your uncle found the device and either moved the artifact, or he is now kidnapped by our opposition." He shrugged. "However, I did plant a tracker on the portal, so hopefully, when we get close, we'll be able to pinpoint its location."

Zane nodded. "Great. Maybe an element of surprise will be just the advantage we need."

Bradley chuckled. "I think our arrival will be a surprise for everyone."

All three settled in for a long ride. After eating from pre-prepared meals from an onboard refrigerator, briefly talking, and getting some rest, Bradley shook each of them awake. He went to the back and pulled out parachutes, handing one to both Zane and Alex.

"What's this?" Alex asked.

"Parachutes, of course. When we land, the opposition could have Iraqi military waiting for us." Bradley grinned. "We don't want to give them the satisfaction." He looked at Zane. "An element of surprise, as you mentioned."

Alex's eyes grew large. "I hardly think that was what he meant." She glanced at Zane, who just shook his head. *This just gets more and more complicated*, he thought.

"Come, Dr. Hadad. I know you have parachuted before."

"Well," Alex said with frustration. "Just because I can doesn't mean I like to."

"Necessary, though," Bradley said with a quick forced smile.

"And how do you know that I can parachute?" Zane asked.

"Not much is private these days," Bradley said. "Don't you agree? There is record of you taking lessons."

"Lessons does not mean proficiency."

Bradley just smiled. "Follow Alex's lead."

Alex stood, shook her head, and began to don her parachute. "Fine" was all she said.

Bradley handed each of them something that looked like a wristwatch. The device didn't display the time, but instead showed a GPS overlay with a blinking dot.

Alex's eyes widened. "That's the marked artifact?"

Bradley nodded. "Should be."

"So, what's the plan?" Zane asked.

Bradley held up his wrist so the two of them could see. "We'll land just east of the ruins. We'll then backtrack and overthrow the contingent with the portal."

"And your confident my uncle is with those with the portal?" Alex asked.

Bradley bobbed his head back and forth. "Pretty confident. His last dig site was near the portal where I exited. I would assume he found the artifact but was likely overpowered before he could tell anyone."

Alex nodded. Zane could see worry on her face.

Bradley checked the attachments of their chutes and led them to the door of the jet.

Alex talked into Zane's ear. "I'm not sure if I'm glad my dad made me learn how to do this or not."

Zane smiled. "You said he wanted you to be prepared for anything."

She chuckled. "I'm not sure this was in his idea of possibilities." She turned as Bradley opened the door.

"Ready?" Bradley asked.

Alex nodded. She stepped to the door, held both sides of the opening, and jumped.

Zane did the same as Alex had done just moments after her jump. He was struck by the sky during his descent. The horizon indicated the day was near dusk, yet that reality, he thought, also should give them just enough time to land and regroup before darkness fell. Good timing, he thought to himself. That should help them go unnoticed. He also knew they could not afford to get caught. How would he explain to anyone how an American civilian wound up in Iraqi territory?

Looking down, Zane saw Alex's parachute open. He pulled his ripcord only minutes after she did. Right before he did so, he looked up and saw Bradley not far above him. Zane was glad they were following so close to one another. That should make regrouping easier.

As they descended, Alex's ability to maneuver her position with her chute impressed him. Apparently, her father's instructions were better ingrained in her brain than she let on. He would never guess many years had passed since she had done anything like this. He did his best to follow her moves.

In a short time, they were all on the desert surface. Zane quickly gathered up his chute and stuffed the fabric back into the chute pack before running to where Alex stood doing the same. Bradley arrived only moments later. They took the packs with them and hid them in some of the ruins and then traveled toward the blinking dot indicated on their wrists—moving as stealthily as they could.

After several minutes of zigging and zagging and climbing over and through rocks and ruins, Alex said, "We're practically *over* the dot. Where is it?"

Bradley leaned in close. "I think the portal should be subterranean. Let's see if we can find an opening that will lead us downward."

After several more minutes, Zane found a small opening, although he initially considered the finding inconsequential. He reluctantly decided to try crawling into the opening, which was barely wider than his shoulders. Shortly after, he poked his head back out of the opening and waved to Alex and Bradley. "This way. Hurry!"

Both came running over through the darkness, which was now full; only a small crescent of moonlight provided ambient light. All three pulled out their flashlights and descended what were clearly manmade steps. These led into an opening, which felt rather large in size, but there were many columns that had collapsed and lay in large pieces on the floor. As Zane scanned this large area, he saw some of the columns still intact and standing. These seemed to be the only structures in this subterranean location that kept it from collapsing onto itself.

"Let's hurry," Zane said as he continued scanning the area with his flashlight. "This place looks pretty unstable to me."

Both Alex and Bradley nodded. Zane pointed toward another opening, and the three of them proceeded in that direction. Apparently, someone had set up camp in this smaller room some time in the past. A cot lay in the corner, but its bedding looked ragged and covered in dust. As Zane walked the perimeter, the blinking dot on his wrist began to blink faster.

"Over here!" Zane whispered loudly.

Alex and Bradley hurried over. "What did you find?" Alex asked. She looked down to see the dot on her wrist blinking very fast as well. "Oh, the portal must be here!"

They each looked around, but no one saw anything. "The artifact *must* be here," Zane said as he scanned the area and turned his flashlight right and left. As he did so, he saw something metal give off a glint as the light hit it. He directed the light where the glint had appeared and then let out a big sigh.

Alex turned to him. "What is it?"

Zane held up a small round metal chip and looked at Bradley. "Here's your tracker. So much for your clever plan to track the portal."

Bradley stood there shaking his head. "I can't believe they found it. I wonder where they've taken it."

"What do we do now?" Alex asked. "I can't believe we came this far for nothing." She sat heavily on an overturned stone column. "And where is my uncle?"

Zane suddenly had an uneasy feeling. "Let's keep our antennas up. I'm not getting a good feeling about this."

"Well, the only out is back the way we came," Bradley said, pointing.

They each filed out, retracing their steps. Once they were back in the night air, they took deep breaths of fresh air. This made Zane realize how much stale air he had been breathing below.

They turned to head back to where they had left their chute packs, then stopped short. Five rifles or handguns were pointed their way. A Bradley doppelganger was staring at them with a strange grin.

"So happy you could join us," this Bradley said. "Come have some tea."

CHAPTER 11

TEA TIME

The gunmen took them to a dig on the far west side of the ruins. Zane felt almost in awe as they traversed the remnants of what was supposedly the ancient city of Babylon. He had always wanted to visit here—just not in this manner, of course. Bradley, Alex, and Zane were led to a large tent toward the outskirts of a dig that was underway. Once they entered, Alex ran to a man sitting with his hands tied behind his back. Dried blood was visible on the side of his face and going up into his hairline. Fresh blood ran from the corner of his lip.

"Uncle, are you okay?"

The man's face lit up when he saw Alex, but his countenance then turned somber. "Alexandria, I'm so sorry I got you involved in this. I didn't know this artifact would prove so . . . dangerous."

Alex kissed her uncle on his forehead and knelt beside him. "It's okay. This isn't your fault. Apparently, I'm involved no matter what. I fear it is I who has gotten you involved. I'm sorry."

The man gave an extremely confused look. He started to speak, but his mouth fell open instead, and his eyes went wide as he apparently noticed the two Bradleys. "What . . . what's going on here?"

The evil Bradley displayed a grin. "Come now, Arvan. It's tea time, of course. I've brought your darling niece to you to celebrate with us." He gave a nod to one of the men in the tent, who gave a slight bow and exited.

The evil Bradley gestured toward the cushions on the floor. "Please. Everyone take a seat." He gestured to another man. "Untie Arvan. I'm sure he's learned his lesson by now. Right, Arvan?"

After being untied, the man said nothing, but rubbed his wrists, which were quite red, likely from struggling to free himself. He gave a brief smile to Alex to let her know he was okay, then turned somber.

The man who stepped from the tent earlier arrived with a tray containing several clear cups of a reddish liquid. Zane assumed this was the tea the evil Bradley had announced. He had expected "tea time" to be a euphemism for something more sinister, but was glad drinking tea had, apparently, become a real event among this group. The tea had a slightly sweet but musky aroma Zane could not at first identify. Once he took a sip, he recognized the taste of saffron immediately. While not his favorite, the tea didn't taste bad either.

There were several minutes of silence. Everyone sipped their tea and looked at each other with expectation . . . and dread—except for the evil Bradley, who maintained a constant grin. Soon, this Bradley gave his cup back to the man who had served them. "There, wasn't that pleasant?" he asked the other four.

No one said anything; each handed their cup back to the server as he came around to each person.

"So, here is how things will play out," the evil Bradley continued. "In the morning, Arvan will tell us where he hid the portal. If he doesn't, I will kill Dr. Hadad."

A gasp escaped the lips of all four. Arvan and Alex locked eyes, which were moistening, but tears did not come. Zane was stunned at how nonchalant this man was with his delivery of such news.

The Bradley who had become their friend gave a confused look. "I thought you already had the artifact. You have her uncle, after all. Didn't he find the portal?"

The evil Bradley gave an annoyed look at Arvan and then turned to his doppelganger. "Yes, he did, but then he hid the device again." He cocked his head and looked at Arvan with contempt. "And apparently placed it where no one else can teleport through."

Zane thought this interesting. Arvan apparently understood the purpose of the portal. Zane wasn't sure if that would have been true before or after Arvan discovered the artifact. Either way, this was a good thing—for the moment. Until morning, at least.

Alex blurted out, "Why should he tell you? You're going to kill me either way. Right?"

The evil Bradley looked at her calmly and replied, again nonchalantly, "Oh, our original intent was to eliminate you. Then none would be the wiser and our plan could continue unabated. Yet . . . " He gave an irritated glance at the other Bradley. "Some have interfered and made that now more complicated. A clean disappearance may prove more beneficial at this point." He shrugged. "Your uncle, however, really holds that choice, and your fate, in his hands at present."

Bradley turned to the evil Bradley. "My lord did not send you. So who did?"

"And which 'lord' are you referring to?" Evil Bradley raised his eyebrows. "You seem to give lip service to one yet serve the other."

Zane assumed he was referring to Bradley being a follower of Yahweh but still appearing to follow Gilgamesh—or whoever Gilgamesh was at this point in their history.

Bradley forced a smile. "Either way, they both want Dr. Hadad alive. Yet you seem to not care if she lives or dies."

Evil Bradley glanced at Alex and then turned to Bradley. "Well, she wasn't important to our plans. Yet . . . " He glanced at Alex again. "I can see now that she may prove useful in our genetic plans." He turned to Zane. "Perhaps both of them." He shrugged and looked at Arvan. "But that decision is now out of my hands."

Evil Bradley stood. "That's enough discussion for tonight. When the sun's rays grace this once beautiful city, decisions will be made."

He left, as did the others of his entourage.

Zane noticed several of the men remained just outside the tent opening. As the firelight outside periodically displayed silhouettes along the tent fabric, Zane corrected himself. Guards were strategically placed around the tent. So much for his thought of trying to escape from the rear of the tent.

Alex and Arvan hugged. "Uncle, I'm so sorry about all of this."

Arvan shook his head. "It's not your fault, Alexandria." He looked down and then back at her. "I rushed things and sought a quick expedition. I hired people I really didn't know to help me on my quest for the grail."

"So what happened?"

"We found a secret subterranean chamber. The room must have been a temple of some sort long ago, but the space was steadily becoming unstable. Yet, there it lay." He smiled. "The artifact looked so beautiful."

Zane leaned in. "What did the portal look like?"

Arvan's eyes widened, almost twinkling. "Magnificent. Its surface is composed almost entirely of crystals, all different colors, roughly in the shape of a square. The device looks so delicate, yet evidently isn't as the artifact has survived all these years.

"Jacques, the one you call Bradley—his accent seemed so different that I didn't question that he wasn't French—somehow knew to immediately look for a tracker on the artifact. He found and removed the hidden device and left the tracker in the ancient temple."

Zane nodded. "Yeah, that's what we found."

"Something must have happened after that," Alex said.

Arvan nodded. "I overheard Jacques talking to some of the others. I didn't know what was going on, but I could tell their intentions weren't good. One night while all of them were sleeping, I moved the artifact. As you can see, Jacques is now very upset about that. I tried to understand what they wanted and even stated I was willing to share the find with them, but he wasn't satisfied."

Arvan looked at Bradley. "So, who are these people?"

"That's a long story," Bradley replied. "At this point, their identity doesn't matter. For all our safety, we need to get out of here."

"How?" Arvan looked around. "There are guards all around our tent." He looked at Alex. His countenance softened and his eyes grew wet again. "I'm going to tell them where I hid the artifact."

"But . . . uncle." Alex's eyes were also watering. "They may kill us no matter what we do."

Arvan kept his voice low. "I know. But I can't take the chance. No artifact is worth your life."

Zane knew they were both right. He felt so helpless, but didn't know what to do.

"We should all at least try to get some rest," he said. "Not sure if that's even possible, but we should try."

They all nodded, mostly from resignation that there was nothing they could do at the moment. Alex laid next to her uncle. Zane heard them whispering but couldn't overhear what they were saying. She was at least getting some time with her uncle before whatever would happen in the morning. For that Zane was grateful, and the thought lingered as he closed his eyes . . . and exhaustion overtook him.

CHAPTER 12

GOING THROUGH THE PORTAL

Zane woke with a pain in his side. His eyes jerked open and he saw evil Bradley—or Jacques—standing over him.

"So glad you could sleep when your girlfriend's life is hanging in the balance."

Zane sat up feeling mad at being kicked awake and embarrassed he had slept so hard without waking at the same time as the others. He glanced at Alex, but he saw only concern in her eyes. She still looked exhausted—just as he had felt last night. This only added to the anxiety he felt about falling asleep when she apparently had not. He scrambled to his feet and walked over to where the others were standing. She quickly squeezed his hand and let go.

Jacques kept the wicked grin plastered on his face. "So, Arvan, everyone's fate is in your hands." The others around them raised their rifles and aimed at all four of them. "What is your pleasure?"

"You're a monster," Arvan said, disgust in his voice.

"Sorry, but your life is inconsequential compared to what is at stake." He shrugged. "We can do this the hard way or the easy way. The fate of all is up to you."

Arvan, quiet for a few seconds, caused the guards to stiffen in their stance. Arvan raised his hands. "Okay. Okay. I will tell you."

The guards relaxed their stances but kept their rifles pointed.

Arvan sighed and looked at Alex, who put her hand on his shoulder and gave a slight squeeze. He turned to Jacques. "It's in another structure on the western side of the ruins."

Jacques turned sideways slightly and, with an overexaggerated grin, gestured with an arm toward the tent door. "Please, by all means, lead the way."

Arvan led as Alex followed. Zane followed her with Bradley behind him. Jacques and the guards, their guns still raised, followed in the rear. Zane kept trying to think of what they could do to turn the tide in their favor, but he came up blank. He wasn't sure if there was a way to come out of this alive.

They passed the hidden opening they had entered the previous day and went about the length of a football field beyond it when Arvan stopped.

Jacques approached. "Where? I don't see anything."

In a condescending tone, Arvan replied, "Well, that's the point, isn't it?"

Jacques pushed a pistol into Arvan's side. "Don't get smart with me, Arvan."

Arvan gave Jacques a hateful look and pointed to a slab of stone leaning against an overturned column. Jacques walked over and gave Arvan a double take. "I'm impressed, Arvan. No one would even consider there is an opening under here." He waved his gun. "By all means, you go first."

Arvan sighed and shook his head. Jacques handed Arvan a flashlight. They each followed behind Arvan. Two guards followed in the rear with lanterns that helped provide additional light. The rest of the guards remained aboveground. Zane realized the chamber they entered looked almost identical to the one they entered yesterday; it had the same stale air as well. Although not smelling bad, the air here didn't smell good, either, but had an aroma similar to that of a musty old house, one which had been shut up for years. Zane wondered if this wasn't part of the same temple they had entered yesterday, just that the area had become divided due to a cave-in years ago.

Arvan led them through a small antechamber into a room that may, at one time, have been regal. There were hints of pigments, long faded, on some walls, although most of the walls were devoid of all pigment and plaster. There on a stone pillar sat the portal, the Sumerian Grail, each side almost square in shape and looking somewhat like an elaborate mirror, though cubical in shape, with two sides open so one could peer through the cube. It seemed to have been placed inside a clear glass cube, evidently to keep it from functioning. Zane was impressed with its beauty. Even from the light of the lanterns, the crystalline colors shone brightly as the light reflected from and refracted through the structure. There were hues of red, green, white, blue, cyan, purple, and even colorless crystals ranging from exceedingly small to almost hand size, in various shapes, with some thin and others rather thick. From looking at the artifact, the crystals seemed to focus their direction inward on one side and outward from the other. Maybe this was how the portal functioned, as a doorway of sorts. Zane couldn't see, though, what would make the device activate.

"It's beautiful," Alex said with a tone of awe. "How does the portal work?"

"This device is a creation of Marduk's," Jacques said. "Only those born of royal blood can activate the crystals."

Alex's eyes widened. "You are *all* of royal descent?"

"Some of us," Jacques said.

"Hmmph," escaped from Bradley. "Depends on what you mean by 'born.'"

Zane assumed Bradley was referring to himself as a person born naturally and of Jacques, who was cloned from his DNA. Apparently, no strong connection existed between the two even though they were likely identical in terms of DNA.

"You can feel superior if you wish," Jacques said as he pushed him over to where Arvan stood. "But my actions are justified."

"Again, depends upon what you mean by 'justified,' doesn't it?"

"Go ahead. Feel superior and more noble. See where that will get you."

Bradley gave him a hard look. "What now, Jacques? You have what you wanted, so what will you do with us?"

Zane found himself wondering the same thing. Would Jacques let them go now that he had the grail? He noticed Arvan and Bradley looking at each other. They seemed to be making some kind of connection. He assumed they were thinking it was three against three. Zane wasn't sure when they would make their move. He kept looking at them to see what they would do.

Jacques looked down as if in thought, his wicked smile now gone. He looked contemplative. Suddenly he looked up.

"Kill them," he said.

The two guards raised their guns and, at that moment, Arvan rushed one and Bradley the other. This took Jacques by surprise, and before he could raise his pistol, Zane rushed him and threw a punch which caused Jacques to lurch backward. One of the guards overpowered Arvan. Bradley knocked out his guard and then lunged for the other, pulling him off Arvan and onto his back. The guard then pushed Bradley off him forcefully with his feet, and this threw Bradley backward into the column holding the grail. The top of the column crumbled as its capital hit the side of the chamber with much force . . .

The glass surrounding the cube shattered and the grail tilted forward and teetered from the column where it had been sitting. Everyone seemed to freeze upon seeing the grail begin its fall. Both Zane and Alex lunged forward, almost simultaneously, to catch the device before it hit the floor. Zane heard Bradley yell "No!"—then felt excruciating pain when his hands touched the grail. One of his last recognitions was that Alex seemed to grab it at the same time he did.

He felt weightless and lost consciousness.

CHAPTER 13

MEMORY LOSS

Zane awoke feeling a tingling sensation throughout his body. Yet with each sensation came pain that caused him to wince constantly. *What on earth happened*, he wondered. He stood and swung his arms and kicked his legs trying to get them back to a normal feeling. As he looked around, he saw some type of an ornate crystalline cubical structure, almost like a mirror, atop a wide pedestal. The room, otherwise vacant, looked beautifully decorated with brilliant colors and pictographs showing some type of tower with a bright light coming from its top tier. Writing—almost hieroglyphic-like, but definitely not Egyptian—which he could not decipher, accompanied the wall mural.

He tried to remember how he got here, but he had no clue. His memory contained nothing before this moment. He stopped and thought hard about himself, but nothing came to him. Not even a name. *What's going on?*

He walked out of the room and down a hallway. After a distance, he heard footsteps, so he ducked into the next available room which, thankfully, was empty. Parading by were men dressed only in loincloths. They looked filthy with what looked like reddish-colored dust over their torsos, and this dust covered their once white loincloths as well. Behind them were other men holding some type of spear. While they also wore only loincloths, these men looked clean and neat compared to the other men in front of them.

So there are slaves here, Zane thought. He looked down at his clothes. His clothing looked nothing like those of the people he had just seen. When he turned, he saw slits in the wall that allowed light to enter the room. When he looked out, he gasped. Birds were flying at eye level. He was in some type of tower!

He looked out again and tried to peer downward. In the distance, he could see a few trees, or what he thought were trees, surrounded by other buildings. Sheer desert was still farther out. But the trees and other buildings looked no higher than his finger. *What kind of place is this?*

Zane attempted to head down the hallway again, but he had to duck into another side room. The pungent smell of the room hit him immediately. He jerked around and looked in horror as he saw bodies stacked on top of each other. They looked exactly like the men he had seen previously. Apparently, slaves were considered disposable labor. Zane once again looked at his clothes and those on these slaves. To blend in better, he knew, he had to change into something. But when he went over to remove some of the slaves' clothing, the smell became so overwhelming and repulsive he couldn't make himself follow through. *Well, perhaps it's best,* he thought. Being identified as a slave was likely not the best solution to his clothes problem.

He heard more footsteps approaching. These were softer, however, than those he heard from the slaves and soldiers. As he peered out, he saw several men—presumably men—dressed in hooded cloaks. *Priests*, he assumed.

The last priest walked somewhat farther behind the others. Zane could see no one behind this one. As this last priest passed, he jumped out, grabbed the man, and placed his hand over his mouth, pulling him into the room with him. He placed a choke hold on the man just long enough for the priest to pass out. As the man fell to the floor, Zane checked for a pulse and found one, although it seemed weak. He breathed a sigh of relief. Killing the guy wasn't part of his plan, but he didn't want to get discovered either.

He quickly stripped the man and put his body with the dead slaves. He wasn't sure what type of turmoil this would cause later, but he hoped he would be long gone by that time. He quickly stripped himself and donned the priest's garments, placing the clothes he had just removed into a large urn he found in the corner of the room.

Zane checked the hallway. No one in sight. He quickly and quietly ran its length to catch up with the other priests and fell in step with them. The garment's deep hood blocked anyone from seeing his face. He smiled. This was a much better option than trying to don slave clothes. He noticed another opening, which they were approaching, that seemed to go outside as the archway looked brightly lit. All he had to do was slow down once he neared the archway and quickly dodge through the opening with no one the wiser.

Yet before he could get there, the entire file of priests began to slow and then stop. Each stepped to the side and genuflected as someone approached. Zane wasn't sure what was happening but mimicked the same motions he saw from the others.

Since he had the hood over his head and was looking down, he couldn't see who had approached. Yet as this person walked by, he noticed these were the legs of a woman. He tried to calm his breathing from his quick trot; he didn't want to draw attention to himself. The woman walked by slowly, moments feeling like eternity. When the priest next to him stood, he did the same. No one moved. He wasn't sure why.

To his surprise, the woman returned and stopped in front of him. She said something, but her words were incomprehensible. She repeated herself, now sounding irritated. He didn't know what to do. Should he remove his hood and look at her, or would that be considered rude? The priest next to him did nothing, so he did nothing as well.

He realized someone else with a hood was standing in front of him. Zane's hood made visibility difficult to see what was going on or who stood there. He heard this hooded one speak, and this voice was masculine. Yet the words sounded similar to what the woman had said.

Zane wasn't sure if this man was talking to him or the woman, but he had a strong suspicion the man's words were directed his way. He felt the man's hand on his head, grabbing the back of his hood. Zane tensed, but the woman then said something in a curt tone. The man stopped and pulled his hand back. Zane felt the man grab his arm instead and pull him down the hallway. He had no idea what had been said or where he was going. For all he knew, he was a lamb being led to slaughter.

The priest dragged Zane into another room. Although his peripheral vision was blocked by the hood, he could tell this room was ornately decorated. A throne, or what he assumed to be a throne, stood positioned near the back wall, and it was flanked by two guards dressed similar to the others he had seen behind the slave procession earlier.

The woman he had heard previously said something in a commanding tone. As far as he could tell, everyone left the room in obedience to whatever command she had given. Yet, in a matter of minutes, he saw another figure approach. While this one also wore a loincloth, the garment was much more ornately decorated, as were his neck and forearm, with pieces of jewelry. The woman bowed slightly as he approached. *Royalty,* Zane guessed to himself.

He heard the man and woman converse briefly, but Zane had no idea what they were saying. Why didn't he understand them? Was he not from here? He thought back to the clothes he wore before. No, he was definitely from somewhere else. *Where?*

The man said something Zane knew was directed toward him, but he did not understand nor know how to respond. The man repeated his request—his tone sounded like a question, but again, Zane remained quiet. He felt his hood jerked from his head.

All three of them gasped.

The man and woman took a step backward, surprise on their faces. Zane's eyes widened. It was as if he was looking into a mirror. Although this man's hairstyle was quite different from his own, the man had his facial features . . . and the woman looked extremely familiar. He just couldn't place who she looked like . . . But he knew, instinctively, that this woman was someone he should know very well.

Before any of them could say anything, the man suddenly went stiff. His arms now went straight and jutted slightly away from his body, and his head leaned back as his eyes rolled backward, with only the whites showing. The man's body shook slightly, then became relaxed. He righted his stance and looked at Zane, but his eyes were now different. They seemed to burn themselves into Zane.

The woman genuflected. "Marduk."

That one name Zane understood. The rest of her words, though, remained unintelligible.

The man cocked his head and spoke. Zane remained quiet and didn't respond. He really had no idea how to respond or what was going on. *Why does this man look like me?*

The man placed his hand on Zane's head, his palm resting on his forehead. Zane felt heat rush through him. The man smiled, but his lips formed a smile of achievement, not of greeting. His expression looked almost evil.

"Now you can understand us," the man said. "Who are you?"

Zane, surprised he could now understand, fumbled over his words. "I . . . I don't know—don't remember. I have no memory prior to my arrival."

"Arrival?" The man looked from him to the woman.

She shook her head as if indicating she knew nothing of what this meant. "He was with the priests in the hallway. Yet his aura was different from the others," the woman said. "His was . . . like yours, my lord."

The man's gaze shot to Zane. "Where did you arrive?"

Zane shrugged. "In the room with the crystalline structure."

The woman gasped. "My lord! Your prophecy."

The man nodded. "Yes, I was thinking the same." He began to pace. "It seems my plan on Adversaria has not gone as planned." He looked at Zane and smiled. "Yet I think we can use him to get back on track."

The name Adversaria sounded familiar to Zane, but he couldn't place where he had heard it before.

"Using his life-giving seed," the woman replied.

Marduk nodded. "Gilgamesh tells me they have the ability now to handle such."

Gilgamesh. Zane knew that name as an ancient Mesopotamian king whom the Bible called Nimrod. *How do I know that?* Yet, he didn't have time to dwell on that question since what the woman said now hit him. *Life-giving seed? What? They want a sperm donation?* Did they know about such things in ancient Mesopotamia? Not according to what he knew. He stopped himself. *What do I know? How do I know about this culture?*

Marduk and the woman stepped away from him and talked in whispers. Zane could hear what they said, however, if he focused on them. It seemed as though he was standing in the right spot in the room for the acoustics to work in his favor.

"Befriend him. See if you can find out what he knows. His memory loss is probably temporary, if he is the one of prophecy."

The woman nodded. "Yes, my lord."

Marduk placed his hand on her upper arm and waited for her gaze to match his. "Summer-amat, Gilgamesh may need to go with him."

Her eyes widened. "Understood. I have plans for how to seal both he and I into the worship you have established."

Zane had to strain and concentrate intensely to hear and understand what they said. Although he heard the words, he really didn't understand what they were talking about.

Marduk smiled. "Good. We don't have much time. I feel the One Who Shall Not Be Named will rise against us soon. We must have the worship engrained . . . "

Zane saw Marduk look directly at him, but it was also more like his gaze went *through* him. He turned to look behind him but saw no one.

Marduk continued to speak to Summer-amat, but his gaze continued in Zane's direction. " . . . in our subjects . . . before . . . that happens."

Suddenly, Marduk went weak and nearly collapsed to the floor. Summer-amat grabbed his arm and steadied him.

* * * * *

Mikael arrived with Raphael just as Marduk was speaking with Summer-amat. After seeing them, Lucifer stepped out of Gilgamesh's body—causing it to go weak.

"Well," Lucifer said, a tinge of anger in his voice. "The Almighty's . . . *reporters* . . . have come back."

"Apparently, none too soon," Mikael replied.

"And when did you start possessing humans?" Raphael asked. "Where is your respect for the Creator's subjects?"

Lucifer all but rolled his eyes. "Oh, please, Raphael. Catch up. These are *my* subjects and I rule them how *I* see fit."

"Manipulate, you mean," Raphael said curtly.

Lucifer gave him a hard stare and then turned to Mikael, ignoring Raphael completely, and forcing a smile. "And what do I owe the pleasure of such an . . . unexpected . . . visit?"

"We told you last time we would be visiting sometime soon," Mikael said.

Lucifer continued his forced smile. "Yes. Yes, you did." He held his arms wide. "And here you are." He leaned toward them. "Not to be rude, but I'm a little busy." He pointed at them. "Want to write your little report quickly and be on your way?" He glanced back at Gilgamesh and then to Mikael. "See what you did? You made him almost faint."

* * * * *

"Gilgamesh, my love," Summer-amat said. "Are you all right?"

Gilgamesh put his hand to the side of his head and nodded. "I will be in a few minutes." He gave a weak smile. "Marduk seems to sap my strength when he leaves me."

"Here." She led him to the throne and had him sit. "You rest, and I'll carry out Marduk's wishes."

Gilgamesh nodded. They smiled at each other and placed their foreheads together for a second or two.

Summer-amat turned, and with a commanding voice said, "Summon Ekmenetet."

A guard outside the entrance suddenly appeared and bowed. "Yes, my queen."

Ekmenetet. Zane knew he should know *that* name as well. But how? From where? He just got here, didn't he?

In a few minutes, a man arrived, also dressed in a loincloth, but looking very neat at the same time. He also wore jewelry, but much simpler in design than that worn by Gilgamesh.

"Take this man to get cleaned, eat, and rest," Summer-amat said. "Present him back to me in the morning."

Ekmenetet bowed. "Yes, my queen." When he looked at Zane his eyes widened, but he did not say anything, instead simply motioned for Zane to follow. As they left the room, two guards followed at a distance.

* * * * *

Lucifer looked at Mikael and then at Raphael. "All finished?"

Raphael gave a sarcastic chuckle. "Hardly. What do you think you are trying to accomplish off world anyway?"

"Try and keep up," Lucifer said, irritation in his voice.

"Well, 'something wonderful'—as you said when we first visited this tower—doesn't really cover the explanation department." Raphael cocked his head. "Plus, how are you able to do anything off world when you are confined to this world?"

This time it was Lucifer's turn to laugh sarcastically. "Ingenuity." He squinted. "Something you obviously wouldn't know anything about."

Mikael shook his head. "Lucifer, you astound me. Your pride will be your downfall."

Lucifer turned to Mikael with disdain. "Oh, spare me, Mikael. You can call it whatever you want." He stood straighter. "But my creation will be . . . magnificent." He pointed between the two of them. "Obviously, I can't make you leave, so stay or leave—I don't care—but I have to go." He forced a smile once more. "Too much to do, you know."

With that, Lucifer disappeared.

Mikael sighed. "He seems to get cockier with time. It's unbelievable."

"Cocky?" Raphael replied. "Insufferable is more like it." He paused, rubbed the back of his neck, and added, raising his eyebrows, "What do you want to do?"

Mikael pointed. "Let's follow Ekmenetet and see what we can find out."

* * * * *

Zane followed Ekmenetet down the hallway through an archway, then down two flights of stairs. As they passed through another archway into another hallway, a convoy of slaves approached. These individuals stepped to the side and bowed as they passed. This made Zane realize a clear hierarchy existed in this place. Evidently even certain servants had a definite degree of status.

Ekmenetet led Zane to a small room. As Zane entered, he saw Ekmenetet say something to one of the guards, who immediately nodded and left. The other guard stood at attention next to the door, the only way out of the room.

Ekmenetet motioned toward a cushion at a low table. Zane sat, not knowing what was going on. As he watched, two burly looking men brought in a large tub, and several women began filling the container with water. Zane felt a little humbled by this act; he knew getting this much water to this level required the hard work of a lot of people.

Next, other women and men brought in several bowls of food items: fruit, small cakes, or perhaps tarts, a flask of water, and a flask of wine. Ekmenetet gestured for Zane to eat as he filled a glass with wine for him to drink. Zane wasn't sure what the cakes were made from, but they did taste good. Hungry, he decided not to ask about the filling; that might spoil his appetite. The wine tasted good as well, although it was a little watered down.

Ekmenetet stood silently as Zane ate. He felt a little awkward eating in silence, but he assumed this was the custom here . . .

Once Zane sat back, quite sated from his meal, Ekmenetet went into motion and had other servants take the remains away, except for the bowl of fruit and the remaining wine and water. Every single crumb was collected and removed.

Another servant entered and handed Ekmenetet a vial of some kind, which he held up to Zane. "Do you like the aroma, or shall I get another?"

Zane took a whiff and smiled. The fragrance from the vial proved quite pleasant. It had an outdoor aroma of pine and sea breeze with just a hint of something fruity. Date came to mind, but he wasn't sure. "That is fine."

After pouring the vial of liquid into the water and stirring the water with his hand, forming a thin layer of bubbles, Ekmenetet gestured for Zane to step into the water. Zane began to undo his robe, but Ekmenetet stopped him.

"Allow me." Seeing Zane start to object, Ekmenetet stated what he wanted sternly, glancing at the guard, but also calmly. "This is the way it is done," Ekmenetet said.

Zane nodded and allowed himself to be undressed. Although quite awkward, he decided to not focus on what Ekmenetet was doing. In only a couple of minutes, he stepped into the tub and submerged his lower half under the water and bubbles, now feeling less awkward.

Next, two women and two men entered and went to work. Zane rolled his eyes as this felt even more awkward than being undressed. He could swear Ekmenetet grinned as he stood watching the scene. Yet after one of the women started to massage his scalp, he relaxed and allowed himself to simply enjoy the experience. After his bath the women laid out cloths on the floor and left. One of the men left and the other had Zane lie down and then massaged a type of oil into his skin, kneading his muscles as well. This relaxed him so much he almost fell asleep before the session was completed. Before he knew it, Ekmenetet was standing over him holding up a fresh tunic for him to wear.

Ekmenetet bowed slightly. "I will come for you after first light. Rest until then."

Zane watched the man exit, but his guard remained, although he did go from being inside the room to stepping just outside the room. There was no door, however. *So much for privacy,* Zane thought. He noticed a cot had been prepared, so he laid down and tried to get some sleep.

Slumber did not come easily. So many questions went through his mind, and at a fast and constant pace. Exhaustion did finally overtake his thoughts, and he fell into a restless sleep.

CHAPTER 14

EXPLORING THE TOWER

Zane saw Bradley careen backward into the column, causing the crystalline portal to tilt and fall from its position on top of the pillar . . . Zane's heart sank. He dove to save the portal, hearing a loud "No!" as he did . . .

Zane sat up quickly as he awoke. He saw a man holding his shoulders, eyes now wide.

"Bradley!" Zane said, seeing the familiar face.

The man simply shook his head and said, "Ekmenetet. I think you were having a bad dream."

Zane nodded, then looked around, confusion overtaking him. He remembered Bradley saying his real name was Ekmenetet, but why did he correct him now? He went by Bradley before—actually preferring the name.

Zane stood and looked around. This room looked about the same size he had been in before. Yet all the dust was gone and there was ample light without the need of a flashlight or lantern. The walls looked clean and not marred by time and weather. Memories came in flashes. The fight, the portal, the pain . . . *Alex*. The woman from yesterday. She had looked exactly like Alex!

He suddenly felt weak and sat down again.

Bradley . . . Ekmenetet . . . handed him a glass of diluted wine and he downed the drink in a matter of seconds.

"What's going on?" Zane looked at this man, who looked to be the spitting image of Bradley. *Did he come through the portal as well?* Zane didn't think so. *But why is he here? Who is he, really?*

"I don't really know. The queen asked that I take care of you and deliver you to her this morning."

Ekmenetet stood and held out his hand, helping Zane to his feet.

"Come sit and have some morning refreshment. We can talk if you wish."

Zane nodded and sat on the cushion where he had sat the night before. In a matter of minutes, two women came in with food, fresh bread, and diluted wine.

Zane motioned for the man to sit with him and eat.

The man shook his head. "I cannot."

"Come on, Bradley," Zane said. "Don't make me eat alone. It's way too awkward." He motioned again for him to sit.

The man sat and nibbled on a piece of bread as Zane ate. "Why do you call me Bradley?"

Zane shrugged. "Well, where I come from, that was the name we called you."

The man cocked his head. "You've met me before?" He shook his head. "But I have never met you. Of course, I've seen you, as you look almost identical to my lord, but you are different from him, yes?"

Zane nodded. "Oh, absolutely." He swallowed a bite of bread. "You may find this hard to believe, but I'm from your future."

"You're from Adversaria?"

Zane paused chewing and his eyes widened. "You know of Adversaria?"

"Oh, yes. It is where our lord Marduk is preparing for the future and where my lord Gilgamesh goes periodically to report to Marduk."

Zane wiped his mouth, no longer hungry. "How long has he been going to Adversaria?"

Ekmenetet shrugged. "Oh, I guess not quite twenty-five years." He sat straighter. "Our lord has almost completed the tower. He's made record time. So, his vision is almost realized."

Zane's gaze jerked right and then left. "The tower." He looked back at Ekmenetet. "*This* is the tower?"

Ekmenetet nodded, looking confused.

"And where is this tower?"

"Babylon of the plain of Shinar, of course." Ekmenetet cocked his head. "You do not know this?"

"I suspected." Zane stood to his feet and looked out the large slits in the wall that allowed light into the room. "How far up are we?"

"As far as the eagles soar," I am told. "I don't know how far that is, but it is quite a distance. On some mornings, we are well above the clouds." He laughed. "It is strange to look down on clouds rather than up at them."

Zane nodded, but not really in response to his statement. "And you know of the prophecy?"

"Prophecy?"

So, that was a no. He decided to move on. "And why did you think me from Adversaria?" Zane asked.

Ekmenetet looked confused again. "From where else could you have come? You look young, strong, and virile—just what Marduk promised my lord he would create."

"And you are to deliver me to your queen?"

Ekmenetet nodded. "Yes. Queen Summer-amat has requested your presence." He stood. "And we should go and not keep her waiting."

Zane nodded and stood. Ekmenetet held up his hand. "After you change, of course."

Another awkward moment as Zane had to be shown how to wrap and tie the loincloth around him. Bradley then gave him another tunic composed of some type of mesh material. The garment didn't really hide anything, but since he now wore a loincloth, he felt somewhat okay with the tunic, for he would at least be cooler than having to wear clothing like that in which he arrived.

Zane followed Ekmenetet back to where he had met Summer-amat previously. Ekmenetet genuflected. "My queen. Here is the one you requested."

Summer-amat rose from her throne and walked toward them. Zane's eyes went slightly wide. Her garment, also mesh, but woven more tightly than his, allowed him to see her figure underneath, just without details. This was obviously a sensual society. He couldn't help but think of Alex as this woman looked exactly like her. He had to force himself to clear his mind of that thought.

"Thank you, Ekmenetet," she said with nearly a dismissive tone.

He bowed and left the room, leaving the two of them alone.

Summer-amat walked completely around him, her gaze making him feel like a *thing* rather than a person.

"Impressive," she finally said. "You look identical to my lord Gilgamesh." She returned to his front. "And what shall I call you?"

"Zane."

"Zane," she said as she looked him up and down again, seemingly mulling over the name. "An odd name, I must admit." She gave a slight shrug. "But if that is what you wish to be called . . . "

He nodded.

"Then so be it," she said as she flashed a smile, which looked genuine, though Zane wasn't sure it was. He knew he would have to be on his guard; he had no idea of her intensions. And he couldn't count on her pleasantries as sincere.

"Shall I give you a tour?"

This question took Zane back; his head jerked back slightly. "Really?"

She nodded.

"That would be great." He had not expected this level of hospitality. Yet he reminded himself this could be a trick to get him to relax his defenses. He would have to remain cautious. But . . . *a tour?* This should provide a great deal of helpful information.

They strolled out of the room and down the hallway as four guards followed them. Zane assumed this was normal procedure since this woman was the queen. Yet he couldn't help but wonder if part of this was because he was in such close proximity to her.

Anyone they encountered along the way stopped and either bowed or genuflected, stepping to the side before they did so. Summer-amat paid them no mind, acting as if they didn't exist. Maybe, to her, they didn't. He nodded a time or two and saw their eyes widen with confusion on their faces.

He guessed they thought him Gilgamesh and did not expect such an acknowledgement from him.

Zane couldn't count the number of ramps and stairs they climbed. Actually, he was surprised the queen could do this much climbing on her own and not once ask to be carried. After all, that is how all the movies depicted ancient royalty—never lifting a finger to do anything for themselves. Yet, he had to admit, this was likely why she appeared so toned. She didn't seem to tire from all the climbing, although he knew he would be quite sore in the morning in his quads and glutes.

They passed many slaves working with their taskmasters closely looking over them. The taskmasters were, of course, the first to see them and give deference. The slaves, seeing the taskmasters bow, would look around and bow with faces to the ground until the two of them passed. The slaves would then return to work immediately.

Once, one slave continued to work. He seemed to be so involved in what he was doing he did not look up to see what was going on around him. Summer-amat stopped and looked at the slave, who continued to work, not looking up. Rather than being rewarded for his diligence, the guard hit him with a whip. The slave jerked around, not understanding what he had done. The man then saw the other slaves. In confusion, he quickly looked around and saw the queen. He immediately bowed with his head to the ground. Summer-amat continued her journey. Zane looked back when he heard the crack of the whip again and saw the guard hit the man two more times and yell, "Get back to work!" *Poor guy. Punished no matter what he does.*

"This is quite the feat," Zane said, using a complimentary tone.

Summer-amat glanced at him and nodded. "It has been a vision of my lord for a long time."

"How long is that?"

She shrugged. "My entire life, actually."

Zane's eyes widened. "Really? How so?"

"Well, it usually takes several reigns for such an achievement as this to be realized. Yet Marduk has promised my lord completion will occur in his lifetime." She smiled. "The portal keeps him young."

"And you?"

She stopped and looked at him. "You think I'm old?"

Zane's eyes widened and he held up his hands, afraid he had offended someone who could have him killed with a wave of her hand. "Oh, no . . . no, that thought . . . never . . . I mean . . . you look . . . beautiful."

She smiled and continued walking. Zane let out a long breath while trying to hide it.

She glanced at him and laughed lightly. "I was betrothed to Gilgamesh when I was incredibly young. I feel blessed. Rather than having an old and wrinkled husband in my prime, he remains in his prime." She paused and then said, with a smile, "Very actively, if you understand me."

Zane tilted his head sideways. "Oh, I think I get you."

"When he is away, you could periodically take his place," she said as she looked into his eyes with a sultry gaze. "No one, but us, would be the wiser."

Zane's voice caught in his throat. "Oh, uh, that is a very generous offer. I'm not sure he would be pleased with that arrangement. I . . . uh . . . would likely have to decline. But, uh, I'm very honored, and flattered . . . at the, uh, offer." *Yes*, he thought, *a very sensuous society indeed.*

She shrugged and kept walking as if the conversation had been nothing of consequence.

Zane let out another slow breath. Had that been a real offer or a test?

At the end of the next ramp, she came to a halt and gestured with a sweep of her hand. "What do you think?"

They had arrived at the top tier, now very flat, even though slaves were working at the edges to complete this level.

"We just have another small tier to go—and then the temple on top."

Zane looked around. He was surprised the slaves worked so close to the edge without any type of safety harness. Maybe they were used to these working conditions, but, more likely, losing a slave was deemed an acceptable working hazard. The thought of all the bodies he had seen the previous day was evidence of that, most likely. This society evidently had the belief that the ends justified the means, at least as long as the ends were what the upper echelon wanted.

"Shall we head back?" Summer-amat asked.

Zane nodded. "What's next?"

She stopped and turned. "A lesson about Adversaria."

CHAPTER 15

ZANE'S TUTELAGE

Zane sat in his room waiting for Ekmenetet. His walk with Summer-amat had taken most of the morning, and she had one of the guards deliver him back to his room where some type of small sandwiches awaited him.

It was uncanny how much Summer-amat looked like Alex. Occasionally she displayed a certain mannerism or smiled in a certain way that reminded him so much of her. At those times, it was hard to keep his defenses up. He only wanted to take her in his arms and rescue her. He thought about that idea and then laughed to himself. To do that, someone would first have to rescue *him*.

But this made him wonder what happened to her. Bradley—Ekmenetet—had warned them not to touch the portal at the same time. He was brought here—to the past. As far as he knew, she wasn't here. At least, she was not with him when he awakened. Although his memory was compromised at that time, he was sure he remembered everything that had taken place since his arrival. If she had come through the portal with him, she would have been in the room with the portal.

Wouldn't she? So where was she? Perhaps she had been taken to the future in the way he was taken to the past. If so, he really needed to get to Adversaria.

Ekmenetet entered and displayed a genuine smile. "Hello, Zane. The queen wishes me to teach you about Adversaria."

Zane nodded. "I have several questions."

Ekmenetet had some type of beer brought in, with bread, as they talked. The taste was not like the beer he knew. It had an earthy taste with just a hint of sweetness. Not his first choice of refreshment, but its coolness helped ease some of the oppressiveness from the heat of the day.

"Did anyone else come through the portal when I did?" Zane didn't know if Ekmenetet would know such a thing—or answer—but he would likely have heard rumors if this had occurred.

Ekmenetet shook his head. "No, I have not heard of anyone else." He displayed a smile. "Just you."

Zane nodded. "Have you ever heard of two people touching the portal at the same time?"

Ekmenetet displayed a shocked look. "Oh no. Everyone is warned not to do such a thing."

"And what would happen if two people did touch the portal simultaneously?"

Ekmenetet rubbed his chin in thought. "I'm not really sure. Something bad, most likely, or why else the warning?" He looked up at Zane. "A question for Marduk, I would presume."

"And what do you know of Adversaria? Have you been there?"

Ekmenetet shook his head. "No, only Gilgamesh is allowed." He bobbed his head back and forth. "Well, except for those selected by Marduk."

"Because of their superior genetic quality?"

Ekmenetet gave him a blank stare. "I don't know what that means. But only the strongest, most handsome, and most virile men are chosen. The women are beautiful and elegant. They are for the royal couple, after all."

"Why?"

He looked at Zane with a blank stare again. "Because only the best is used for Marduk's plan. He is creating a man that will become his rival." Ekmenetet grinned and held up his index finger. "Though not his equal, mind you. No one can match Marduk." His smile vanished. "But he will be superior to any other man so he can rule the world with great wisdom, charisma, and ability."

"And why does this have to be done on Adversaria?"

Ekmenetet shrugged. "I can't say for sure, but I have heard that time is different there somehow. More is accomplished in a single year than one hundred years for us." He shook his head. "I don't know how, but Marduk has created a society more advanced than ours. Only there can Marduk's plan be achieved."

"And what about me? What will happen to me?"

Ekmenetet's eyes widened. "You are equal in every way to lord Gilgamesh. You will be taken to Adversaria to help fulfill Marduk's plan." He shook his head. "I don't know the details, but I understand Gilgamesh has had to alter Marduk's original plan somehow." He gestured to Zane and smiled. "I think *you* are the answer he has been looking for."

Zane assumed that was because of what Bradley had said about cloning techniques that had to be initiated. Yet he wasn't sure if that had happened yet, since they were just getting started. He paused in thought. On Adversaria, they would have worked on this for more than two thousand years. Perhaps they were running into problems already.

"Are you all right?" Ekmenetet asked.

Zane came out of his thoughts. "Yes. Sorry. I was just thinking."

He nodded. "About?"

Zane didn't answer directly, but had a question of his own. "How exactly do I fit in?"

Ekmenetet smiled. "Well, if done here, I feel you would have the pleasure of siring many children."

Zane's eyes went wide. "What?"

"Marduk has done it before. Many children are sired, and only those of superior breeding stock are allowed to continue."

Zane's eyes remained wide. "And what happens to the others?"

"Oh, they are sacrificed to Marduk, of course."

Seeing the look on Zane's face, Ekmenetet looked confused. "Have you not been a part of this before?"

Zane shook his head.

"These actions are so common with the worship of Marduk. At select times, men and women are free to engage in as much pleasure as they wish. Any children of such ordeals are offered to Marduk. Doing so is considered a privilege."

Zane felt repulsed. Shock must have shown on his face.

"Oh, don't worry. If you wish to be with men, that can be arranged also." Ekmenetet smiled. "Marduk is more concerned with your happiness than how you wish to express your pleasure."

Zane held up his hands and waved them. "No, no. Stop. Just . . . stop. I've heard enough."

Ekmenetet gave him a curious look. "I don't understand. Is this not how you worship?"

Zane shook his head. "No. No. We believe such acts are reserved for one man and one woman."

Ekmenetet just stared at him. "Really? Well, that seems rather . . . limited." Giving a shrug, he added, "Well, if that is what you believe, I won't try and persuade you otherwise." He paused. "But . . . "

Zane cocked his head. "But what?"

"You may not then like what Marduk will have planned for you. Although . . . " He paused once more. "I'm not sure if the choices and techniques on Adversaria will be different." He struck a pensive look.

"Just tell me, Ekmenetet."

"Well, I've heard your life-giving seed is important to Marduk's plan. They will obtain it somehow." He gave a small grin. "Might as well enjoy the process."

Zane stood and began to pace. This was certainly not what he bargained for. He would have to think of a way to delay this idea of his "usefulness" as long as possible. Maybe he could fulfill what Bradley had said. Destroying Adversaria earlier rather than later was beginning to sound necessary.

Ekmenetet watched him pace. "I'm sorry I have upset you. That was not my intent. I just thought this might excite you. I never considered it would not." He sat in quiet for several seconds. "Can you explain why this upsets you?"

Zane turned and looked at him. His question seemed genuine, so he returned to his seat. "Ekmenetet, I do not serve Marduk. I serve the one you would know as Yahweh."

Ekmenetet's eyes grew wide. He pressed his index finger against his lips. "Shh, Shh!" He quickly glanced at the door to see if the guard had heard anything and would respond. After letting out a long breath, he responded, in a whisper, "That name is forbidden here! Please, for your safety, do not use it!"

Zane furrowed his brow. "Why? He is truth, and that needs to be proclaimed."

"All I know is that when Marduk hears this name he goes into an angry fit and the person who spoke the name is slain." Ekmenetet leaned in. "And that person doesn't have to be in Marduk's physical presence for him to hear the words."

Zane's eyes widened. Obviously, Marduk would be against someone being a believer in Yahweh, but that last part was something he had not expected.

"How is that possible, Ekmenetet?"

"When Marduk is not within lord Gilgamesh, I assume he can hear anywhere. Speaking that name brings his wrath upon the speaker."

If Ekmenetet had heard the name of the true God, Zane reasoned, then perhaps he would be curious to know something about him. Zane tried to think about the time period in which, he seemed reasonably certain, he found himself, and how he might make a connection.

"Ekmenetet, have you heard of Melchizedek?"

"Oh, yes. He is the ancient one from before the beginning of the world from water."

Zane took that to mean Ekmenetet understood Melchizedek existed before the worldwide flood. So that would mean Melchizedek was likely Shem, one of Noah's three sons. He knew many biblical scholars had attributed this connection to the two.

"And who does he serve?"

"Oh, the One Who Shall Not Be Named. Marduk does not like him either."

Zane smiled. "I'm sure. And what does Melchizedek believe?"

Ekmenetet shook his head and gave a slight shrug.

"He also believes one is coming, but this one will be stronger than Marduk—stronger than the one Marduk is trying to create. This is why Marduk is trying to build such a human, to build a counterfeit to the true One who is to come."

"More powerful than *Marduk*?" Ekmenetet cocked his head. "Seems hard to believe."

"I'm sure it does. But there is a prophecy that Marduk may strike the true One's heel, but the true One will crush Marduk's head."

Ekmenetet's eyes grew wide. "Really? Melchizedek teaches this?"

Zane nodded. "And the holy Scriptures, the writings of the One Who Shall Not Be Named, teach this. Does Melchizedek make sacrifices?"

Ekmenetet nodded. "They seem different, though, somehow."

Zane nodded. "Yes, they represent the giving of themselves to the true One. Marduk's sacrifices are demanded to *force* people to serve. The sacrifices such as Melchizedek offer are to show they are willingly giving themselves to the service of the true One. That's a big difference. Plus, their sacrifices also represent a prophecy of the One to come who will sacrifice himself and make atonement for the whole world."

Ekmenetet's eyes widened. "Well, keep all of this to yourself." He paused, looked around once more, and lowered his voice. "Such words could get you killed." He stood. "Is there anything I can do for you?"

Zane looked at him and shook his head. He wasn't sure if his words convicted or offended Ekmenetet. The resemblance between this man and Bradley was uncanny. While he knew Ekmenetet was the same man as Bradley—they were from different times—his nature had not changed. He gave a reassuring smile. "No. Thank you for the information you provided me. And . . . I hope you ponder the information I provided you."

Ekmenetet bowed. "I will send in some refreshment and some water to wash your face and feet."

Before he left, Zane called to him once more. "Ekmenetet, do you know anything about the workings of Adversaria?"

Ekmenetet cocked his head as if not understanding the question.

"I mean, do you know how much more advanced they are, how they live, what power source their culture uses, how many live there?"

He shook his head. "As I said, I have never been there. My lord has not revealed those details to me. I am sorry."

"No, no. That's fine. I was just wondering." He chuckled. "I guess I'll find out soon enough."

Ekmenetet smiled and gave a slight nod. "Yes, Zane. I guess that is definitely true."

He turned to leave but then turned back once more. "I'll be back in the morning for you."

Zane found himself alone except for the guard outside his door who never said a word. He thought about what he had learned from Ekmenetet and what Bradley had told him. Knowing Ekmenetet would go to Adversaria at some point, he pondered the bigger question: was his being here an accident, or something that became part of history? Had he become part of one of those *Back to the Future*-like movie events he had seen, where his presence in the past would change his future—or was his being here actually part of his timeline?

Zane had always been something of a science fiction media connoisseur. He recalled a line by Captain Janeway of the TV series *Star Trek Voyager:* "The future is the past, the past is the future, it all gives me a headache." *Indeed,* Zane thought. He rubbed his temples.

CHAPTER 16

PREPARATION FOR THE QUEEN

The end of the third week since Zane's arrival at Babylon had come, but he had seen very little except for his room and the top of the tower, where he often came and sat in the early mornings or late afternoons, and sometimes at night. The temperature got way too hot during the day to stand outside for any length of time. The fortitude of the slaves was something he admired deeply. How they managed such heat and still exerted the needed effort for the extreme manual labor they had to endure, he could not imagine.

On this day, he was sitting with Ekmenetet on top of the tower in the early morning, still knowing little more than what he learned the first few days after his arrival. Gilgamesh and Summer-amat had only seen him once after his first encounter with them. While it was obvious they were scheming something that included him, he was unsure what that something was or how they planned to achieve their objective.

He kept asking Ekmenetet questions to try and find out what was going on, but Ekmenetet either didn't know or kept the information to himself. Ekmenetet had become his shadow, replacing the guard who had been outside Zane's door when he was in his room, and who followed him everywhere—never speaking, of course. At least Ekmenetet spoke and kept him company. Zane also found it interesting that Ekmenetet always slept on the floor just away from his bed. When asked why, he stated he liked being on the floor since it was cooler. Apparently, the hardness of the floor didn't bother him. Ekmenetet's actions in this way brought back a memory of what Bradley had said when he slept the one night in the hotel room: "I'm used to sleeping on the floor. It'll be like old times." *Was this what he meant?* Zane had a feeling Ekmenetet would become a key player in whatever was going to happen, and the two of them would remain together—somehow.

"Look," Ekmenetet said. "They're putting the columns of the temple in place." He turned to Zane. "I don't think it will be long now until the temple is complete. Likely complete by the next full moon."

Zane did a mental calculation. That would be about three weeks from now. "And what do you think will happen then?"

Ekmenetet's eyes went wide. "Oh, quite the celebration will be held, I'm sure. Much feasting, sacrificing, and religious rites."

Zane knew "religious rites" was a euphemism for all the sensuous rituals the priests and priestesses took part in, all in the name of Marduk.

"I know a very beautiful priestess."

Zane shook his head. "Thank you. But no thank you."

Ekmenetet shrugged. "Your loss. Not many can attain her. She has already asked about you."

Zane's eyes went wide. "Why?"

He smiled. "She thinks you're quite handsome. Plus, since you look like lord Gilgamesh, being with you will be a boon for her. Her prominence will be further elevated in the eyes of others."

Zane shook his head. Again, that made him feel like a *thing*. He half chuckled to himself. *Reverse discrimination*. Marduk had completely blinded these people to the truth of Yahweh and his principles. They didn't even speak his name.

"And what else will occur?"

"Not sure, but my bet is you will be sent to Adversaria along with lord Gilgamesh."

Zane gave a slight nod and stared at the temple construction. He wondered if Alex would be there. *Where else can she be?* If she wasn't here, then she had to be there, didn't she? Although, he knew, there was no assurance of that. Bradley had said no one ever saw them again. Did that mean she could be trapped somewhere in subspace? Was she now an unknown energy source in the cosmos? His eyes watered and he blinked rapidly. No, he wasn't going to entertain that thought.

Yet, would she be there in Adversaria past, or in the Adversaria present when they left Earth? Would they both be in Adversaria, but on different timelines? He shook his head and stood. He could not get lost in this thought paradox.

Ekmenetet followed his action.

"Let's go back," Zane said. "It's getting pretty hot out here in the open."

Over the next three weeks Zane had little to do but talk with Ekmenetet, so he talked his companion into doing exercises with him. Not much convincing was needed, however, as Ekmenetet seemed thrilled; this gave him something to do as well. They wrestled, did push-ups, sit-ups, and any other calisthenics they could think of. They also ran. Ekmenetet seemed to enjoy this the most. After their first race of running up and down many stairs and inclines, the next morning Zane could hardly move. Yet Ekmenetet convinced him to continue the exercising. By the beginning of the third week, Zane felt he was almost as fast as Ekmenetet. Almost, but not quite. Ekmenetet always won.

It seemed these activities helped the two of them become friends. At least Zane felt like that was what they had become. This also allowed him to talk more about God and the difference between Marduk and Yahweh—while not using the latter's actual name, of course. Zane also knew Ekmenetet had loyalties that went deeper than their friendship. If Gilgamesh asked Ekmenetet to kill him, there was no doubt Ekmenetet would do so. Maybe Ekmenetet would not want to, but he would most likely follow through with the deed. Still, Zane appreciated Ekmenetet's camaraderie, and he prayed that his words and explanation of Scripture would—could—have a lasting effect on Ekmenetet's life.

* * * * *

At the end of the third week, Summer-amat appeared in his doorway as he and Ekmenetet were having breakfast. Ekmenetet's eyes went wide, and he immediately genuflected. Zane stood and gave a bow. He always found he had to force himself not to stare at her and to remind himself that Alex would not emerge from her persona no matter how much his mind wished it. He had to keep reminding himself who this woman really was.

Ekmenetet stood and bowed slightly. "My queen, is anything of concern?"

She kept her air of aristocracy as she spoke. "There are many things that are of concern to me, but you are not one of them."

Ekmenetet bowed again. "Thank you, my queen. That is good to hear."

She gave a half smile and focused on Zane. "You are needed tonight at the temple dedication. Ekmenetet will prepare you." She turned back to Ekmenetet. "You know what to do."

Ekmenetet nodded. "Yes, my queen."

"Prepare him, and have him brought to the throne room."

"Very good, my queen."

As she turned to leave, the afternoon sun coming through the doorway highlighted her figure under the sheer robe she wore. Zane forced himself to look away.

As soon as she left, Ekmenetet ran to the hallway and flagged down the first two guards he saw. He said something to them and they scurried away in opposite directions. Zane was surprised Ekmenetet had this much authority. Yet he reasoned that if the guards heard his words were directives of the queen, they would move as fast as possible.

In short order, the tub was again brought into the room and filled with water. One of the women brought a vial of the oil to make the bubble bath. Zane again undressed and stepped into the water. While the oil did not produce many bubbles, he was glad for the few generated.

For the most part, this was a repeat of the first bath he received before he met with the queen. He had only been given enough water for a sponge bath of sorts since then. This true bath allowed him to feel clean. He missed that about his former life. Showers here were nonexistent, and baths were a rarity. Although, he was sure, the queen received baths quite frequently. Remaining clean, evidently, was a status symbol.

Although the man who gave him the massage last time did the same this time as well, he added some herbs Zane could not identify to the oil.

"What is that for?" Zane asked the man.

The man's eyes went wide, and he looked at Ekmenetet in nearly a pleading manner.

"He is not allowed to speak as he performs his duty."

"What?" Zane said, unbelief in his voice. "Your customs are so strange to me, Ekmenetet. I'm not sure I'll ever understand them."

"I will answer your question. The queen expects you to not only be clean but to look perfect as well. These herbs will be massaged into your skin, and you will have an even, tanned appearance."

A bronzer of some type, Zane surmised. When the man was done, Zane noticed his skin now had an even tanned appearance from the top of his head to, even, between his toes! This time the man stayed and made some other type of concoction as Zane donned his loincloth. While similar to the previous one when he had visited Summer-amat, this one looked more ornate in design.

The male servant gestured for Zane to sit. He dipped some type of stylus into a black liquid and brought the stylus toward Zane's face. Zane grabbed the man's forearm to prevent him. The servant's eyes went wide. Both he and Zane looked at Ekmenetet.

"You can relax, Zane," Ekmenetet said, patting his shoulder. "This is part of the ritual for tonight. This is how the queen expects you to be adorned."

Zane scrunched his brow. "Really? With *eye* liner?"

Ekmenetet smiled. "It is only kohl. Even our lord Gilgamesh uses this." Ekmenetet put his hand on Zane's, which held back the servant's hand. He gave gentle pressure to move Zane toward releasing his grip. "Please, let him finish."

Zane let go, and the servant continued his work, though cautiously.

Ekmenetet continued, "This will highlight your eyes, make the white of your eyes stand out, and enhance your presence." He smiled. "You will look almost royal."

The servant then took a different stylus and worked on his lips. Zane rolled his eyes as Ekmenetet smiled at him.

Shortly thereafter, just as the male servant finished and took his implements and paints away, a woman servant entered with some items on a type of pillow, set them on the table, and left.

Ekmenetet retrieved a pendant from the pillow and placed the chain around Zane's neck. The pendant appeared triangular in shape and rested just above the center of his pectoral muscles. It was roughly the size of a silver dollar, made of silver, and had three crystalline inlays of green, purple, and red.

Next he was given another decoration, also of silver, which looked to be shaped like a serpent, and this wrapped around his forearm. The serpent's head, also triangular-shaped, had two clear crystals, looking like small diamonds, which seemed to form the serpent's eyes. Zane wasn't sure, however, if that was what they were.

Ekmenetet stepped back and looked at him with a satisfied nod and smile.

"So, how do I look?" Zane looked around, but there was nothing in the room for him to see his reflection. He wasn't sure if he looked good—or ridiculous.

Ekmenetet nodded. "The queen will be pleased."

Zane hoped so. He only had Ekmenetet's word for it. Yet, he was sure, Ekmenetet understood their customs and had to be sure the queen would be impressed.

By the time they left for his presentation to the queen, the sun lay low in the sky. Zane found the scene almost humorous as those meeting them in the hallway would give him a second look and fall to their knees.

Ekmenetet chuckled. "They're not sure if you're lord Gilgamesh or not, so they bow in deference just to be sure."

Zane felt a little awkward over all this. Yet, after several had bowed or genuflected, he could see how something like this could become addictive and make one feel superior to others—whether they were or not.

When they arrived at the throne room, Summer-amat was talking to someone. They both entered and waited patiently. Once Summer-amat dismissed the one talking with her, she turned and Ekmenetet genuflected and then rose.

"My queen, I present Zane to you."

Ekmenetet took a step backward, bowed, and turned to leave.

"Stay, Ekmenetet."

He turned, bowed, and stepped to the side as she approached Zane.

She did what she had done before: slowly walking around him, looking him up and down. Again, this made him feel less like a person and more like a possession. Yet, for all intents and purposes, wasn't that what he was?

"I think I like you better this way." She smiled as she continued to gaze at him. "Your muscle tone is very good."

"Thank—"

She quickly held up her hand to cut him off. Apparently, he was not to speak until spoken to.

"You will accompany our lord Gilgamesh to Adversaria tonight. He has an . . . assignment for you to fulfill." She looked at Ekmenetet and then back to Zane. "I'm told you do not wish to participate in our religious ritual tonight." She looked him up and down again in a somewhat sensual manner. "No one has ever refused such an offer." She shrugged. "Yet no one can force one if they are unwilling."

Zane glanced at Ekmenetet, who stood motionless and expressionless. So, Zane's initial thoughts were true. Even though they had become what he would call good friends, his loyalty definitely lay with Summer-amat. Yet, Zane surmised, in some ways he could not really blame him.

Summer-amat ran the back of her fingernail down his chest. "Yet, one way or the other, you will succumb once you reach Adversaria. You can give of yourself willingly or perhaps with a little struggle." She smiled again. "Either way, you will submit—and maybe even like it."

"And after?"

She shot him a hot look for speaking without her permission. Her expression then relaxed and she displayed a wicked grin. "That . . . Zane . . . is up to you. Will lord Gilgamesh find you helpful or resistant? He may think you're worthy to give of yourself again. Or . . . " She turned away from him. "Not."

Zane swallowed hard. That gave him pause and a lot to think about. But he didn't have much time to come up with a plan.

Summer-amat turned back to Ekmenetet. "Accompany him behind us to the temple. Be sure he drinks the ceremonial elixir." She smiled. "Maybe he'll be more accommodating in Adversaria if we get him in a good mood." She laughed and looked at Zane. "You're welcome."

At that moment, Gilgamesh entered from an archway on the opposite wall from where they were standing and stood next to Summer-amat. Although dressed more regally and with finer clothes and jewelry than himself, Zane still felt like he was looking in a mirror. The experience was uncanny and made him feel ill at ease. How was he to get on this guy's good side?

Gilgamesh also walked around him in a way similar to Summer-amat's manner. He squeezed several of Zane's muscles, however, and said, "Hmm." He then had Zane open his mouth and inspected his teeth. Zane wanted to deck the guy but knew that would certainly end any chance he had of either a plan or a life, so he endured the humiliation.

Gilgamesh suddenly turned. "Come!" he commanded. The light caught one of the jewels, and this drew Zane's gaze to the pendant. Although looking similar to his, this one appeared larger and thicker. The colors in his were clear, blue, and cyan. He wondered if there was some significance to the colors, the stones, or even the pendant itself.

Gilgamesh and Summer-amat led the delegation, followed by two guards, Zane and Ekmenetet, and then two more guards. Zane wasn't sure if this was protocol or if he was considered dangerous.

Maybe both, he thought.

CHAPTER 17

CEREMONIAL RITE

Many people lined the hallways that the procession entered and passed through. Each person genuflected or bowed as the royal couple passed. They would then fall in line behind the procession as the ever-increasing conga line advanced upward through and around the ziggurat to the top tier where the temple stood.

By the time they reached the temple, a large crowd had assembled behind them and filled the area in front of the temple, evidently eager for the ceremony to begin. Zane and Ekmenetet followed the royal couple to the very front of the temple. Here, a large statue of Marduk stood; it was, Zane guessed, about three times his height as well as width. The statue's composition looked to be pure gold, but he assumed gold overlay was most likely used, although he couldn't be certain of that. The statue's golden color contrasted brilliantly against the pure white of the temple and gleamed from the light of the flames of the fires which had been lit.

As Zane's gaze turned upward, he noticed that, in the arms of Marduk, the portal had been placed. Its crystalline structure glowed and twinkled from the fires in front of the temple. Two huge bronze bowls each contained a bonfire whose flames rose higher than Zane's head. Thankfully, they were placed higher up, on the temple steps. He could feel their heat from where he stood, but the temperature from their flames was not intolerable.

On either side of the temple stood musicians, and he could see the priests and priestesses looking out from the temple toward the audience. Only stringed instruments were playing: a quiet but haunting melody.

Zane stayed with Ekmenetet at the base of the stairs of the temple as Gilgamesh and Summer-amat climbed several stairs onto a platform stationed in the middle of the stairway going into the temple. This allowed them to approach closer to the crowd and at a height at which all could see them. Gilgamesh raised his hands and the music stopped immediately.

"My people. This day, Etemenanki, my temple, forming the link between Heaven and Earth, is complete."

The people cheered, the noise rising to a cacophony of sounds as their yells, whistles, and applause echoed off the temple walls. Gilgamesh held up his hands again and the noise came to an abrupt stop. The echo died a couple of seconds after the people themselves ended their cheering.

"I go to Adversaria to fulfill Marduk's plan," Gilgamesh continued. "You have all been a part of his plan and your achievement today will go down in history as the day Marduk paved the way for the downfall of the One Who Shall Not be Named."

More applause could be heard, but fewer clapped this time.

"But before that moment, we first want to celebrate this victory by becoming one with our gods through our giving of ourselves to them. Let the priests and priestesses lead the way."

At that moment, the musicians began to play. A driving beat seemed to rise out of the music, imperceptible at first, but, in crescendo fashion, rising in prominence and penetrating the very core of everyone present. As the priests and priestesses descended the steps, their bodies swayed and moved to the beat of the drums. The men removed their cloaks revealing bare torsos and loin cloths that left little to the imagination. The priestesses did the same. While their bodies were more covered, their clothing appeared sheer, and the light of the flames revealed almost every detail of their lithe figures underneath. The free-flowing fabric around them fluttered in the breeze making their appearance almost ethereal and enticingly sensual.

One priest, also dressed provocatively, passed a goblet to Gilgamesh. He drank and passed the chalice to Summer-amat who did the same. Gilgamesh then held the goblet high and poured the rest into his mouth. Some ran down his beard and dripped to the surface of the platform. The crowd roared in applause and whistles. Gilgamesh then kissed Summer-amat passionately.

The music increased in volume as the drumbeat intensified causing the crowd to become visibly restless. Priests and priestesses went through the crowd passing out a liquid which everyone devoured hungrily. At times the priests and priestesses would put the liquid in their mouths and then feed the potion to individual members of the crowd—seemingly indiscriminately to both men and women. This caused the crowd to morph into a mob of sensual frenzy.

Once Gilgamesh and Summer-amat entered the temple, all inhibitions vanished and the people rushed to the temple, clothes dropping and left strewn along their path. The liquid apparently worked fast; the lusts were fueled at a feverous pace.

Zane was glad that what was happening inside the temple was there and not outside, where he would have to view their passionate lusts. He looked around; only he and Ekmenetet were left outside the temple.

He looked at Ekmenetet. "Don't let me stop you. If you want to enter, go ahead."

Ekmenetet smiled. "I value my life more than my pleasure."

Zane cocked his head. "What is that supposed to mean?"

"I am to look after you until Gilgamesh comes out." He held up a goblet. "At some point, you will be made to drink this elixir."

Zane sat with a thud on the steps. Ekmenetet sat beside him.

"Zane, you are a man who behaves differently from any man I have known. Do you not enjoy pleasure?"

"Well of course I do. But I'm not an animal that disrespects the other person and treats them like property."

Ekmenetet cocked his head. "But they are all willing."

"Are they?"

Again, Ekmenetet gave him a curious look. "You think they aren't?"

"Oh, some more than others, I'm sure. But why are they given the elixir?"

"It enhances their pleasure."

Zane shook his head. "No, the potion dulls their inhibitions. Most—not all, I know—would be ashamed to initiate such an act in the sight of everyone else. Gilgamesh knows this. Marduk knows this. The elixir makes them worship in this way. They are not really giving themselves in the worship of Marduk, he is forcing them to this way of worship by dulling their inhibitions and inciting their lusts. That is not really worship. It's enslavement."

Ekmenetet sat staring at Zane for several seconds. "Your words, though strange, seem to have merit."

"Recall what we talked about before: the difference between giving oneself to worship versus being made to worship."

Ekmenetet nodded. "And this is being made to worship?"

Zane nodded. "The One Who Shall Not Be Named, as Gilgamesh calls him, would never do something like this to initiate worship." He tapped Ekmenetet's chest. "He wants this, your heart." He tapped Ekmenetet's upper thigh. "Not your lust." Zane looked him in his eyes. "He wants devotion, not a one night's stand. Truth, not deceit."

Ekmenetet nodded. "Your words strike to one's core." He shook his head. "Marduk's words have never elicited such a feeling in me before."

"Marduk's words and actions elicit an addiction of lust from his followers. The words and actions of The One Who Shall Not Be Named elicit true freedom. Don't settle for addiction when freedom is within your grasp."

At that moment, Gilgamesh and Summer-amat returned.

Gilgamesh laughed. "Why are you out here all alone when pleasure is in your grasp?" He gestured toward the temple. "Go. The fairest priestess of all is at your beck and call. Enjoy all that she can offer." He smiled. "She is trained in many ways of pleasure. You won't be disappointed."

Zane gave a slight bow. "A very generous offer, but I am fine where I am."

"Nonsense." He looked at Ekmenetet. "The goblet."

Ekmenetet gave Zane a look that said he was sorry. He handed the goblet to Gilgamesh.

Zane held up his hand. "I'm quite fine, thank you."

Gilgamesh's temperament went from jolly to anger; likely, no one had ever refused him before. He pointed at Ekmenetet and looked at Zane. "If you don't drink, then it means Ekmenetet has failed in his duties and will have to pay the consequences."

Zane gave a quick glance at Ekmenetet, who now displayed fear in his eyes, then turned back to Gilgamesh. "What consequences?"

Gilgamesh gave a wicked grin. "We haven't yet paid a tribute sacrifice to Marduk. I'm sure Marduk would be pleased with such a one offered to him to demonstrate the importance of loyalty to those who may think they would question theirs."

Giving Gilgamesh a stern look, Zane held out his hands to receive the goblet. Gilgamesh smiled and handed the chalice to Zane, who took a gulp and handed the goblet back, coughing a few times. He was definitely not used to the taste of this potion.

Gilgamesh held up his palm. "Oh no. You must drink all of the elixir."

Zane looked at the goblet and surmised it contained a pint if not more. He hesitated and looked at Ekmenetet, who shook his head slightly. What choice did he have? He put the goblet to his lips and chugged the contents as fast as possible. The elixir didn't taste horrible, but it had a bitterness that intensified the more he drank. He knew the others didn't drink as much as he did—and he had seen how they acted. Yet many of their inhibitions were likely already diminished as beer had freely flowed long before the ceremony began.

Once all the contents had been drunk, Gilgamesh took the goblet and laughed. "There now. That's better, isn't it?"

Zane did start to feel a little dizzy. Ekmenetet had to steady him several times.

Gilgamesh laughed even more. He turned to Summer-amat. "I know you've wanted to kiss him for a long time. Go ahead. I'm sure he'd like that."

Summer-amat stepped forward and ran her fingertips over his torso. Zane tried to focus on something else but found doing so difficult. Her touch sent sparks of electricity through him. His body was telling him to give in, to enjoy himself. She kissed him. He began to feel a warm and tingly sensation throughout his body. She pressed in harder and, for a moment, he did the same. Her kiss was enjoyable; all he had to do was simply give in to his feelings. Yet his thoughts reminded himself of what he had just told Ekmenetet. He was being forced to worship, and this action was not true worship. He broke the kiss and pulled away.

"No! This is not right."

Summer-amat stepped back in shock. She turned to Gilgamesh with a look of disbelief.

"No one has ever refused the gift of my wife. She is not a gift that is freely offered to many."

"She is yours and should be yours alone."

Summer-amat gave him a curious look, but Gilgamesh looked angry.

"I give her to whomever I deem worthy. Clearly, you are not." He paced on the stair for a few seconds. "Maybe you're not worthy for any of Marduk's plans." Gilgamesh leaned in. "Maybe *you* would be the better sacrifice to Marduk."

Summer-amat took Gilgamesh's arm. "My darling. Don't let him destroy your happy mood. Marduk brought him to you so your plan, and his, can continue. At least take from him what Marduk needs and then decide if he is worthy to continue to serve you or not. If a sacrifice is needed, better on Adversaria so all can see your devotion to Marduk."

Gilgamesh looked at Summer-amat and slowly began to smile. "You are wise, my queen." He kissed her and Summer-amat turned it into a more passionate kiss than Zane thought should be displayed in public. Gilgamesh stared at Zane. "See what you have missed?"

Gilgamesh turned to Ekmenetet. "Fetch the high priest. He needs to witness our departure."

⁎ ⁎ ⁎ ⁎ ⁎

As Mikael observed Ekmenetet bow and rush up the stairs of the temple, he turned to Raphael. "All of this is disturbing on so many levels."

Raphael nodded. "So many." After a pause, he added, "I can't believe the Creator is allowing Lucifer to do all this—especially his work off world." He placed his hand to the side of his head. "I mean, he's playing around with time itself!" Raphael shook his head. "Why would the Creator even allow such a thing?" He produced a frustrated sigh. "And then to allow Lucifer to forbid Yahweh's name from even being uttered . . ." His voice trailed off, then he uttered, "These poor people."

Mikael put his hand on Raphael's shoulder. "While this takes us off guard, that is not true of Yahweh." He smiled. "I think he is giving Lucifer just enough of what he wishes so the final outcome will ultimately yield what our Creator wants."

Raphael squinted. "Say that again."

Mikael smiled. "Lucifer's pride does him in every time. Yahweh's will always wins in the end, no matter how Lucifer tries to thwart it."

Raphael nodded slowly. "Yes, that is true. But I have a hard time seeing how this is going to turn around."

Mikael shrugged. "I can't say I see it either. Let's go report to Ruach, and then we'll see what he says. He's probably already working on a solution."

＊ ＊ ＊ ＊ ＊

Gilgamesh watched Ekmenetet rush up the temple steps and then looked back at Zane. "I see your air of superiority. You will not feel that way for long."

Zane shook his head. "I do not feel superior to you at all. Not agreeing to your customs does not make me feel superior."

"Hmph. We'll see. My people on Adversaria can get from you what we need. If you cooperate, then maybe I'll let your life continue. Think about that—and see who is more superior."

Zane sighed. "I don't—"

Before he could finish, Ekmenetet was quickly bounding down the stairs with a priest in tow who was trying to look presentable before meeting his king.

The priest bowed. "My lord, I did not know you wished to leave so quickly after the start of the ceremony."

Gilgamesh did not justify his request or apologize for his interruption. "I must get to Adversaria with this one." He gestured to Zane.

Zane gave an inward sigh. *He could at least say my name.*

The priest looked from Gilgamesh to Zane and back, then bowed. "Yes, my lord. Of course." He motioned for them to follow him as he approached the statue of Marduk.

The priest positioned Zane near the statue, in front. Zane looked up and saw the crystalline structure directly above him. He looked at Ekmenetet and gave a brief smile with a slight nod. Ekmenetet returned the same. Zane wished he had more time with this one. He felt Ekmenetet stood on the verge of making a decision in favor of Yahweh. Would he now? He certainly hoped so.

Gilgamesh said goodbye to his wife. "Until we meet again."

She nodded and kissed him on his cheek. "Until then." She put her hand on his cheek. "Not to worry. I'll prepare our people for the next step."

"Remember the words of Marduk."

She nodded. "Yes, I will prepare before He Who Shall Not be Named does anything against us. I know time is short." She smiled again. "Do not worry. I'll be sure all is ready."

Gilgamesh nodded and stepped next to Zane. He turned to the priest, who gave a nod.

The priest lifted his hand. "Lord Marduk, hear my prayer. May you lead lord Gilgamesh safely to your abode of preparation for your most holy work. May he and you be successful."

Gilgamesh touched the statue of Marduk. Zane wasn't sure how that activated the portal, but everything suddenly went white like a bright light enveloping them. He saw a flash of something like lightning, felt pain charge through his entire body, and lost consciousness.

CHAPTER 18

SURPRISING NEWS

Mikael closed his eyes. This had to be his favorite spot. The babbling sound of the brook was always so mesmerizing and peaceful. He felt he just had to come to this boulder next to this brook in Eden every so often to rejuvenate himself. Upon hearing soft footfalls approaching, he opened his eyes and before noticing who was approaching, watched as one of the most beautiful butterflies slowly moved its wings as it rested on his leg.

"Hello, there," Mikael said. "My, you're glorious."

As its delicate wings moved, they caught the light and appeared to twinkle. Although practically sheer, the wings contained tiny blue crystalline-like structures that refracted the light. Mikael knew they weren't actual crystals as that would make this tiny, beautiful creature too heavy to fly. He marveled at the creativity of his Creator.

Raphael laughed as he approached. This apparently startled the creature as it took flight. Mikael felt sad seeing it flit away.

"I always know . . . Woah!" Raphael said, coming to an immediate halt, as a host of these butterflies took flight from flowers across the brook looking just as delicate as these wonderful, tiny creatures. As they took to flight, they looked like tiny firework displays as they twinkled with each flutter of their wings.

"That was amazing," Raphael said. "I always know where to locate you when I can't find you in the angel dimension."

Mikael smiled. "Well, you just witnessed why. But, I fear I've become too predictable."

"From what I hear," Raphael said, "Eden will one day be filled with many our Creator will bring from Sheol." Raphael grinned. "You may have to share your boulder."

Mikael sat up and looked around. "Well, this beauty is too wonderful to keep to ourselves forever." He looked at Raphael. "I'm happy to share it." He stood and adjusted his sword. "I'm assuming you came with news."

Raphael nodded. "Lucifer may have miscalculated."

Mikael's eyebrows raised. "Do tell. What happened?"

"Gilgamesh is dead."

"*What?* When?"

"Apparently not long after we last visited. He was to take Zane Archer to Adversaria through the portal outside the tower temple. It seems Zane disappeared, but Gilgamesh fell dead."

"Does that thwart Lucifer's plans?"

Raphael shrugged. "Maybe. Maybe not. I think another visit is warranted. What do you think?"

"Hmm. Very likely," Mikael said. "It seems we need another conversation with Ruach." He looked at Raphael. "Did Zane make it to Adversaria?"

"Ruach is the one who told me about Gilgamesh, but he didn't really comment on Zane Archer."

"Maybe because, if Zane's teleport was successful, he likely went into the future on Adversaria."

"You think Ruach will let us visit the future state of Adversaria?"

Mikael gave a slight smile. "That's the exact question I want to ask him. Come on. Let's go find out."

Both angels disappeared together.

CHAPTER 19

ARRIVAL

Hearing voices, Zane moved slightly, then stopped. The pain, severe, caused his muscles to freeze. He opened his eyes and groaned. All he knew was that he was lying on a marble floor. *Why?*

He heard footsteps and then voices. He couldn't force himself to turn his head to see whose they were.

"There he is, just like you said." The woman chuckled. "Bradley, you're a genius."

Bradley. Zane knew he should know that name, but all that came to him was a blank. A big blank. He could remember nothing—not even *his* name. *What's happened to me?*

The man and woman helped him sit up. He groaned again. As he looked at the woman, he froze. *She's so beautiful.* He should know her. He *did* know her, he was sure, but couldn't place her. *How could I forget someone so beautiful?*

He looked at the man, who also looked familiar—somehow. "I should know you." Zane tried to talk normally, but he felt as though his words were coming out as nearly incomprehensible. He knew what he was saying, but his ears were hearing his words as slurred.

"Yes, Zane, you do know me." The man helped Zane to his feet and tried to steady him. "Probably not this instant, but your memory will come back soon."

The woman came up to him. "Are you all right, Zane?"

Zane just stared at her.

The woman glanced at the man. "What's wrong with him?"

"Temporary memory loss. Remember? That happened to you as well."

The woman nodded. "Oh yes. I forgot."

Zane looked from one of them to the other while trying to understand what was going on. *Memory loss?* He remembered he had that happen before—at some type of tower. Is that where he was again? He looked around. *No, this looks different. Quite different.*

The man smiled. "Zane, this is Alex. Remember Alex?"

Zane looked at her again. "Alex?" he whispered. "So . . . beautiful." He fell back to the floor.

The woman gave a concerned look. "Bradley, I think there's more than just memory loss here."

The man nodded. "Yes. They probably made him drink the ceremonial elixir." He shook his head. "Looks like he has two things to sleep off."

"Well, let's get him out of here before we get discovered. That'll dash all our hopes."

They both pulled Zane back to his feet and wrapped their arms around his shoulders to steady him. Zane looked up, pointed, and announced in a slurred tone, "Portal. Marduk." He glanced around. "Different. Bigger."

The woman gave the man a curious look. "He's really out of it, Bradley."

The man patted Zane's arm. "Yes, this statue of Marduk is even larger than the one in Babylon. There, the statue was in front of a temple. Here, the statue is displayed in this large glass room." He looked around. "Which we need to get out of as soon as we can."

Zane tried to walk a bit on his own and ease the burden he was putting on these two, but he had drunk too much of the elixir. He looked at one of them and then the other. "You . . . two . . . friends?"

"Yes, Zane, we're all friends," the woman said. She pulled forward to keep him moving. "We need to get to the monorail. Can you do that?"

"Monorail?" Zane scrunched his brow, then gave a bright smile. "Are we at Disney World?"

The woman looked at the man and rolled her eyes. "How long will he *be* like this?"

"He should be okay once he sleeps the effects off," the man said. "Hopefully by morning he'll be coherent."

"I feel fine. Just fine," Zane said, his speech still slurred. He tried to concentrate heavily to say his words clearly, but his body just would not respond the way he wanted.

"Yes, I'm sure you do," the man replied. "Probably a little too good."

Zane grabbed the man's face and stared into his eyes while trying to focus. "I know you. You're Ek . . . " He wrinkled his brow. "Ekmen . . . " Zane patted his cheek. "Friend. Good friend."

Zane knew this man was a friend—someone he knew before now. But the name was different. He knew this man as someone different. Didn't he? He felt so frustrated. Why wouldn't his mind work?

Both the man and woman got him to an escalator not far from the glass room they had left. Zane felt secure between the two of them. He knew his mind was foggy, but he felt confident that these were good friends. He just wasn't sure who they were. He did his best to remember—but couldn't.

The vastness of this place reminded him of a mall he used to visit. *Mall? Yes, mall.* Yet he couldn't remember the location. Only a vague memory could be conjured. All memories seemed to be jumbled inside his head. Pieces of memories would emerge every so often, but without context.

The woman pushed on his upper shoulder. "Stand straight, Zane. We can't draw suspicion to ourselves."

Once down the escalator, they made their way out the door and then down the street a short distance toward a monorail station. Zane saw a sign: Adversaria Monorail Complex.

"Ad . . . ver . . . sar . . . i . . . a." He looked at one of them and then the other. "I'm here."

The man laughed. "You made it, buddy. Just like we talked about."

Zane smiled and pointed with his head. "Here you come, buddy."

His male companion furrowed his brow, but then made them all veer to the right and toward a restaurant outdoor seating area.

"Where . . . we going?" Zane asked. He pointed with his finger over his companion's shoulder. "Monorail . . . that way."

"What's wrong, Bradley?" The woman asked.

The man had Zane sit at a bistro table as he and the woman sat as well.

"Two other Bradleys coming down the sidewalk."

The woman jerked to look, but then turned back to not look; her eyes were wide. "Are they on to us?"

Zane smiled. His eyes went wide in an attempt to match hers. "Your eyes are big . . . beautiful."

The man picked up a menu and held it up, blocking his face. Zane noticed the two men who looked like this man walk by.

"Look," Zane said, poking his companion. "You're now over there." He blinked his eyes and tried to focus. "Two of you."

The woman reached and pushed his pointing finger down. "Don't point. We don't want them to notice us."

As the two men walked on, a waitress came by. "Can I get you anything?"

The woman shook her head. "No, thanks. My friend just needed to sit for a minute."

"Well, my manager gets upset if you sit here and don't order."

The man with him stood. "We understand. Sorry for the inconvenience. We'll be out of your way."

The waitress looked annoyed but nodded and walked off.

The man and woman got on either side of Zane and the three of them walked down the street to the monorail station.

"That was close," the woman said as she turned her head to look behind them. "Do you think they were looking for us specifically?"

The man shook his head. "I don't think so. As far as I know, they didn't know Zane was coming today. Otherwise, they would have had guards posted at the portal."

The woman nodded. "Just coincidence, then?"

The man gave her a glance. "Let's hope."

Once inside one of the monorail compartments, the two sat Zane next to the window, the woman sat next to him, and the man sat across from them. Zane leaned his head against the window and tried to stay awake to look at where they were going and listen to what the woman and man were saying. Yet focusing proved difficult.

What he could focus on, however, was impressive. As they left the city proper, he saw several extremely abstract-looking skyscrapers, other monorail systems going here and there throughout the city, and all buildings looking modern and surrounded by picturesque locales. They passed over water, near beautiful parklike areas, and there were even mountains in the distance.

They were only on the monorail for a short distance, or so it seemed. Zane knew that, because of his loopy state, he wasn't sure how long the trip actually took.

Both the woman and man again stood on either side of him to help steady and guide him. Yet, by this time, he felt better able to assist and less of a burden on them. While thankful for their support, Zane tried to walk on his own—but kept stumbling. He was still a little too dizzy from the elixir.

"Don't try and walk by yourself, Zane," the woman said, now sounding a little annoyed. "You'll draw attention to us. Just let us help."

Hearing her tone, Zane complied. He didn't like that tone from her.

They zigged and zagged through several blocks, went through a small park of some kind, and then to a building complex. They entered what looked to be a back entrance, up an elevator, and then to a room that looked spacious and neat.

Zane didn't get a chance to see much of this place, however, as they whisked him into a bedroom and set him on a bed.

"You go rest, Alex," the man said. "This has been an exhausting day for you. I'll get him undressed and into bed."

"Okay. I hope he's coherent tomorrow. We really need to plan. We don't have much time."

The man nodded. "I understand. There's nothing we can do until he sleeps this off."

Zane felt his shoes come off. He raised his hand. "I'm fine. Really." He then felt his body collapse onto the bed, which felt soft, comfortable. That was all he remembered as he slipped into unconsciousness.

CHAPTER 20

REUNION

As he slowly woke, Zane heard noises like pans clinking together. He raised his head to listen more closely. His surroundings slowly came into view. He was on a bed, apparently in some type of bedroom. Filtered light came into the room through the shade, which had been drawn. He slowly sat up; his head would not let him raise up any faster. His hands went to his head, which felt like he had just awakened from a hangover.

Memories came back in spurts. He remembered being in Mesopotamia and going through the portal. But something must have happened as he didn't remember being with Gilgamesh once he was through the portal. He cocked his head in thought. *So what happened to him?* Looking up, he saw a familiar face enter.

Zane squinted. "Ekmenetet?"

The man smiled. "Good morning, Zane. I haven't heard that name in a long time."

Zane thought about that. "But I was with you yesterday."

The man chuckled. "An explanation that needs an explanation."

Zane shook his head slightly. "My head hurts too much to comprehend that statement."

Bradley motioned to him. "Come. Let me give you some pain reliever that will help your headache."

After taking the tablets given him, Bradley patted his shoulder. "Get a shower and clean up. We'll have a long talk over breakfast. Sound good?"

Zane nodded.

"I'll put some clean clothes on your bed for you to change into. Breakfast should be ready by the time you get dressed."

After he left the room, Zane undressed and stepped into the shower. The warm water helped him wake up, and the massage the water produced at the base of the back of his neck helped release the tension there, allowing his headache to ease somewhat. Inside the shower was a mirror. His eyes widened when he looked at his face. He definitely needed to get the makeup off! He had to scrub his face and eyes several times for his face to look like himself again. By the time he finished his shower and dressed, his head felt much better and his thoughts were clearer.

As Zane walked from the bedroom, he saw Bradley putting an omelet on someone's plate.

Zane stopped short. "Alex?" He remembered another woman from yesterday, but his thoughts were such a jumble until now. That woman had been *his Alex,* and he had not even recognized her!

She stood and smiled. "Hi, Zane." She came over and gave him a hug. He reciprocated. Feeling her arms surround him elicited such joy. He gave her a soft squeeze; he was overwhelmed at being able to feel her touch again. He couldn't express how happy this made him to know she was fine. He looked into her eyes as she released the hug. His eyes watered. "I had no idea what happened to you. You've been here all this time?"

Alex nodded. "Come to the table and eat. There's a lot for us to discuss and catch up on."

"Here's an omelet and some fruit," Bradley said as he set the plate on the table. "Sit and eat."

Zane took a bite and closed his eyes. "This is so good. The food of ancient Babylon wasn't bad, but having something familiar is nice."

Bradley laughed as he sat with them. "I'm sure."

After a few more bites, Zane looked at Bradley. "How did you get here? You were left in Babylon."

Bradley smiled. "It's a long story, so let me try and explain."

"Please do," Zane said.

Bradley took a bite and swallowed. "If you recall, when you and Alex touched the portal back in your original timeline, you both disappeared."

Zane nodded. "I woke in ancient Babylon. I met you there and you went by the name Ekmenetet."

Bradley nodded. "Yes, I know you feel all that was just yesterday for you." He took another bite of food. "Now, when Gilgamesh had you come through the portal, something went wrong."

Zane's eyes widened. "The lightning."

"Exactly."

"What was that?"

Bradley shrugged. "Not sure. My guess is that because the portal had to send you here to the future Adversaria and Gilgamesh to the current Adversaria, the device malfunctioned."

"Malfunctioned?" Zane looked from Bradley to Alex. "What kind of malfunction?"

"Gilgamesh was killed."

Zane's eyes widened. "Really? Then what?"

"Well, Summer-amat covered that up, of course. She had Ekmenetet and the priest take care of the body so no one would know. That's when she claimed Marduk had made him the sun. She found out she was pregnant, made her impregnation seem supernatural by saying the sun's rays of Gilgamesh—the sun, through the power of Marduk—is what made her pregnant. She put steps in motion for her and her son to become gods as well and worshipped by her followers." He shrugged. "Of course, Ekmenetet was sent to Adversaria to find you before all that was put into place. But as you know, history bears out her efforts were successful."

Zane finished his omelet and started on his fruit. "So why are you speaking of yourself in third person?"

Bradley shook his head. "I'm not Ekmenetet. Ekmenetet came through the portal not long after you did. Yet, as you now know, you came to this time frame, and he came through much earlier in Adversaria's timeline. The two of you did not overlap until he came to your timeline on Earth."

Zane cocked his head. "So, if Ekmenetet came to my time-line, then you're . . . a clone?"

"Yes, Zane, that's correct."

Alex put her hand on his forearm. "But he's a good clone."

"Yes, Ekmenetet made sure of that," Bradley said. "He oversaw my creation."

Zane stood. "I need a moment to process." He walked to the window and looked out. "Wow."

Alex stepped beside him. "Impressive, isn't it?"

"Unbelievable." Zane had never seen anything like this. Not only were the buildings more modern than he had ever seen, people seemed to be traveling not only on monorails but in some sort of bubble-like structure moving from place to place. Everything looked so efficient.

"Have you enjoyed living here?" Zane asked, turning to Alex.

She smiled. "I would have liked being here a lot more if you had been here also."

He wrapped his arm around her shoulders. "I'm sorry you had to wait for so long." He smiled. "At least you had Bradley."

She laughed. "Well, that's a story unto itself."

Zane's eyebrows raised. "Do tell."

She patted his chest. "Another time. You need to finish with Bradley. You need to understand all of this. We are under a time pressure, and we need you up to speed."

"Time pressure?" He looked at her with great concern. "Alex, what's going on?"

Alex took his hand and guided him back to the table. "Just hear him out."

Zane sat and looked at Bradley. "Okay, fill me in. What happened when Ekmenetet came through the portal?"

Bradley shook his head. "He didn't find you. At the time, he didn't know you arrived in a future state of Adversaria."

Zane looked at Alex. "And what happened back when you entered the portal?"

"Well, when there is simultaneous touching of it, as we did, apparently the portal sends one person forward and one backward."

Bradley nodded. "Yes, that is likely why no one sees them again. Evidently, they have to go back through the portal together." He held up his hand. "I know all this is hard to process."

"Really?" Zane said with a bit of sarcasm. He shook his head. "Sorry. It just seems so convoluted."

"Well, if you had tried to go back to your timeline, it likely would not have worked. But because you were coming to where Alex was, the portal was trying to realign itself, so to speak."

Zane rubbed his temples. "This is all so confusing."

"Time travel and wormholes always are," Bradley said with a smile.

Zane chuckled. "Stop acting like you know how it all works."

"Well," Alex said, "we've had a little over a decade to figure this out."

Zane's gaze shot to hers. "What?"

"Zane, I've been here eleven and a half years."

His eyes widened. "But it's been only six weeks."

"Yeah, six weeks for you," Bradley interjected. "But multiply that by one hundred, and you get how long being here has felt to Alex."

Zane put his hand on her forearm. "Alex, I'm so sorry."

She gave a weak smile. "Well, in some ways, my stay was likely better than yours. I got the scaled-up version. You got the scaled-down version."

Zane smiled and laughed. "I got the Flintstones and you the Jetsons."

That made Alex laugh. How he had missed that laugh. "That's quite the analogy." She bobbed her head. "But somewhat accurate."

After the laughter settled, Zane suddenly froze. "Wait a minute. I now understand what happened to us." He tilted his head slightly. "Sort of." He turned to Bradley. "But how are there so many of you—and who is the real Ekmenetet?"

"As you know," Bradley said, "Ekmenetet originally lived in Mesopotamia millennia ago."

"I know. I was with him just a day or so ago."

"Although time is a lot faster here than on Earth, aging is actually much slower than on Earth." He pointed at Alex. "Although she has been here over a decade, she hasn't even aged a year."

Zane grinned. "Just as lovely as ever."

Alex smiled as she developed a tinge of red in her cheeks. Zane thought that made her even more lovely.

"After Ekmenetet made me, he went to your world," Bradley said. "He thought you would get sent to Adversaria, and I was to meet you and help you figure out how to destroy this world. Yet, lo and behold, Alex came instead of you."

"Trust me," Zane said with a chuckle. "You got the better deal."

Bradley smiled. "I'm not touching that one."

Zane laughed. "So what happened then?"

"Well, I did some digging, looking through the archives to see what happened in the past under those circumstances, although such an event was a definite rarity. I read all I could about how the portal was supposed to work."

"And?"

"And based upon what Ekmenetet had told me . . . " He pointed his finger between himself and Alex. "We calculated the time you would likely arrive here."

Alex jumped in. "And we were right!"

Zane smiled. "And I'm grateful." He looked from one of them to the other. "So, what now?"

Alex raised her eyebrows. "Well, if we're going to keep with our television analogies, think of *The Bodysnatchers*."

CHAPTER 21

NOT AS IT SEEMS

Zane stood again and went to the window. He turned back and looked at Alex. "Can we go for a walk or something?"

"Overwhelmed?" Bradley asked.

Zane nodded. "Something like that." He looked from Alex to Bradley and back. "Look, I know you're under a time pressure for something. But I really need some air."

Bradley looked at Alex. "You two go and have some time together. We can discuss more when you get back. Maybe a breather is better anyway."

Alex smiled and stood. "Sure." She held out her hand. "Come on, Zane." She turned to Bradley. "We'll be back soon."

He nodded and began to clear the table.

As they left the apartment—if that was what the place was supposed to be—Alex went to the stairs and headed up instead of down.

Zane stood still for a moment. "Don't we want to go downstairs?"

Alex shook her head. "No, you'll see. Come on." She looked up and then back at him. "We're near the roof, so we only have to climb a couple of floors."

Zane went with her. Once they opened the door to the roof, Zane was taken aback. There was an infinity pool on one side, a small garden area next to some patio furniture, and some type of portal located on the other side of the roof.

Alex stepped onto a round pad and sat on a small seat. She patted the seat next to her and invited Zane to sit. "Don't worry. This will be fun."

Once he sat next to her, she pressed a button and a force-field of some type enclosed around them.

"We call this a sky car," Alex said, smiling.

The car lifted and took flight, giving them a three-sixty view around them. Being so high in the air was a little unnerving, but Alex seemed totally relaxed.

She rubbed his knee and gave a slight squeeze. "It's perfectly safe. Believe me. I've done this hundreds of times. We're on an invisible track plotted by computer." She pointed to other sky cars in the air. "Each of these is on a separately programmed track, so none of them can crash into each other."

She gave a smile and he smiled back. While unnerving, he trusted her and, after a few minutes, began to enjoy himself. She pointed out various landmarks, parks, lakes, and buildings. In the distance, from where they had come yesterday, stood a large ziggurat-shaped structure, similar to the one in Babylon, but much more modern with reflective glass on each floor.

Zane looked up. Although faint in the sky above, he clearly saw a couple of planets and a galaxy.

Alex smiled. "The sky is spectacular at night. We'll have to come back sometime at night for you to see."

"This is all remarkable, Alex. Seems you've enjoyed being here."

Alex cocked her head. "Well, things here are not as great as they look."

"What do you mean?" He looked down and back up again at both picturesque views. "It all looks pretty great from here."

Alex nodded. "Yes, on the surface all is wonderful." Her countenance changed and she became more solemn. "The details of how this society works is very dark."

Zane didn't know what to say. "Dark? What goes on here?"

"As you know, this whole city is designed for one purpose."

Zane nodded. "To produce, basically, the Antichrist, I presume."

"Exactly." She pointed to a park below. "You can sort of think of this place as a movie backdrop. In a way. There are a lot of extras who make this world feel like a wonderful place. Their main job is to make society work. You need waiters, chefs, entertainers, and the like. But don't move your eye off of the main purpose."

"So, what are the inner workings?"

"Summer-amat and Gilgamesh still run Adversaria." She bobbed her head. "Or, rather, one of their clones."

Zane scrunched his brow. "But Bradley said Gilgamesh died."

Alex nodded. "Yes, but he has been cloned—many times. As well as she."

Zane's eyes widened, then he nodded. "Well, I guess that makes sense, in a bizarre way." He shrugged. "They would want to be the ones to rule the world in the end, I suppose."

"I think so. At any rate, every so often they create a new clone. When they do, they incorporate other genetic attributes to enhance themselves."

Zane nodded. "I see. That makes sense." He shook his head slightly. "From their agenda—their point of view—anyway." He paused and looked at Alex. He suddenly wondered: wasn't she in danger since she looked like Summer-amat? "So, how many clones are alive at one time?" He put his hand on her upper arm. "Are you in danger?"

"I don't think so. At least not yet." She took a deep breath and looked at him. "In the beginning Gilgamesh had children here with the . . . " She motioned in a form of air quotes. " . . . superior breeding stock brought here. His travels made him infertile, and so cloning began."

Zane nodded. "That's what I had heard."

"But when the portal became unusable, many clones were made to first help build a society to sustain things here and to combine genetic factors for superior clones. Therefore, there are duplicates of many people here. That's how I can be somewhat anonymous. Plus, I am not registered in their database." She smiled. "My arrival was fortuitously untracked, thanks to Bradley."

She developed a sad look.

"Alex?" Zane said in a hushed tone. "What is it? What else is wrong?"

"Once someone is considered not contributing anymore, they are disposed of—a sacrifice to Marduk." She swept her arm to the scene below. "That's why Adversaria is still just a city. The population doesn't exceed a certain capacity. Adversaria is a city on an uninhabitable planet protected by a forcefield."

Zane thought about that as Alex pressed on. "Though morbid, that does make sense from their perspective. If they believe the ends justify the means, they would not see that as wrong even though such an action is—on so many levels."

He took her hand. "So what is the pressing news you needed to tell me?"

"A new clone for Gilgamesh will be produced in the next few days." She looked at him and took his hand. "We need you to take the clone's place."

Zane's eyes widened. "What? Why?"

"We need you to have access to everything. Only the new clones have unlimited access. The old clones just become a part of society until their usefulness is deemed to no longer be of benefit, or they are just considered too old."

"And what do you mean by 'everything'?"

"There are only three people with access to the power source for Adversaria: Gilgamesh, Summer-amat, and a scientist named Farzad."

Zane nodded. "I remember Bradley mentioning him."

Alex still had a pensive look.

"And the catch?" Zane asked. "I know there has to be one or you wouldn't have that concerned look."

"For the new clones to be effective, they must have the memory of the previous clone. Otherwise, they would not be effective."

"And getting this infusion of memory will be dangerous?"

Alex kept her pensive look. "While that is a concern to me, Bradley assures me receiving their memories will not be detrimental or harm you. Although . . . "

Zane raised his eyebrows.

"You will know how he thinks, and how he and Marduk communicated." She grimaced. "I fear such memories will be a very dark experience."

Zane nodded. "I see. But that will give us knowledge of their ultimate plan."

"Yes," Alex said. "That is another reason for doing this."

"But that's not your main concern."

Alex shook her head. "No." She grabbed his hand. "Zane, if you recall, Bradley said there is another faction trying to produce a perfect human."

Zane nodded. "And that has what to do with this?"

"We feel this faction will try and achieve the same thing. New Gilgamesh clones don't happen often. They will likely try and make their move as we make ours."

"Okay." Zane shook his head. He wasn't understanding the downside. "So we have to be concerned about someone trying to usurp me once I'm in place?"

Alex shook her head. "Once the memory is transferred to the new clone, the memory of the old clone is wiped so they can't remember anything, and then they are just a member of society."

Zane tried to understand, but found himself still failing.

"Oh, Zane, only one person will have their memories intact. Either you come out with both your memories and the previous clone's, or you come out with no memories at all."

Zane swallowed hard. "But you're confident this can work, right?"

"Bradley thinks so. But doing so is still a risk."

"Worth taking?"

Alex's eyes watered. "I just got you back. I don't want to lose you again."

Zane gave a weak smile. "If Bradley thinks this will work, we have to trust him, right?"

"I guess." Her words were hushed and weak.

"So if this works, then their plan is destroyed since their perfect human would no longer be . . . perfect, right?"

Alex nodded. "That's the thought, anyway."

He lifted her chin and looked into her eyes. "A double win." Seeing her eyes water, he added, "Plus . . . " He gave a little smirk. " . . . I can find out which version of Summer-amat is the better kisser."

It took a few seconds for his words to process. She chuckled and poked him in his side. Zane gave an "umph."

"And how are you going to compare?"

Zane gave a smile and looked into her eyes. "Well, I do need a baseline, don't I?"

She gave a slight nod. "That's the scientific thing to do."

He leaned in. She did not move. Their lips touched and he leaned in farther, wrapping his arms around her torso and making the kiss linger for several seconds.

CHAPTER 22

PLANNING

As Zane and Alex stepped back into the apartment, Bradley was sitting with someone at the dining table.

"Grant!" Alex exclaimed as she stepped forward and gave the man, who rose from the table, a hug and kiss on his cheek. "It's so good to see you."

"And you, as always, Alexandria."

Zane was unsure about this guy. He seemed way too familiar with Alex.

Alex turned and gestured for Zane to come over. "Zane, this is Grant. He's a good friend and a scientist here who works on teleportation, among other things. Grant, this is Zane."

They shook hands.

Grant smiled. "Ah, the long awaited one."

Zane furrowed his brow.

Grant chuckled. "Alex has been telling us about you for a decade. It's nice to finally get to meet the savior of us all."

Zane's eyes widened. "Wow. That's a lot to live up to."

Grant looked from Zane to Alex. "You did tell him, right?"

She nodded. "But not the details. I'll leave that to you."

Grant gestured for all of them to sit.

Zane noticed a paper on the table. The document looked incredibly old—ancient, even. "What's that?" Zane asked.

Bradley smiled. "This is what Ekmenetet brought to Adversaria with him, and what he taught us about The One Who Shall Not be Named."

Zane's head jerked back slightly. "Really? Where did he get such a document?"

"From someone he called Melchizedek."

Zane's eyes widened. "What?"

"After you went through the portal," Bradley said, "Ekmenetet visited Melchizedek and had a long talk with him. Melchizedek told about the One to come and gave Ekmenetet a copy of these writings about him."

Zane reached for the document. "May I?"

Bradley nodded and gently moved the paper toward him.

"It's ancient Akkadian," Alex said. "Quite remarkable both historically and content-wise."

Grant pointed to the document. "It tells of creation, the flood, and what was to come prophetically." He smiled as he gently touched the document. "We have all learned from these teachings and have believed in the true One."

"And we owe our transformation all to you, Zane," Bradley said with a large smile.

Zane looked up from the document and over at Bradley. "What do you mean?"

"Well, if you hadn't been so open and sharing of your faith with Ekmenetet, he would not have visited Melchizedek, would not have brought this with him, and we would not know the truth."

"I know he said a believer brought knowledge of the truth to Adversaria, but I didn't know he was referring to himself," Zane said.

Grant nodded. "He brought the document and its knowledge, but it was only due to you."

"Who all knows about this?"

Grant looked from Bradley to Zane and back. "We teach the message to humans who are brought through the portal." He shifted in his seat as though he was nervous. "We have to be careful, though, as sharing this could get us all killed if they don't believe or if they report what we're doing. Bradley and Alex shared this message with me." His eyes watered. "And I'll forever be grateful. I pledged myself and my talents to their cause."

Bradley shrugged. "Most are unhappy with what has happened to them—that is, being brought here against their will—so this gives them hope for their future and most readily believe." Zane noticed Grant nodding in agreement to this statement. "For some," Bradley continued, "we have to time our delivery just right to be sure they are in the right mood to hear such news."

Zane nodded. "Makes sense. And the clones?"

Grant looked at Bradley and then Alex but didn't say anything.

Zane looked at all three. "What? You don't talk to the clones?"

Alex put her hand on Zane's upper arm. "It seems the clones are soulless. Somehow, their cloning process makes them less than human. They appear human, act as if human, but are more or less genetically programmed to mimic human behavior and emotions." Alex developed a sad look. "If you look into their eyes, you see an eerie blankness. Something not human."

Bradley stepped in. "I think they're soulless because they are made here on Adversaria, and Marduk didn't want them to be able to switch their allegiance."

Zane thought about that. What Bradley said made sense in a morbid kind of way. He looked at Bradley. "But aren't you a clone also?"

Bradley nodded. "Yes, I will likely cease to exist with the rest of Adversaria."

Alex reached out and put her hand on his. "Bradley, you're different."

"You believe," Grant added.

"Yes," Alex said with a nod. "You believe in the true One just as much as we do."

Bradley gave a small smile. "Yes, but what you see in me is just the charisma Ekmenetet placed in my genetic programming." He looked at Zane. "That is why Ekmenetet was originally cloned and some of his genetic material deemed worthy. Summer-amat thought he had strong charisma."

In thinking back, Zane realized Ekmenetet did display a great deal of charisma. "He *was* able to be on Summer-amat's good side no matter what seemed to occur," Zane said.

"Bradley," Alex said, "you are more than just programming. I can feel it."

"So can I," Grant said.

Alex knelt next to Bradley. "When I look into your eyes, I see kindness. They are more human than those of many humans I have encountered."

Bradley smiled. "You are kind. I hope you are correct. Either way, the success of this mission is still highly important." He looked at Zane. "I promise, Zane, I will do all within my power to be sure you are successful."

"Well, speaking of that, how exactly am I going to be . . . successful?"

Grant smiled, got up, and retrieved a file. He sat down and pulled out a disc which he turned on. This caused a holographic blueprint of some kind to spread across the table. "Here is where the awakening of the clone will happen."

Zane leaned in. "Looks like where the Marduk statue is located."

Grant nodded. "Once the clone is made . . . " He pointed to a room not far from the glass room that housed the statue. ". . . it is brought in a pod and placed before the Marduk statue. The current Gilgamesh clone then lies in another pod so his memories can be transferred to the new clone."

Bradley then added to Grant's narrative. "We feel this other faction will teleport their version of Gilgamesh, the one they feel is now the perfect human specimen, to replace the clone which Gilgamesh has developed. The memory download will then go to their clone and not to the clone developed by Gilgamesh and Summer-amat."

Grant pointed to the map again. "Best I can tell, they will likely do that from here." He pointed to a room around the corner from the glass room housing the statue. He looked up. "It has all the technology and capability they need to accomplish that."

"And where do I come in?" Zane asked, looking from Bradley to Grant.

Bradley smiled and placed his hand on Grant's shoulder. "Due to Grant's expertise in teleportation, he will intercept the matter stream and replace the essence of this perfect human this other faction has created with . . . yours."

"So timing is very important," Alex interjected.

Zane nodded. "I see. And what can go wrong?"

Alex swallowed hard and looked at Grant.

Grant gave a forced smile. "Several things, unfortunately."

Zane's eyes widened. "Such as?"

"This faction cannot know of our actions, so we have to be extremely secretive. If I don't intercept the matter stream at the right time, we may lose you."

"*Lose* me?" Zane looked from one of them to the other. "What does that mean?"

Grant wiped his mouth with his hand and ran it through his hair. "Like we said. Timing is extremely important. If I'm too early, your matter stream will be replaced. If I'm too late, your matter stream will dissipate." He grimaced. "Either way, we lose you." He held up his hands. "I'm working on a mitigation strategy so that we can retrieve you and rematerialize you so we don't lose you entirely. Yet . . . even in that case, our mission would still be a failure."

Zane sat quietly for several seconds as what Grant and Bradley said sunk in. Alex rubbed his arm. "Are you okay?"

"Wow." He forced a smile. "I would have preferred a more robust plan."

"We are taking as many precautions as possible," Bradley said. He pointed to the map again. "If the faction will be in this lab . . . " He tapped his finger on the digital map. ". . . which is most likely, I'll be across the way, here." He moved his finger to the lab diagonal from the previous lab. "That way, we'll be in close proximity but out of the way. Cameras will be placed in all the labs on this floor just to be sure we're not surprised."

Zane nodded. "And if we're successful? What then?"

Bradley raised his eyebrows. "Well, you get all of Gilgamesh's memories—"

Zane held up his hand to cut him off.

Bradley stopped and cocked his head. "Yes?"

"I get how a clone would receive memories as they go from one program into another, but how are they transferred into a *person's* brain?"

Bradley shook his head. "It's not the type of programming you're thinking of. This is genetic programming. They are, in every way, at least physiologically, like any other human."

"Yes," Grant said. "The brain is somewhat like a computer. Yet a neuro-interface is scheduled to be installed into the pod so the transfer into your brain will work correctly. Think of it as a type of capacitor. It will give your brain a few extra microseconds to process and store the memories."

"And what will happen if, for some reason, the interface is not there? For whatever reason."

Grant paused in thought. "I surmise you may not get all the memories of Gilgamesh stored. I don't think there will be any concern in regard to safety, but not getting all of his memories could definitely hinder our mission."

Zane nodded. "So, consider that we're successful. What does that achieve for us?"

"If you get all of Gilgamesh's memories," Grant said, "you can then expose those who are part of this faction because you will receive the memories of the perfect human clone that this faction has created as well." He smiled. "Double bonus." His smile faded. "Well for us, at least. Likely more bad memories for you." He grimaced. "Sorry." Grant gave a slight shrug and smiled again. "Also, as the new, official, Gilgamesh, you gain access to the power station, and you can then destroy the exotic matter stream within the power station—thereby destroying Adversaria."

Zane looked at Grant. "All I can say, then, is don't screw up your timing."

Grant grinned. "That's the plan."

CHAPTER 23

WAITING

The next few days proved more of a waiting game for Zane rather than him doing something useful. Bradley and Grant went about getting things ready. They were afraid to have Zane help them as they felt his presence would draw too much attention to what they were trying to deceptively accomplish. While that was a little frustrating, not helping Grant did mean Zane got to spend more time with Alex, which was okay by him. Yet being inside for so long made him increasingly antsy. At least in Babylon he was able to exercise during his days of waiting.

Zane stood at the apartment window in the late afternoon on the third day after he had met Grant. He looked over at Alex who sat deciphering more of the ancient Akkadian document Bradley was letting her study.

"Alex, can't we go out and eat, or sightsee, or something?" Zane asked. "Anything at all would be fine by me. Just let me get out of this room for a little while."

Alex looked up from her reading. "Well, Grant did say to stay low."

181

Zane gave her a pleading look. "But you did say there are many clones of almost everyone here, right?"

She nodded.

"Well, won't that cover us, then? Would anyone really notice us?"

Alex cocked her head. "Well, perhaps if we stay on this side of the lake and away from the downtown area, we may be okay."

Zane smiled and put his hands together while pointing them at her. "Great. I'll take those restrictions. Anywhere. You lead. I'll follow."

Alex stood and gave him a smirk. "Well, that's the way it should always be, isn't it?"

Zane laughed. "I won't even argue with you on that." He put his palms together and placed them under his chin in a type of pleading gesture. "Just, please, get me out of here."

Alex came to the window and pointed to a building on the lake's edge that had some type of spire with a blinking light. "They serve sushi there."

Zane's eyes lit up. "Really? That would be great."

As they turned to leave, Zane added, "Without the creepy guy that stares at us, right?"

Alex laughed. "Had forgotten about that. But, yes, I certainly hope so. Besides . . . " She smiled. "I have no car to explode."

He opened the apartment door. "Seems like we're safe then."

This time they took the elevator to ground level.

"I thought we'd walk this time," Alex said. "Okay with you?"

"Absolutely. Movement is what I need right now."

Once outside, Zane breathed in deeply and then exhaled. "Ah, much better."

Alex smiled as she took his hand and they walked together. "I hate to break this to you, but the air is the same air whether inside the building or outside."

He furrowed his brow. She looked up. "We're under a dome."

"Really?" He looked up. "Wow. I don't see a dome, but the sky is breathtaking." He pointed. "Let's stop at the bench over here so we don't trip or look silly walking with our noses in the air."

He led Alex to a bench along the path beside the lake but didn't let go of her hand. A long time had lapsed since he had held her hand; he wasn't going to let go so quickly.

"Is that the Milky Way galaxy?" he asked. "Never thought I'd see such a view of our own galaxy."

Alex nodded. "I know. This place does have magnificent wonders despite its evil heart. Not sure where we are exactly, but some say we're on the outer limit of one of the spiral arms of the galaxy, which tend to curl upward, so we can have a view of the galaxy more face-onward rather than sideways as we have on Earth. And maybe because the nearest sun from here is only the size of a dime, things look brighter in the sky."

Zane looked at her. "So, the need for a dome."

"Exactly. Outside this city is a barren wasteland devoid of oxygen, heat, life."

Zane looked over the lake. "But the view seems to go on, way past the city."

Alex pointed to a place just past where they were headed to eat. "See that wharf?"

Zane nodded. "What about it?"

"The dome ends just past there."

His eyes widened. "Really?" He turned her way. "Optical illusion?"

"Something like that." She pointed across the lake. "See the mountains in the distance?"

Zane nodded. "Uh-huh. Quite beautiful."

"They're also past the forcefield."

"So you can't get there from here?" Zane asked.

"Whatever generates this dome makes the city look larger than it really is." Alex shrugged. "To seem less confining, I suppose."

"Ever been outside the dome?"

Alex shook her head. "No. But I'm told that is where people are sent when deemed no longer of use to society."

Zane wrinkled his brow. "But that means . . . "

Alex nodded. "Yes. Instant death. They become a sacrifice to Marduk." She gave a forced smile. "A privilege and an honor—they say." She stood and pulled him to his feet. "Let's go before our thoughts get too morbid."

He gave a weak smile, put his arm around her shoulders, and walked with her down the path along the lake to the restaurant.

They passed several people and couples on their walk. Many were faces he had not seen before, but some were clones of Bradley, Grant, Summer-amat, and Gilgamesh. Yet no one paid them any attention. Everything seemed rather surreal, even a little eerie, to see a society composed of so many clones.

"How did you get used to many others looking like you, and how do you know who is who?"

Alex smiled. "It took some getting used to for sure. The clones have rings of different colors so others can recognize their status, or order."

Zane glanced at her hand but didn't see a ring. "And yours?"

"No ring means yours is being constructed." She gave a slight shrug. "That makes explanations easier when others ask, but this fact is well known by others so they don't typically comment."

Zane nodded. "I see. And for me?"

"The same. You have no ring for the same reason. If someone happens to check the database, they will have to assume the newest clone in the database is you. This allows us to be anonymous and not be registered."

This made Zane realize their existence here was a continuously precarious one. As they drew closer to their destination, Zane suddenly realized what he had identified as a spire was actually the sword component of a large swordfish, which formed the restaurant building and seemed to be composed of geometric shapes. The composition of these shapes formed the fish, and it ranged from purple to blue to white—as the colors of a swordfish would. Very unusual, he thought, but ingenious and beautiful as well.

To his surprise, they were seated in the eye of the swordfish, and this proved to be a lookout from the restaurant over the lake and city proper. With all the lights of the city and the outline of the lake, the view produced a great ambience.

Their meal came in several courses. Zane was glad because this made their time together longer. Alex's laugh was as intoxicating as ever. Despite their circumstances, he was glad they could still find things to laugh about.

"Alex, I'm so sorry you had to endure a whole decade here before I arrived." He took her hand. "I feel awful about that."

"Well, me being here isn't your fault. Besides, the situation has given us plenty of time to come up with a detailed plan. Once Bradley figured out your arrival time, we were able to match upcoming events with your arrival."

"Speaking of Bradley, how did he get that name here? Ekmenetet took that name after arriving on Earth."

Alex smiled and took a drink of water. "Well, evidently Ekmenetet is quite the schemer."

Zane cocked his head.

"I just mean he's the one who planned all of this: his coming to Earth, his getting us involved, the creation of his clone here and naming him Bradley—that's why he chose the name Bradley back on Earth—how the clone Bradley here was to find you . . . " She bobbed her head. "But found me instead, and . . . " She lowered her voice substantially. "The plan for destroying Adversaria."

Zane smiled. "And we became pawns in his scheme."

Alex took her index finger and pushed on his hand. "All thanks to you."

"What did I do?"

"You told him about truth and who is the essence of truth."

Zane's eyes widened. "So, you're saying you being on this planet for a decade is my fault."

"Absolutely."

"But, I, uh . . . "

She laughed. "I'm kidding. Although . . . " She smirked. "There is truth to that statement." She smiled again. "But when you stop and think, we have become a big part of God's ultimate plan." She shrugged lightly. "Kind of exciting, don't you think?"

Zane nodded just a bit. Any plan with her in it was exciting to him.

She sat up straighter. "Want to walk off dinner?"

He nodded and stood, helping Alex to her feet. She put her thumb on the pad at the corner of their table and a display read, "Thank you for your payment."

As they walked out of the restaurant, Zane asked, "If you're anonymous, how did you pay for dinner?"

"Oh, my thumbprint is linked to Bradley's. So is yours now, by the way." She shrugged. "Not sure how he managed that, but that's why I don't eat out very often. Fewer chances of getting caught."

Suddenly, Zane felt as though he had put her in danger with his selfish desire to go out. "Oh, I didn't even consider the consequences of us going out like this."

She looped her arm through his. "Not to worry. I'm sure all will be fine. I've done this before." She smiled. "Just not often." She pulled on his arm to move him toward the small wharf area. "Come, let's walk."

The night was quite pleasant. Certain shrubbery and trees along the path were highlighted with lights, and this provided a beautiful ambience for their stroll. Lights along the dock highlighted the area from the water. They sat on a bench at the end of the dock and gazed across the lake toward the city proper.

Alex leaned her head on his shoulder. That made him smile. While their separation had been a relatively short time for him, a long time had passed for her to not be with him. He was glad she had not gotten over him—he was definitely not over her.

"In some ways, things are nice here," Alex said. "The city is beautiful, life is not frantic, and things are peaceful for the most part." She paused, then added, "I wonder if the Kingdom will be like this for us."

Zane looked down at her and smiled. "Well, it most certainly could be, I suppose. I know our future will be spectacular."

"I think I would have loved being here if not for the undercurrent of darkness that seems to pervade everything."

"Undercurrent?"

As if on cue, a holographic image of Marduk appeared over the lake, looking as large as one of the city's skyscrapers. The golden image almost glowed while surrounded by the darkness and hovering above the dark waters below it. The goldenness of the statue complemented the lit ziggurat towering just across the lake. The view was beautiful and impressive—but also a reminder of who was in control here.

Alex nodded toward the hologram. "Does that answer your question?" She gave a slight shrug. "I get this feeling of impending doom." She sat up and looked at him. "It's hard to describe. I didn't feel the ominousness at first, but the longer I'm here, the more I feel an uneasiness. Like a growing evil getting larger and larger."

"Until everything here goes 'poof!'" Zane used his hands to demonstrate his words.

Alex nodded slowly. "That's why you're here." She smirked. "Mr. Poof-Man."

"Hey, now! Wait a minute. I'm not sure I'm on board with that name."

Alex held up her hands. "You're the one who said it first."

"Well, you don't have to capitalize on the phrase."

Alex laughed, stood, and reached out her hands. "Okay, take me home. It's getting late."

Zane stood, kissed her on the forehead, and wrapped his arm around her shoulders. "Yes, ma'am."

They walked quietly for several minutes as they traveled the path along the lake back to their high-rise. Zane thought about what Alex had said. He glanced at the city. *Beautiful. Just like the Adversary to make a counterfeit of what was to come and fill the wonderment with evil.* He looked again at the giant hologram over the lake. *And just like him to make something evil look beautiful.*

As they drew near their destination, Alex patted his chest. "You've been quiet. What have you been thinking about?"

"Oh, just what we have to do here, and if everything will work out in the end."

She glanced up at him. "I'm sure it will. After all, what can go wrong with Poof-Man in charge?"

He poked her in her ribs, and she laughed and pulled away from him. He attempted to grab her, but she escaped his reach and ran for the door of the building, laughing all the way.

Zane ran after her.

CHAPTER 24

PREPARATION

When Zane woke the next morning, he found Grant already at the dining table eating breakfast with Alex and Bradley. He guessed he had been more tired than he realized to sleep through both Grant's arrival and Bradley's cooking breakfast. And all three were laughing at something.

"There you are!" Bradley exclaimed. "Here, sit down. I have pancakes."

"Pancakes?" Zane sat with eyebrows raised. "You should have woken me."

"I thought about it," Bradley said as he placed a plate of pancakes and sausage in front of him. "But I wanted you to get your sleep."

"After all," Grant said, "we have a lot of work to do today."

"That's true," Alex added. She put her head in her hand and propped her elbow on the table. "We'll just watch you eat until we get down to business."

Zane smiled. "That desperate for entertainment, huh?"

Alex's eyes gleamed as she spoke. "Well, we haven't seen someone eat like that in over a decade."

"Hey, now!" He waved his fork at her. "Where's the love here?"

Bradley patted his shoulder. "Don't worry, Zane. I'm sure we can find it somewhere around here."

They all laughed. Alex stood, took her plate, and gave Zane a kiss on his cheek as she walked by on her way to the kitchen.

There was a knock at the door.

Zane stopped chewing and looked from Bradley to Grant. "Expecting someone?"

"Yes," Grant said as he stood. "I asked Marla to come by."

"Marla?" Zane looked at Bradley. "Who's Marla?"

"Someone to help us. She works in the cloning facility."

As Zane finished his last bite of pancake, he pushed his plate aside and stood to greet her.

Alex stepped from the kitchen. "Hey, bestie. Give me a hug." She gestured to Zane. "Marla, this is Zane."

Zane gave a slight wave. "Hi, Marla. Good to meet you."

"Same here." She gave him a hug. "No sense being shy. We're all family anyway, right?" She pointed upward and smiled. Zane nodded his understanding and returned her smile.

Bradley gestured for her to sit, and the others did so as well. Zane offered Alex his seat and pulled a chair from the balcony for himself.

"So, Marla," Grant said. "What's the word?"

Marla leaned in and grinned. "You're not going to believe it." She panned their faces to increase the anticipation.

Alex pushed on her shoulder. "Come on. Don't leave us in suspense."

"Yeah," Grant said. "You're grinning, so your surprise has to be good, right?"

She gave a shrug. "Well, I think so." She turned to Alex. "I hope Alex does."

Alex put her hand to her chest. "Me? How does this involve me?"

Marla turned to Zane. "Your coming could not have been timed better. I just learned that there will be a double cloning ceremony."

Bradley looked at her with eyes wide. "You mean . . . ?"

Marla nodded. "Yep. Both Gilgamesh and Summer-amat will have new clones at the same time." She sat up straighter. "I don't think this has happened before. At least, not as long as I've been here."

"And how long is that?" Zane asked.

Marla shrugged. "Oh, about one thousand years, give or take a few."

This took Zane back, but then he realized that was only about ten years on Earth.

"We've had them close before," Marla continued. "But never simultaneously."

"And what makes them do so now?" Zane asked.

"I'm not sure. But rumor is, they both feel this may be the last time they have to be cloned."

"No," Grant said with a tinge of regret and unbelief. "That doesn't give us much time."

Zane looked from Grant to Marla and back. "Why? What do you mean?"

Alex placed her hand on his forearm. "If this is true . . . " She looked at Marla, who gave a shrug. "Then after a short time of evaluation, they would likely be sent to Earth to get set up for gaining power."

Bradley interjected. "So you have to destroy the power source as quickly as possible."

"Yes," Marla said, holding up her hand to display her fingers. "The sooner the better."

Alex's eyes went wide as she grabbed Marla's hand. "Marla . . . no!" She gasped and looked at Marla. "When did you get the black ring?"

"A few days ago."

Everyone looked solemn. Zane felt confused. "Sorry, but I'm not sure I understand," he said.

"Marla's ring just changed to black," Alex said. "Black is the color just before a person is considered expendable."

Zane's eyes widened. "I know you said each clone wears a different colored ring to distinguish them."

Alex nodded. "Yes, but as one clone is considered no longer needed, the clone with the black ring is . . . " She did air quotes. "Offered to Marduk. Which means she is sent outside the city forcefield. Then all the colors change to indicate who is next to be eliminated based upon their perceived usefulness."

Bradley jumped in. "The human is the last to be eliminated."

Marla gave a forced smile. "I'm now the only . . . me . . . here."

"You always were one-of-a-kind anyway," Grant said as he smiled, reaching over and squeezing her hand. "Besides, they could still decide they need another clone from you for something."

Marla tilted her head. "I've never seen that happen."

Bradley shrugged but looked sad. "Yet there's no reason it couldn't happen."

Marla waived her hand with a dismissive gesture. "Enough about me. We have to work on getting things ready for both Alex and Zane."

"Double cloning does add complications we hadn't planned for," Grant added.

"Yes," Marla said, "but the decision to do so solves the problem of Summer-amat becoming suspicious of Zane's actions after he becomes the new Gilgamesh."

"Granted." Grant still looked perplexed.

"What's the matter, Grant?" Alex asked, matching his worried look.

"I have two matter streams now to prepare for. And I can't do both from the same lab." He turned and looked around. "Bradley, where's the floor plans we were looking at the other day?"

Bradley pointed to the hutch in the corner. "Upper drawer on the left."

As he walked over, Alex removed the other dishes from the table and took them to the kitchen. Grant displayed the plans over the table and pointed out, to Marla, the decisions they had reached the other night.

She nodded in agreement but bit her thumbnail at the same time. "It's a good plan, Grant." She tilted her head back and forth slightly. "Or, *was* a good plan." She glanced at him and then pointed at the blueprints. "Where you said our 'competitors' are located is the only other lab that has the capability to pull this off. Once they do their part, we have to take them out." She panned each of their faces. "Quietly."

"And we—you—do that how?" Zane asked.

"We go old school," Marla replied.

Zane raised his eyebrows in anticipation of what that would be. "What, like blow darts or something?"

Marla smiled. "Stun guns."

Zane's eyes widened. "Stun guns is old school?" Back home, Zane knew the closest thing they had to that was a taser or maybe a bean bag launcher. Of course, with their technology so far advanced from anything on Earth, he supposed an advanced piece of technology on Earth would be considered old school here.

"We'll have to be precise and accurate, though," Bradley said. "We can't miss a single one or we risk drawing attention to ourselves and the whole thing will be a bust." He shook his head. "We can't afford to blow this. This is our only—and last—chance for success."

Everyone nodded.

"What happens if you do get caught?" Alex asked.

Bradley looked at her and said, with force, "As the new rulers, you'll have no choice but to execute us."

"What?" Alex's expression was one of horror. "I can't do that!"

"And you'll have to eliminate them as quickly as possible," Bradley added. "Before anyone has a chance to investigate and discover what we were really up to and that you two were also involved."

Alex looked at Zane with eyes wide, filled with unbelief. Zane, though, knew Bradley was right. They may have no other choice if their whole mission for being here was to come true.

All looked solemn for a few minutes. Finally, Grant spoke up. "Wait a minute."

Everyone looked his way.

"We can't use stun guns. If we're caught, as we just stated, then their bodies will be evidence against Zane and Alex."

Marla put her hand to her chin as if in thought. "Good point, Grant." She shrugged. "So, new school it is."

Zane cocked his head. "And that means . . . ?"

"Phasers."

His eyes went wide. "Like in *Star Trek*?"

Marla gave him a blank stare. "Don't understand the reference, but they're an extension of the stun gun. The first shot stuns and the second shot will vaporize—not a trace remaining."

Alex looked uncertain. "That seems so drastic."

Marla put her hand on Alex's shoulder while giving her a sympathetic look. "I know, Alex. But whether you want to admit it or not, this is war. Not one that we started, but one we have to win."

Alex nodded but gave Zane an anxious look. He reached over and squeezed her hand for support. This was all becoming more dangerous than anyone had anticipated.

Zane leaned over and whispered. "Think about them just going 'poof.'"

Alex gave a chuckle and shook her head. She looked back at him with an adoring smile.

That was a look he would definitely fight for.

CHAPTER 25

GETTING PREPARED

Quietly, Zane opened the door to the lab. Empty. As he and Grant walked in, Zane heard several pieces of equipment making noise and saw various lights blinking.

Grant looked around. "The technicians must have stepped out for a few minutes. Watch the door."

"What if they come back?"

Grant shrugged. "Just stall them. I won't need long to install the cameras."

As Grant got to work, Zane stood at the door looking out the glass window down the hallway as best he could. He saw a few people, but they simply walked by. Yet each time, his heart rate skyrocketed. He breathed a sigh of relief each time they passed the door.

Zane became startled by a person suddenly appearing and grabbing the door handle. Yet the guy turned back when someone called to him. Zane turned and plastered his back to the wall, trying to recover from his adrenaline surge. He saw Grant approaching.

"Come on, let's go," Grant said.

"But someone is out there about to come in."

Grant patted his shoulder. "It's okay. Just be yourself."

Grant opened the door and walked out. Zane followed.

The man, outside the door talking to someone, suddenly turned. "Can I help you?"

Grant smiled. "I was looking for Benson, but I just realized he was transferred to the lab down the hall."

The man nodded. "Yeah, he was transferred last week." He pointed. "Just down the hall on your left."

Grant began walking and held up his hand. "Thanks. Have a great day."

Zane looked behind him. The man turned and entered the lab. Zane turned back and let out a long breath.

Grant looked at him and laughed. "Relax, Zane. If you're relaxed, so will they be. If you act tense, they will suspect something. Be confident in what you're doing, and they will accept what you say."

"That's easier said than done."

Grant stopped and faced him. "Look, Zane. You're a scientist. They are scientists. Just be geeky, and they will reciprocate." He raised his eyebrows. "Got it?"

Zane nodded. Understanding the concept was easy, but following through wasn't that simple.

"Good. Let's get this done."

Grant confidently entered the next lab. A man working on a pod turned with an expectant look.

"Hey, Benson. I was told you had a light out, so I've come to fix it."

Benson laughed. "Drew the short straw, huh?"

Grant laughed with him. "Something like that." As Grant headed to his task, he added, "This is Zane—somewhat new. I thought you could explain your work to help him acclimate."

Benson held out his hand and Zane shook it.

Zane pointed to the pod. "So what are you working on?"

Benson smiled. "I'm putting in a neuro-interface. Familiar?"

"Somewhat. I think I understand the concept, but how is the transfer actually accomplished?" Zane smiled. "Grant tells me you're the best at this."

"Well," Benson said, "I don't like to brag, but I think so. I've made many improvements to the process."

Zane's eyes widened. "Do tell."

As Benson went through the process, Zane kept glancing at Grant, who installed the camera as he replaced the light fixture. Zane understood some of what Benson was telling him. Hearing the confidence Benson had in the process made Zane feel more confident their approach and process would work.

"So, where do you apply the electrodes for the transfer to occur properly?"

Benson turned and picked up a mannequin head and placed it in a pod. "This step is pretty important. I've marked where they are to be attached here. When I train people, I use this so they can see their placement, and then I have them practice on a head without markings so I can see if they've properly placed them."

"Impressive." Zane picked up the mannequin head and held it up, turning the replica back and forth. He nodded. "You're very thorough, Benson." He smiled. "No wonder you're the best."

"All finished! We need to go," Grant said.

Zane handed the mannequin head to Benson. "Thanks for the demo. Very impressive."

"Sure, not a problem," Benson said. "Not often I get to tell someone about my work." He laughed. "And them actually wanting to hear the details."

As they walked out of the lab and farther down the hallway, Grant patted Zane on his shoulder. "Very good, Zane. Smart thinking holding the head up for the camera to see."

"Just tell me the camera was on."

Grant nodded. "Yep. Now you can practice how to put the electrodes on very quickly and accurately."

Zane nodded. "And teach Alex the same."

It took them most of the morning to get all the cameras installed. Most of the other rooms were not labs, so they were not all occupied. They had to wait a few times for the room to become empty, but usually not very long. The trickiest room was the glass room where the statue of Marduk was housed.

As they stood outside the door to the glass room, Zane looked at Grant. "How are we going to put cameras here when everyone can see into the room?"

Grant smiled. "I've made plans for that."

Zane squinted. He had no idea what Grant was talking about.

Grant pulled something from his pocket, looked around, and pointed the device at the ceiling inside the glass room. One of the lights suddenly blew.

"Now what?" Zane asked.

"We wait."

Zane felt nervous just standing around. Those who came by, however, didn't pay them any notice. They seemed to be in their own world.

Grant's communicator sounded; he tapped it. "This is Grant."

A man's voice stated, "We have a light out in the glass room. Please repair."

Grant smiled at Zane and then responded. "On it."

Zane's eyes widened. "And how did you accomplish that?"

"I got myself assigned to maintenance duty today." He grinned. "Good idea, right?"

"So, the light in Benson's lab was legit?"

"Believe it or not, it was. I didn't have to sabotage that one—and see how well that turned out."

Zane shook his head. "I think you may be a little too confident."

Grant smiled and gestured for Zane to follow him into the glass room. As Grant got to work, Zane looked at the statue, which looked almost identical to the one he had seen in Babylon. The stance of Marduk looked the same, with his arms crossed across his chest, but the statue itself must have been at least three times larger. He had to admit: the size and detail were very impressive.

The portal was also larger and impressive. The device was cube-shaped like the original and seemed to have the same colored crystals. Being larger, the artifact had more layers of crystals. Even though not activated, the lights in the room caused the light to reflect and refract through the crystals making them look like they were actually glowing. This caused the colors to be reflected on the ceiling in a nearly kaleidoscope effect.

It wasn't long before Grant completed his work. "There," he said, looking up. "Done, and you can't even see the camera." He patted Zane's arm. "Ready for lunch?"

They went to the first floor to a type of cafeteria. Zane had never seen a design similar to this one before, except maybe on a show like *Star Trek*. At a holographic computer terminal, one selected their meal choices, and those choices were assembled in a matter of minutes in a type of chamber where the food just seemed to appear. The meal was ready for pickup at another counter.

They walked out onto a large patio with many tables and seating arrangements. Grant pointed. "There's Marla."

They went over and sat with her. She smiled at Grant and said hello to Zane. The two were obviously close, and Zane suspected something more existed between them, even if they didn't admit it.

Marla took a bite of salad and pointed her fork at Grant. "Everything done?"

He smiled and nodded. "And no issues." He nodded toward Zane. "And Zane here worked like a pro, allowing us to get electrode placements on camera."

Marla's eyebrows went up. "Very good, Zane. I'm impressed."

Zane chuckled. "I had a good teacher."

She looked at Grant and smiled. *Yeah*, Zane thought. *There's more than just friendship between them*. Their gaze at one another lingered.

Zane smiled. "And what about you, Marla? Everything go okay?"

His words brought Marla back to reality. "What? Oh, yeah. Everything went fine. No hiccups."

"Does that mean we're all set?"

Marla nodded. "I think so. My sources feel confident about the lab this rogue faction will use. We feel they don't know about our plans."

Grant added, "We just have to get everyone in their positions on cloning day."

"And exactly when is cloning day?" Zane asked. He wondered why he had not asked that question earlier. It was perhaps the most important question of all.

Marla smiled. "One week from today."

Zane swallowed hard. That made the reality tangible. Was he up to the task?

He had to be, didn't he?

CHAPTER 26

PRACTICE MAKES PERFECT

The next couple of days for Zane and Alex were spent learning how to attach the electrodes of the neural interface to their correct placement. After they watched the video feed of the mannequin head several times, they attempted the feat and then compared their placements with the video. This became a time-consuming and laborious effort.

They took a break two afternoons later and sat at the dining table.

The door opened and Bradley walked in. "How's it going?"

Alex sighed. "I don't know if we will ever get this right. Checking the video feed after each attempt is eating up way too much time."

"Hmm," Bradley said as he sat down a grocery bag. "I may have an idea." He went to the hutch in the corner, came back with a marker, and handed it to Zane. "Use this to mark where the electrodes should go on Alex's head," Bradley said. "I'll then use those markings to make the same marks on your head."

Alex's eyes widened. "Then all we have to do is compare the placement to the mark." She looked at Bradley and smiled. "You're a genius, Bradley."

He gave an exaggerated shrug. "That's what I keep telling everyone, but . . . "

She laughed. "Well, I'll back you up next time."

He laughed with her and took his groceries to the kitchen. Zane got to work to put the correct markings on Alex's head. "There," he said. "Now we can really get to work."

Bradley came out and looked at the marks on Alex's head and made the same placements on Zane's. He patted Zane's shoulders. "Now off you go to practice."

Both laid on the floor in the living area and attempted the feat. After a few tries, Bradley walked over.

"I hate to be the bearer of bad news," he said.

Zane stopped what he was doing and looked up from the floor. "Are we doing something wrong?"

"Well, the space between your face and the top of the pod will be barely enough room for you to get your hands up around your face. You both have your elbows way up in the air." He shook his head. "If you learn this way, you'll likely fail when the time comes to do it the same in the pod itself."

Zane sat up and sighed. "Great. We're back to square one."

"Not exactly," Bradley said. He looked around and pointed at the balcony. "The balcony chairs. Their backs are rounded. We can tip the chairs over and put them around your head. If you bump them out of place, then you know the attempt wasn't successful."

Alex pointed at Bradley and smiled. "I told you: you're a genius."

Bradley grinned. "Just validation, I guess."

Zane shook his head and went to the balcony. "I'll get them. I'm not sure your head can make it through the opening."

Bradley first looked shocked, then laughed with both of them.

For the rest of the afternoon, both Zane and Alex worked to attach the electrodes properly. In the beginning, their elbows always moved the chairs. Zane started by not worrying about the placement until he could attach them anywhere on his head without moving his chair.

They were still practicing when Grant and Marla arrived. Grant came over between the two of them and just stared. He laughed. "I would ask what you're doing, but I'm afraid to."

Zane lifted his chair and peeked up at him. "Very funny."

Grant laughed again. "It looks like you have snakes sticking out of your head."

Zane rolled his eyes. "Thanks for the encouragement."

Grant bent down and patted his chest. "Anytime, buddy."

Alex lifted her chair. "Bradley, check my placement. I feel good about my attempt this time."

Bradley came over and knelt next to her. "Let me see . . . " He checked each placement while saying "uh-huh" each time. He smiled. "Congratulations, Alex. The placements are perfect."

She beamed. "I didn't move the chair either." She sat up. "I'm stopping now on a good note. I'll practice more tomorrow."

Zane lifted his chair. "While you're here, check mine."

Bradley leaned over. "Uh-huh, uh-huh, uh-uh . . . uh-uh, uh-huh . . . uh-uh." He grimaced. "Sorry, buddy, but three were off. Just slightly, but off."

Zane sat up. "At least I didn't move the chair. I'll work more on placement tomorrow."

Bradley patted his shoulder, stood, and extended his hand to pull Zane to his feet. Zane righted his chair and brought it to the dining table where the others were sitting. He removed his simulated electrodes as he sat.

"How'd you do?" Alex asked.

Zane shook his head. "Still need more practice. Doing this is really harder than it looks."

Marla patted his arm. "Don't get discouraged," she said. "This is only your second day. Even those who can see where to place the electrodes don't get their placements right the first time. You're doing great."

Alex rubbed his arm. "It's not a competition. Don't turn it into one."

He leaned in and gave her a kiss. "If I have to be trumped, I'm glad it's by you."

Alex chuckled and shook her head. She turned her attention to Grant. "So where do we stand?"

"All in all, pretty good, I think," Grant said. "All the cameras are installed. I was able to add sound to the video feed as well."

"That will prove helpful," Marla added. "Easier to course-correct when we know what they're saying rather than just guessing based on their actions and reactions alone."

"Benson put a neural link into each pod." Grant smiled. "I convinced him to do that as a just-in-case scenario."

"He wasn't suspicious about that request?" Bradley asked.

Grant shook his head. "I convinced him that since he had to work on them now, anyway, he might as well put everything in so he won't need to work on them again later. Plus, they can then use any pod, any time, for any reason." He smiled. "Benson thought that was a good idea."

"Good job," Bradley said. "Maybe you should have been a lawyer."

Grant laughed. "Maybe I will be when I get back to Earth."

Bradley patted his arm. "I wish that for you, buddy." He stood and went to the kitchen.

Grant became solemn and shook his head. "He's, like, one of my best friends—and I forget he's a clone," he said to the others. "He just doesn't act like a clone."

"I know," Marla said. "He knows how you feel. Knowing everyone else will likely go back to Earth, but he won't, is hard for him."

Grant shook his head. "I think he will. He has to." He paused, then added, "He just has to. He acts more human than many of the humans in this place."

Bradley returned with a tray of drinks. "How about iced tea for everyone?"

Everyone took a glass. Grant held his up. "Here's to Bradley, the best friend anyone could have."

"Hear, hear," the others said as they clinked glasses together.

Zane added, "And whose head will hopefully soon get through the balcony door."

Bradley and Alex laughed. The others gave him a *What?* look—then laughed as well.

Zane could have sworn Bradley's cheeks reddened. He wondered: *Can clones physiologically react that way?*

After the laughter died, Marla looked at Alex and then Zane. "There is another significant piece of information the two of you need to know."

Zane raised his eyebrows. "Oh, did Grant propose or something?"

Marla's expression froze for several seconds. "What? No, no. Nothing like that." She playfully slapped Zane's arm a couple of times. "What made you say that?"

Zane mock defended himself and laughed. "Hey, it doesn't take a genius to see you two like each other—a lot."

Marla's expression changed suddenly. "It doesn't matter."

Zane stopped laughing. "What? Why doesn't it matter?" He glanced at Grant, who also had a saddened look. *What's wrong with these two?* Zane thought. *They're perfect for each other.*

"Remember, we won't be on Adversaria for much longer," Grant said. "Then we'll each go to our separate timeline." He shrugged. "Or that's what we believe." He glanced at Bradley, who nodded.

"So what's the timeline difference between you two?" Zane asked.

Marla said softly, "About nine hundred years—give or take."

"You can see," Grant said, "by the time our lives overlap, I'll cease to be."

"I'm sorry," Zane said, regretting his teasing and bringing up something painful.

After a long silence, Zane spoke up again. "Wait a minute. That's Adversarian years from when you two got here, right?"

They nodded.

"Grant, how old were you on Earth when you got here?"

"Thirty. Why?"

"And, Marla, you were . . . ?"

"Twenty-five." She scrunched her brow. "What are you getting at?"

"So, if we look at the timeline difference between when the two of you arrived here, we would take your age, Grant, being thirty, add nine hundred to that, but then subtract your age, Marla, being twenty-five, and then add how long you have been here—which is one thousand years. That gives us one thousand, nine hundred, and five years." He chuckled. "But those are Adversarian years. That's only slightly more than nineteen Earth years!"

Grant and Marla looked at each other, their mouths open slightly.

Zane grinned. "I'm not sure how the portal will send you back. But however you are sent back, there will only be nineteen years between the two of you." He shrugged. "More time than between most couples, but not unheard of either. Either way, you should be good."

Grant took Marla's hand. "There's hope for us, Marla."

She nodded, leaned over, and kissed Zane's cheek. "Thank you, Math Boy."

Everyone laughed.

Alex leaned in. "Two nicknames now. Wow."

Zane pointed his index finger at Marla. "Wait just a minute!"

Alex leaned in and gave him a kiss. "You're wonderful."

"I like *that* nickname."

She grinned and laughed again with everyone at the table.

Marla soon formed a T with her hands. "Sorry, Math Boy here got me off topic."

"Oh, yeah," Zane said with a chuckle. "You said we needed to know something."

"The ring from the previous occupant of the pod will remain in the pod when they are teleported out. So you will need to put this ring on before you exit the pod. Your ring will turn purple, and you will automatically be registered as the new Gilgamesh and Summer-amat. The ring of all subsequent clones will then change to the lower color statuses."

Alex gasped. She realized something.

Zane's attention jerked her way. "What's wrong?"

"That means someone will have to be offered to Marduk."

Marla nodded. "Unfortunately, yes." She looked at Alex. "And I'm sorry, but that duty goes to Summer-amat."

Alex swallowed hard. "I'm not sure I can banish someone like that, clone or no clone."

Zane took her hand and gave a slight squeeze.

"Alex," Marla said softly. "It has to be done. And you have to show no emotion when you do so."

Grant nodded. "Summer-amat would act as if such an act did not phase her in the least."

"You will be the first Summer-amat since the original from Babylon who will not be soulless on Adversaria," Bradley said. "Still, you have to remember she would do such a thing without batting an eyelash."

Alex swallowed hard but nodded. "I will pray about it."

Zane gave her hand a soft squeeze once more. He wanted to show his support; he didn't know what else to do. He wondered if he could take this burden from her. Yet taking that responsibility would change a tradition that had existed for thousands of Adversarian years. That would likely be a dead giveaway that something was amiss.

Yet the realization the two people were soulless clones was somewhat comforting—at least in his mind. He glanced at Alex, who had a pensive look. Evidently, such an act seemed just as wrong in her eyes as if the individual was fully human.

A thought came back to him that Marla had expressed earlier: *this is war.*

CHAPTER 27

FAULTY INTEL

Marla checked Zane's connections and nodded. "They're spot-on, Zane. Good job." She then removed the next chair and checked Alex's. "Same. Perfect." She helped both to their feet. "I think you're both ready." She glanced from one to the other. "Feel ready?"

Both nodded.

"As ready as we'll ever be, I'm afraid," Zane said, forcing a smile. He was ready. He felt ready—but apprehensive at the same time.

The door burst open and Grant came rushing through. "Our timeline is wrong. The cloning ceremony is at dawn."

"What?" Marla shook her head. "No, all my sources said the ceremony was to be held at noon." She looked at her watch. "This doesn't give us nearly enough time." She looked back at Grant. "Are you sure?"

Grant nodded. "Benson just told me. He's preparing the pods now."

Marla began to pace. "But now is when we expected him to prepare the pods. Then we would have all morning to get everything in place." She shook her head and looked at Grant. "We can't do anything until he's done."

Alex looked from one to the other. "Is he trustworthy? Can we bring him into the loop?"

"Not enough time," Grant said as he shook his head. "I like the guy, but I don't really know where his loyalties lie. After all, he's a clone, so I'm not sure we can afford to trust him. Not without enough background checks. And we just don't have time for that."

"This could work out to our favor."

All turned to see Bradley entering from the bedroom.

"What do you mean?" Grant asked.

"Think about it. We didn't know which lab our rivals would choose. Now we know they have to choose the lab Benson *isn't* using." He bobbed his head. "Yes, we now have more pressure on us, but this yields a more definite outcome."

Alex looked at Bradley and smiled. "Bradley . . . "

Bradley held up his hand. "Yes, yes." He looked at Zane. "And my head still fits through the balcony door."

Zane chuckled. "I'm not arguing to the contrary this time."

Bradley grinned and turned to Grant. "So what now?"

"Well, we pull an all-nighter and get things ready."

Bradley nodded. "Okay, everyone. Pack your backpacks. I'll get some nutrition bars and we can have them on the way."

In only a short time, everyone was back at the dining table. Grant and Bradley went over the checklist of what they needed to ensure they had everything.

Grant looked up at each of them. "Well, guys, this is it. Good luck to us all."

"Grant, we should pray," Bradley said.

Grant looked resistant at first, likely feeling they didn't have time, then nodded. "You're right, Bradley." He bowed his head and began a short, heartfelt offering. "To you who indwells us, we ask for your protection and wisdom as we prepare to achieve what we feel is your desire. Guide our actions and our motives. Amen."

Everyone else added "Amen."

As they headed to the door, Alex said, "I think the sky cars are the better bet. The teleporter will register our departure and arrival, and the monorail has too many stops."

Grant nodded. "Good deduction. Okay. Let's go."

They headed up the few flights of stairs to the roof. Thankfully, no one else was there when they arrived. All five of them stepped onto a round pad and took a seat. Alex chose the location. A forcefield came over them and the sky car took off.

Bradley passed out nutrition bars and Grant pointed at the hologram over the lake. "As soon as the Marduk hologram dissipates, the ceremony will begin." He looked at his watch. "That gives us ten hours to get everything done."

All nodded as they ate in silence. Zane looked around as the craft provided a total surround view. All looked beautiful from here. The golden glow of the statue over the dark water of the lake . . . the city lights of the skyscrapers in their geometric shapes, and of the shops across the lake . . . the night sky with a brilliant view of a galaxy . . . some type of moon next to another planet . . . and some type of nebulae in the far distance—all of these were things to greatly admire. Soon all of this would be gone, a distant memory. The beauty was an evil beauty, though. The heart of this place was against everything Zane believed in and stood for. He reminded himself that was important to remember.

The craft landed on top of the ziggurat, the main city skyscraper—the hub of the entire city and the location of the

Marduk statue. Having no guards always surprised Zane. Security did exist throughout the city, but mainly to ensure all went as planned and to always carry out Gilgamesh's orders. Since everyone was supposed to be here, no one considered that there could be other agendas. A proverb from Scripture came to Zane's mind; it seemed apropos: pride goes before destruction.

They found a place on the roof to stay until everything was clear. They sat in patio chairs under an umbrella. Zane had to chuckle. Even clandestine operations were posh here. Grant looked at the video feeds from all the rooms on his computer tablet. Zane looked over and saw Benson still working in his lab.

Zane pointed to one of the screens. "Is this the other lab? Where are the folks that should be there?"

Grant shrugged. "I don't know. I would have thought they would need as much time as we do."

They heard voices from around the corner. All looked at one another wide-eyed. Grant motioned for everyone to move around the potted shrubbery that lined one side of the roof's edge. Thankfully, there was just enough space between the large urns and the roof edge to hide.

The voices became louder as they heard footsteps get closer.

"So, where is Jamison?" one of the men said. "We can't get this done without him, and we're running out of time."

"Don't be so hard on him," a second man said. "He was caught off guard just as much as we were about the timeline. He'll be here. Just give him a few minutes."

Zane heard the first man drop down into one of the chairs. "Well, he'd better be. If we miss this opportunity, I'll—"

Just then, Zane got a cramp in his hamstring from the position he was tucked into. He grunted, then caught himself. He turned over and straightened his leg to try to get the cramp to ease. Although painful, he forced himself to not make a noise except for the first grunt, when the pain caught him off guard.

"What was that?" one of the men asked.

Zane heard a noise from the man pushing his chair back as he stood. The sound of footsteps came their way. Everyone froze. Grant slowly pulled his phaser from his backpack. Taking these guys out may have to occur earlier than anticipated.

Zane then heard the other man. "There's Jamison now."

He heard the footsteps of the man who approached go back the other way. "Well, it's about time."

Zane heard the craft land, a quick exchange of greetings, and then the fast gait of footsteps back inside the building.

Everyone breathed a sigh of relief.

"How's your leg?" Grant asked.

Zane nodded. "Okay now. Sorry about that. The pain took me off guard."

They went back to the patio chairs and sat. Zane walked around a little longer to return his leg circulation to normal.

Grant looked at the video feed again. "Benson seems to be finishing up." He picked up his backpack. "Okay, everyone. Show time."

As they got in the elevator, Grant pushed the elevator button for the floor above their destination.

Zane raised an eyebrow.

"Just a precaution," Grant said.

Zane nodded but didn't comment. Doing so made sense. Likely Benson would use the elevator to leave, and they couldn't risk the elevator opening and them being in the car.

As the doors to the elevator opened, Grant slowly peeked out and then motioned for all to follow. They went to the stairwell and down one flight of stairs. Grant looked at the video feed once more. The lab they needed was empty, and the three men they encountered on the roof were now in the other lab beginning their work with their pod.

Grant slowly opened the door to the hallway, peeked out, then quickly ducked back into the stairwell. "He's still waiting for the elevator," he said.

In about one minute, they heard the ding of the elevator. Grant opened the door slowly and peeked in again. "He's getting in." After a few seconds, Grant motioned for the others to follow.

They slowly snuck down the hallway to the lab Benson had left and breathed a sigh of relief once all of them were inside. After each unpacked their backpacks, Bradley and Marla began working on the pod. Grant worked on another device. Zane wasn't sure what this piece of equipment was for, but Grant hooked the device up to the end of the pod and started doing some type of calibration. Lights glowed on and off as he worked.

Zane and Alex sat as they watched the three of them work. He wished they could help, but he knew the two of them would just be in the way. Let the experts do the expert stuff, he reasoned.

As Zane quietly waited, he closed his eyes and imagined himself putting the electrodes in the right place. That was his job. To be sure he did that correctly, he spent time practicing mentally. That was all he could do for now, so he spent his time doing so. Suddenly, another thought came to him. He was supposed to remember something else. He opened his eyes, his mind in a panic. *What am I supposed to remember?*

The sound of a large falling washer jerked everyone's attention to the pod. Grant quickly reached down and recovered the metal ring as Alex went to the door and looked out, just in case the sound had been heard by someone. She looked both ways and shook her head indicating no one was coming.

As Zane watched Grant put the washer back in place, what he needed to remember came back to him. *The ring.* When the clone teleports out of the pod, the ring will remain. He had to put the ring on his finger. Put on the electrodes, then put on the ring. *Electrodes. Ring.*

Alex scooted her chair over and put her hand in his. They smiled weakly at each other. At least they were in this together. As time went on, Zane could feel himself becoming more and more anxious.

To do something, Zane picked up Grant's tablet and looked at the video feed. He could see them all in one frame and the other lab in another. The other group in their lab seemed to be doing similar work on their pod.

Suddenly, Zane saw movement in another frame. Three Bradley clones, seemingly out of nowhere, appeared in the glass room. Zane surmised they came through the portal. There was no other explanation.

"Uh, guys," Zane said. "We have company. Three Bradleys just entered through the portal."

Bradley swung around. "What?" He looked in thought for a few seconds. "Their timing can't be a coincidence."

"You think these are the three Bradleys from Earth?" Zane asked.

Bradley nodded. "Likely. I had hoped Ekmenetet would have prevented them from coming back." He tapped his chin rapidly with his index finger. "If they don't delay the ceremony, we'll be fine."

"But won't we be okay since they'll have memory loss until tomorrow?" Zane asked.

Bradley shook his head. "Clones don't have memory loss. Only humans do. But if they wait until after the ceremony, they'll basically be reporting the problem to you."

Zane nodded. "And we can let them search as much as they want, and they won't find us because we'll be Gilgamesh and Summer-amat."

"Right," Bradley said. "We have to stall them somehow. I don't want the present royal couple to know of anything they know. That information could cause them to delay the ceremony and put all of us in jeopardy."

Alex looked at the tablet. "Where are they going?"

Zane looked up and locked gazes with Bradley. "To the receiving room."

Alex looked from Zane to Bradley. "Well, that can't be good." She looked at her watch. "The royal couple will be there in about two hours. What do we do?" she asked.

Bradley started searching shelves. "Help me find green paint of some kind."

Zane started looking but wasn't sure why. "What's your plan, Bradley?"

"The clone looking like me who serves the royal couple has a green ring. They will know that. If I can deceive them for at least a short while, I'll get them to another room."

Zane paused and looked at Bradley. "How?"

Bradley kept looking. "Early breakfast. I just hope they fall for the ruse."

Zane looked at his watch. "At this hour?"

Marla snapped her fingers. "There's a bakery not far from here that opens pretty early." She turned to Grant. "Can you finish up without me?"

He nodded. "Not much choice." He nodded his head in thought. "But I'm pretty close to finishing. It'll be close, but doable, I think."

Bradley pulled something from a cabinet. "Here. Ask the bakery to put powdered sugar on the tops of the muffins, or whatever you get. Then, sprinkle this on top. The sugar will mask the taste, and this agent should knock them out for several hours."

"But won't you get caught?" Alex asked.

"I'll go down the stairs and out the back. When I return, I can act official and say I'm providing breakfast to visitors." She gave a slight shrug. "It should work."

She put the bottle Bradley gave her in her pocket and then headed out the door, cautiously looking down the hall, and then was gone.

"Voila!" Alex exclaimed. She held up a bottle containing something green. "I'm not sure what this is, but it might work."

While she and Bradley worked on the ring project, Zane looked at the video feed again and turned up the volume slightly. His eyes widened. "Bradley. Bradley, are you almost done?" His voice was almost in a panic.

"Yeah. Why?"

"One of the guys is talking about going out to get coffee or something to eat."

Bradley's eyes widened. He looked at Alex. "I can't let them leave. I've got to go."

"But the ring is still tacky," Alex said.

"It'll have to do," Bradley said. "I'll be careful and try not to touch anything. They just have to see my ring, not inspect it."

Alex nodded, but she looked worried as Bradley hurried out of the room. Alex came over and sat next to Zane. "Turn up the volume."

The posture of the other Bradleys stiffened when Bradley entered their room.

"Who are you?" one of the clones asked.

Bradley held up his hands so all could see his ring. Yet his doing so looked natural and as though he was the proper Bradley who served the royal couple.

"You have arrived so early," Bradley said. "We were not expecting you. Security told me the portal activated, so I came to investigate."

Zane knew that was a lie but hoped these clones didn't know that.

"We have an important message for the royal couple. We think an imposter has come to Adversaria. They must be warned."

"Oh, absolutely," Bradley said. His words were quite convincing, Zane thought. "But surely you don't expect me to wake them at this hour?"

Two of them shook their heads. "No," one said. "But we must speak to them as soon as they can see us."

"Of course, of course. Without question. But you must be tired and hungry."

"I was just going out to get something," another responded.

Bradley gave a dismissive wave. "Don't bother. I've arranged some refreshments and beverages for you."

One of them stepped forward. "Why would you do that before you even knew who we were?"

Bradley smiled. "Well, for someone to come this early, your arrival had to be important. And then knowing you would have to wait a few hours . . . " He shrugged. "It just seemed the appropriate thing to do. We don't want guests to think we are inhospitable, do we?" Bradley gave a slight chuckle.

The clone's stance seemed to relax a bit after that.

Bradley gestured to the door. "Just follow me a couple of rooms over and you can rest and enjoy an early breakfast there. We're having it brought in."

Another suddenly had a questioning look. "Why not here?"

"Oh," Bradley said with a sense of disbelief. "Here in the royal receiving room?" He shook his head. "The royal couple expects this room to remain spotless. I'm sure you don't want to upset them before you deliver your important news to them."

The man cocked his head. "Well, no."

Bradley smiled. "Good. Now in the other room, if things get a little . . . messy, no problem. We can have the cleaning crew take care of that room when they come on duty." He walked to the door. The others followed. "We'll send for you just as soon as the royal couple arrives."

Bradley showed them to the other room and opened the door. "Refreshments will arrive momentarily." He held the door open for them as they entered. Zane saw one of the men enter but linger near Bradley, which seemed to make Bradley nervous. He saw Bradley reach for something, and a cart of food came into view. Apparently, Marla had left the cart at the door rather than entering.

"Ah, perfect timing," Bradley exclaimed as he wheeled the cart into the room.

The gaze of the man near Bradley went from Bradley to the cart with their breakfast. The man took the cart containing muffins and a carafe of coffee, or some kind of hot beverage, and pushed their breakfast into the room. Each man took a muffin and poured themselves a cup of the hot drink. The three decided to sit back and put their feet up. Bradley left the room and rejoined the others in the lab.

Coming to the nearest chair, Bradley sat with a thud. "Wow, that was a little intense."

"What do you mean?" Zane asked. "You handled those clones like a pro."

"One of them kept staring at my finger. I thought he was going to demand to examine my ring." He pointed at Marla. "Thankfully, the food arrived just in time, and he lost interest in my ring."

Marla fanned herself. "Well, I've gotten my exercise for the day." She looked over at Grant, still busily working. "How's everything over there, Grant?"

Grant turned and smiled. "I think we're ready. How are we on time?"

Marla looked at her watch. "We have about forty minutes. My guess is those prepping for the ceremony will arrive in about ten."

Zane looked up from his tablet. "And it seems our Bradleys are now sleeping soundly." He looked at Marla. "They went out quick. How much of that stuff did you use?"

She handed the bottle back to Bradley a bit sheepishly. "I didn't know how much to add, so I was . . . quite generous with it."

Bradley held up the bottle, now half empty. "Very generous."

CHAPTER 28

BODY SWITCH

All stood around Zane as they watched the video feed on the tablet. The Bradleys were still asleep, the group in the other lab making final preparations, and people were arriving in the glass room. First, several workers came in and placed seating arrangements for the royal couple, brought in two pods, and finally carried in two tables draped ornately for the clones' memory transference.

Shortly after, the royal couple arrived and sat.

Grant patted Zane's shoulder. "Okay, Zane. It's time to get in the pod."

Zane went over and began to climb into the device, but Grant stopped him.

"Sorry, buddy. But you have to remove all your clothes before you get in."

Zane stared at him to see if he was being serious.

Grant shrugged. "That's just how it is, unfortunately. We have to stick to their process and rituals."

"Uh, we'll be over here out of the way," Alex said.

That made Zane feel better. He wasn't ashamed of his body, but getting undressed in front of people felt odd. He removed his clothes as quickly as possible and climbed into the pod. The surface felt cold to his skin. He tried to ignore the sensation, but found that difficult, giving several grimaces and gasps as he settled in.

Grant leaned over him. "You'll feel yourself go weightless. When you feel your weight return, you'll be in the glass room. You should be able to recognize that through your viewport here." Grant patted the part of the lid composed of glass. "Then, as fast as you can, put on the electrodes—and then the ring."

Zane nodded. "Got it."

Grant started to close the lid, then added, "Don't forget to act royal."

Zane got a serious look, then said sternly, "How dare you talk to me like a child. Just do your job as instructed." He gave a wide smile. "Like that?"

At first, this took Grant off guard. He smiled when he saw Zane smile and then chuckled. "Yeah, something like that."

Zane tried to relax as Grant closed the top of the pod. He kept telling himself he could do this. No, he had to do this. All their lives were at stake. There was no room for error.

He could still hear everyone speaking, but their voices were now muffled. He heard Grant tell Bradley and Marla to prepare to invade the other lab and put Alex in position.

Zane saw flashes of light and then heard Bradley yell, "Now! Go, go, go!" Zane wanted to know what was going on, but at the same time, he saw everything go white and he felt weightless.

It's happening!

He felt his weight return. All felt the same as before. Was he back in the lab or in the glass room? As he looked up, he saw a kaleidoscope of color on the ceiling. *The glass room.* He closed his eyes and worked to get the electrodes in place. Since this was how he practiced attaching the electrodes while at the apartment, he kept to the same routine. Shortly, it was accomplished! He forced himself to calm his breathing as he put his arms by his side. His hand touched something. *The ring.* He grabbed the piece of jewelry and quickly slipped it on his finger. He willed his heart to slow, and he further forced his breathing to a normal rhythm.

He heard muffled voices but couldn't really tell what was being said. A few words came through: "Marduk" . . . "lie down" . . . "start the process."

Suddenly, a force seemed to flood into his mind like a tsunami. The emotions were overwhelming. Zane gasped and his body tensed. Multitudes of memories with their intense emotions flooded his mind. . . . He had a lust for power which was inhibited by Melchizedek and even by Yahweh. He sought power, and Marduk came to him with an offer and opportunity. . . . He could not refuse because the gift from Marduk included everything he wanted: power, influence, immortality. . . . Then came all the trips between Adversaria and Earth, all that had been put in place and what was to be accomplished. All these memories created a very dark feeling—but an immensely appealing one at the same time.

By the time the memory transference was completed, Zane was breathing hard. He had to force his breathing to calm again. His heart rate slowly returned to normal. While he felt like himself, he felt different at the same time. There was a power struggle going on inside him. He realized he could simply ditch their original plan to destroy Adversaria and become the ruler, the true ruler, that everyone was looking for. He could likely rule the world. The thought was overwhelming.

But no. *That is a lie.* There was only one truth, and he had to follow it. Didn't he? Something kept telling him there were other options now open to him that he could take advantage of. Yes, these thoughts were all extremely tempting.

Before he could come to terms with his thoughts, the lid opened. Two priests looked down at him while holding an ornate robe for him to wear and preserve his modesty. He sat up, turned so his back was to everyone, and let his arms slip into the garment and over his shoulders. The Bradley with the green ring quickly came around and secured the robe in his front.

Zane turned and everyone genuflected. He gave a slight smile. This reminded him of the experience in Babylon when those not knowing if he was Gilgamesh or not bowed to him. He found these actions almost enjoyable. He had to fight against this thought and not take all their actions to heart.

Zane walked to the throne chair and sat. "Remove the pod I exited and prepare for my queen."

Several of the priests did, helping the previous Gilgamesh to his feet, his ring now green rather than purple. This clone genuflected and then spoke. "I pledge my allegiance to the new Gilgamesh. My memories are now yours. Yet I continue to serve. May you still find use of me for Marduk's greater purpose."

Zane pointed to a place to his right. The clone bowed, walked over, and stood there. "The offer of your memories is accepted, but we are all in Marduk's hands for what further use we will be in his service."

Zane knew that was what this clone had said to his predecessor, so he felt saying the same words was needed for this one as well. The words would at least provide a tinge of hope to this clone who, though once royalty, would now have a life filled with mediocrity.

The clone nodded. "Yes, my lord."

Zane heard noise down the corridor behind the glass room. Some turned to look, but Zane refocused them. "Prepare for the queen's arrival. That is precedent."

The priest put the female clone on the ornate table, placed the electrodes on her head, and connected them to the pod that contained the new clone that had been placed there before the ceremony began.

Zane stood. All genuflected with their eyes looking at the floor. *Good*, he thought. *They won't notice the transference.* He raised his hands. "Marduk, we give you praise . . . " Zane saw a flash of light. No one stirred, so the event seemed to go unnoticed. " . . . for our new queen which you provide to us today." He remembered what other clones had said and then thought how to give Alex additional time to get her electrodes connected. He talked slowly, regally: "Everyone here is excited to see the fulfillment of your vision and willing to do whatever is required for it to succeed. I am sure truth will reign true to the end."

That last sentence caused some to glance up quickly. He knew no clone had ever said those words, but he had to end his praise by giving it to the One who truly deserved it.

Once the priests hooked the clone on the table to the pod which now contained Alex, he noticed a slight movement in the pod. She likely was being overwhelmed with the memories that now flooded her brain. He hoped she could handle them. Some, Zane knew, were quite dark.

Zane also assumed this to mean that Grant, Marla, and Bradley were successful in overthrowing the rebel faction.

Otherwise, he surmised, Alex would not have been teleported into the pod.

After a few minutes the pod opened. Alex sat upright. Zane was surprised she did not try to inhibit her modesty. This reminded him of the original Summer-amat in Babylon who used her sensuality as a power play and not as something to be kept to herself. She stood and was wrapped in the sheer robe the priests draped around her and secured in front. Zane stood and held out his hand to guide her to her throne chair. His eyes widened. *She's not wearing her ring!*

As soon as she sat with him, the priest turned to close the pod, but Zane stood suddenly in his place. The priests turned in shock and quickly genuflected. He knew he had taken them off guard. He just hoped they had not seen the ring before they turned back around.

"Because this is the first time both Summer-amat and I have been renewed together, I want our admiration of her to be extended, as she is well worth the adoration," Zane, as the new Gilgamesh, said.

"Praise be Summer-amat and Gilgamesh our lord. Praise be Marduk," the priests said.

As they said this, Zane walked toward the pod and turned. He quickly reached a hand into the pod behind his back. His fingers found the ring and he closed his hand around the small piece of jewelry. Casually, he walked back to the throne chairs, stood in front of Alex, and presented the ring to her behind his back so no one would see. He heard a slight gasp and then felt the ring being slipped from his fingers.

"You may rise," Zane said in a commanding voice. "Marduk appreciates your dedication." He sat in his chair.

Once all were standing, Alex looked at the head priest. "Bring the clones no longer of relevance."

The priest bowed and exited the glass room, then returned with two individuals—one man and one woman. Zane noticed the rings on their fingers glowed. Now that he had previous memories, he knew this was the signal of who was no longer considered useful to Marduk's purpose. Because of the glow, they could not hide their status. The clones did not resist but allowed themselves to be led directly next to Marduk's statue under the portal.

Alex stood and walked to the statue, placing her hand somewhere on the idol's right leg. Zane saw several of the crystals reposition themselves. He tried to hide his surprise as no one had mentioned the portal could do that. But these actions did make sense in that something had to be altered to change where the person would be deposited once teleported. Zane knew they would be deposited outside the city's force-field where they would suffocate and die. Clones were clones, but they were also flesh and blood; they needed oxygen to live. Apparently, outside the forcefield dome there was no air, so their death would be quick.

Alex looked at the couple. "Marduk thanks you for your service. From Marduk you came, to Marduk you return." She then touched the statue in a different position and a beam of light shot from Marduk's eyes and surrounded the couple, who then disappeared. All that remained were the robes they had worn. Zane noticed the priests also retrieved the rings the couple had worn; these were now clear with no color to them at all. Zane assumed this was to allow the rings to be used again.

Zane again had to force himself not to be surprised at what had just occurred. This was no ordinary statue but was some-how integrated with the portal. While the portal sent people between Earth and Adversaria, the statue evidently sent people through the forcefield and onto the planet's surface. Since they were considered sacrificed to Marduk, this was clearly a visual representation of that fact. The beam came from the Marduk statue, and not the portal, as if to signify Marduk himself had accepted them as he looked down upon them.

Alex held out her hand. Zane rose and took her hand in his. They walked to the opposite side of the glass room where an archway formed and led down a long tunnel to a balcony on the side of the building. Zane had not known about this archway and balcony until the memories were downloaded into his mind.

Once they arrived at the balcony, a large crowd that had gathered below began to cheer and whistle. Both waved to the crowd; its noise grew still louder. After several seconds of waving, they turned back and walked to the glass room. Zane knew a large celebration would now be held for the citizens of Adversaria. Yet, he knew, based upon the memories of the previous clones, this celebration was just a way for everyone to drown their disappointment in being moved to a lower notch in the clone priority list.

Deception seemed to exist in almost everything done here. He and Alex would have to move forward cautiously.

Once back at the glass room, they proceeded to their receiving room without additional comment. Workers jumped into action to get everything removed from the glass room and back to normal. The Bradley with the green ring ran around them, opened the door of their receiving room, and closed it behind them.

Both went to their respective chairs and sat.

Alex, Zane noticed, let out a long sigh.

CHAPTER 29

THE NEW GILGAMESH

Alex looked pensive.

"Are you all right?" Zane asked.

She put her palm to her forehead and shook it back and forth. "No. No, I'm not." She looked at him. "Zane, there are so many things that are not right."

He took her hand. "I know. But you handled yourself quite regally. I don't think anyone could tell that sentencing the clones to their death upset you." He smiled. "And neither did that display of coming out of the pod."

Alex's cheeks blushed slightly. "I knew that was what was expected. I thought I was going to faint. Never have I ever displayed myself like that in front of strangers." She looked in his eyes. "But that's not the half of our problems."

Zane squinted. "What else went wrong?"

Alex's eyes widened. "Oh, just about everything."

Zane's eyebrows raised. "I did see a white light just before I was teleported to the pod in the glass room. What was that?"

"Stun gun fire."

Zane's mouth fell open. "From whom?"

"One of the ones from the other lab. Somehow, they had been informed of our actions. He just missed Grant. If he had come a few seconds earlier, you would have missed your window." She shook her head. "Anyway, Bradley was able to get him with his phaser as he yelled at us to go to the other lab."

"Then what happened?"

"Marla was able to shoot the guy in the other lab and then get me into the pod in time for Grant to send me right after he got to the lab. But I heard someone else come into the lab."

"Do you know who?"

Alex shook her head. "No, but I think the visitors may have been the three Bradleys who arrived from Earth."

"What makes you think *that*?"

Alex shrugged. "I can't think of who else it would be." She placed her hand on his forearm. "But for them to know, they would have had to be tipped off."

Zane sighed. "So our first mission is to solve a conspiracy."

Alex twisted the corner of her mouth and nodded. "Seems to be."

At that moment they heard a knock and saw Bradley stick his head in. Zane noticed the ring on this Bradley was green. Now that he had Gilgamesh's memories and those of all his clones, he knew this man's name was Cyrus.

"Come in, Cyrus," Zane said.

Cyrus entered and bowed. "Forgive me, but we have a couple of issues you should be made aware of."

"A couple?"

"I'm afraid so, my lord. May I bring some individuals in?"

Zane gestured for them to enter. Along with Cyrus came the three Bradleys from Earth, then Bradley, Marla, and Grant.

Zane gave a quick glance at Alex whose stance had now stiffened. Neither of them had expected this. Something had definitely gone wrong.

"My lord," Cyrus said. "These three have come from Earth to alert you to an issue they have discovered."

Zane gestured for them to step forward.

One of them spoke for all three. "My lord, we have been led to believe that the twenty-first century duplicates of my lord and queen have made their way to Adversaria without escort."

"What?" Zane tried to sound surprised and greatly angered. "How is that possible? You were to bring them back here so we can utilize the new retrovirus to incorporate their genetic material into our own." He slapped the arm of his chair. "This was Marduk's plan. Why have you not followed through with his plan?"

The man bowed. "My lord, I am sorry. Due to unforeseen circumstances they both touched the portal simultaneously."

Zane jumped to his feet. "They what?" He was nearly yelling as he said it. "You idiots! Why did you let that happen?"

The man bowed again. "I'm sorry, my lord. Such an event was unforeseen."

"How do you know they are here, then?" Alex interjected. "We don't know what the portal does when they touch the device simultaneously."

Zane sat. "That is true." He looked at the man. "Explain."

The man looked nervous. "I'm sorry, my lord. We would like to at least search and see if either of them is here."

Zane looked at Alex. She shrugged. He turned to the man. "Granted."

"Thank you, my lord."

Zane waved his hand at the other three. "And who are these others?"

The man pointed at them. "These three tried to sabotage your ceremony."

"That is untrue!" Marla said emphatically as she tried to break away from the other Earth Bradley, who was now holding her.

Zane held up his hand to indicate silence. "Cyrus, please explain what happened."

"My lord, these were found in one of the nearby labs. We feel they were trying to do something to hinder your ceremony."

"And what would that be?" Alex asked.

Cyrus shook his head. "I do not know, my queen. Yet I think these are the rebels we have been trying to catch."

Alex's eyes widened. "You mean the perfect clone to replace my lord Gilgamesh?"

Cyrus nodded. "Yes, my queen."

"And you think they succeeded?" Alex looked at Zane. "You feel my lord can be improved upon?"

Cyrus's eyes widened. "Oh no, my queen. My lord is definitely more perfect than any other clone here." He looked from those in the room back to Alex. "I just mean, these are the ones who felt they could make a better clone than could our lord Marduk."

Zane sat up straighter while trying to look irritated. "And where is this other Gilgamesh clone they were using to usurp me?"

Cyrus looked down. "We did not find him, my lord."

"Then how could they be those you indicated? How could they sabotage my ceremony if they have no . . . " He did air quotes around his next words. "Perfect Gilgamesh clone."

Cyrus now looked uneasy. "My lord, we feel they attempted this, but their timing was off, surprised by these three from

Earth interrupting their efforts, and the matter stream was unsuccessful."

"We would never!" Grant said. "We are loyal."

"Quiet!" said the Bradley clone holding him as he punched Grant in his stomach.

Grant bent over in pain and gasped for breath.

Alex held up her hand. All stopped and looked at her in expectation. "This is quite serious, and we cannot deal with this lightly."

Zane looked at her. "And what do you imply, my queen?"

"We should question them ourselves. These three from Earth have other important work to embark on."

Cyrus bowed. "My queen, please allow me to do that for you."

Alex shook her head. "I require you to go with these three and be sure their needs are met. If we have an imposter in Adversaria, we need to root them out as soon as possible."

"But—"

Alex held up her hand and made her words more stern. "I have spoken."

Cyrus bowed again. "Yes, my queen." He didn't look happy, but Zane knew Cyrus had no choice but to obey. He motioned for the Bradleys to follow him.

The Bradley who had spoken before added, "My lord, I don't want to leave you unprotected here."

Zane stood straighter, drew up a confident look. "Are they armed?"

"No, my lord."

"Are you saying I can be overcome by these . . . insurrectionists when they are bound?"

"No, my lord."

"Away then."

The man bowed. "Yes, my lord."

As soon as the four of them left, and the door was secured behind them, Alex let out a long breath. "Well, that was fun. What on earth happened?"

"Zane?" Bradley asked. He looked very unsure.

Zane smiled. "It's me, Bradley."

Bradley devised a quick test. "What was the last thing you said to me yesterday?"

"I bet your head still doesn't fit through the balcony door. Does it?"

Bradley sighed and then smiled. "I must say. You really took to your part quite well."

"Blame that on Grant."

Grant's eyes widened. "What?"

"You're the one who told me to act royal."

Grant laughed. "Yes, I guess I did. Very good job, by the way."

Zane went on. "Now to Alex's question: What happened?"

"To be honest," Marla said, "I'm not sure." She gestured to Zane. "One of the guys from the other lab tried to take us out just before you teleported to the glass room. Bradley here took him out." She gestured to Alex. "You and I went to the other lab. I was able to take the second guy out and get you into the pod just as Grant came in. He then had just enough time to teleport you before the Bradleys from Earth stormed in."

"But how did they even know you were there?" Zane asked. "This was something not even on their radar."

"It is curious," Grant added. "When did . . . what was his name? . . . Cyrus? . . . come to the glass room?"

Zane thought about the question. "I'm not sure. I really didn't pay him any attention until he helped me get dressed after I came out of the pod." He looked from one of them to the other. "You think he is the culprit?"

Marla grimaced. "I can't see who else it would have been."

"But how would he have known?" Zane asked. "Plus, he didn't seem to think we were not the clones expected."

"But," Alex said, "he did seem to feel you were not the perfect clone expected."

Zane turned and looked at her. "So, you think he was involved in that conspiracy?"

She shrugged. "Makes sense to me."

"That's what I was thinking," Marla said. "Since the plot failed, he now wants to pin the suspicion on someone else so he won't be a suspect."

"But how do we prove that?" Grant asked. "Right now, it's our word against his, and he has the support of the three Earth Bradleys."

Alex pointed at Bradley. "Your ring, Bradley. Exploit what you did with the Earth Bradleys when you had your ring green. You can blame that on Cyrus."

Bradley cocked his head for a moment as if he did not understand. Slowly, a grin came across his face. "They won't be so happy if they know they were drugged once they got here," he said.

Marla suddenly looked excited. "Right. And they only saw Bradley, who had a green ring. So why would he drug them?"

Grant laughed. "Because he didn't want them to find out his plot against lord Gilgamesh."

"Yes, you three have defended my honor," Zane said with a smile. "I will have to replace Cyrus for his untrustworthiness."

"You will need another to replace him," Alex said.

He looked at her and smiled. "Indeed. Who better than the hero—Bradley?"

CHAPTER 30

CROSSING THE DOUBLECROSSER

Cyrus entered the receiving room with the three Earth Bradleys. All bowed.

"And what have you found?" Zane asked.

"Nothing, my lord," Cyrus said with a sigh of resignation.

"It's been three days," Alex said. "Surely you've had time to search all of Adversaria. I know the city's large, but it is not vast."

One of the Earth Bradleys stepped forward. "My queen, we have searched everywhere without finding anything."

"Someone could be hiding them," Cyrus said.

Zane's eyebrows raised. "Oh, and you have evidence of this?"

Cyrus shook his head while looking downcast. "No, my lord. Not yet."

"Not yet? So you hope to find evidence?"

"Yes, my lord. Of course."

Zane cocked his head. "And why do you think you will find something when these three fine gentlemen have not?"

"Uh, I mean, my lord . . . they must be here somewhere."

Alex looked at Zane and then back to Cyrus. "Maybe you are biding time to fabricate something, as you did for these three men at our cloning celebration."

Cyrus's eyes grew wide. "My queen? I . . . I have not fabricated *anything*."

"Oh, really?" Alex displayed an air of condescension. "Well, we have done our own investigation these past three days."

"Yes," Zane said. "And the facts seem to indicate you did fabricate, and you made these three men here with you part of your conspiracy."

"What?" Cyrus shook his head emphatically. "No, my lord. No. Never."

Zane looked at the man who had spoken to him the first time. "Please tell us what happened when you first arrived here on Adversaria."

The man cleared his throat. "Well, we arrived very early, my lord, so your servant here provided us with something to eat and drink until you were awake so he could make our presence known to you."

Cyrus looked at the man as though he was crazy. "I did no such thing."

The man bowed slightly. "Pardon me, my lord. The man we met could have been another clone. All I know is he wore a green ring. I just assumed he was your servant. Perhaps the man was another."

Zane looked at Cyrus sternly. "And how many clones have a green ring?"

"Oh . . . only one, my lord," Cyrus said, his voice cracking.

Zane could tell Cyrus knew he was being backed into a corner. His eyes darted right and left as his mind tried to think of a way out. He looked from the man to Zane. "But, I never—"

Zane ignored him, not letting him finish. He looked at the man again. "And who presented you to us? I do not recall us meeting."

"No one, my lord. We were apparently drugged."

Alex sat up straighter. "What? Someone here drugged you? Who?"

"A man who looked like Cyrus and wore a green ring."

Alex stared at Cyrus.

He held up his hands. "No. No, my queen! I would never!"

"Perhaps this is why we could never find the clone behind the revolt against us who tried to usurp lord Gilgamesh's rightful rule." She pointed her index finger at Cyrus. "It was you!"

Zane grabbed the arms of his chair and leaned forward. "So you attempted to replace me with your so-called 'perfect' clone? When that failed, you saw your opportunity to get rid of all evidence by waking these three men who you had drugged earlier just in case you needed them to cover up your scheme."

The other two men grabbed Cyrus's arms and held him fast.

"What are you doing?" He looked at Zane. "No, my lord. That is not true—not how it happened. I have been loyal."

"Everyone is loyal," Zane snapped. "Until they are not." Zane looked at the man who did the speaking for the three. "Bring in the others."

The man opened the door. Bradley, Grant, and Marla stepped in.

Cyrus pointed. "Them! *They* are the ones who tried to usurp you. They were in the lab." He looked at the men holding him. "These are the ones you found in the lab."

"Because you told them," Grant exclaimed.

"Of course you would say that," Cyrus said with contempt.

"Wait!" Zane held up his hand.

Cyrus turned. "My lord?"

"Just how did you know they were even there?" Zane cocked his head and waited in anticipation for an answer.

Now Cyrus looked like a caged animal, one looking for a way out but not finding any. "I . . . I was just walking by and saw them. I then ran and told these men."

Alex leaned forward. "To see them, you would have to be late for our ceremony. How could our trusted servant be at our ceremony and see them in the lab at the same time?" She squinted. "You are lying to us."

Cyrus shook his head and struggled to get free. He pointed again. "*Those* are your culprits!"

Zane pointed at them as well. "These three 'culprits,' as you call them, were the ones defeating those you were helping to try and overthrow your lord. These are the heroes. *You.* You are the enemy."

The man standing next to Cyrus spoke. "And what shall I do with this man?"

Zane shrugged. "I give you free reign to use your imagination."

The man smiled and bowed slightly. "Thank you, my lord. You won't have to worry with him any longer."

The two men turned with Cyrus between them. The third man spoke. "And what shall I do with his ring, my lord?"

Zane looked at Bradley. "You, clone looking like Cyrus, what is your designation?"

"Bradley, my lord." He bowed to Zane.

"Since you are my rescuer, so to speak, do you wish to take his place as my servant?"

Bradley bowed again. "Indeed, my lord. Doing so would be my honor."

"Come forward."

Bradley walked up and stood in front of Zane as Zane motioned for the other clone to bring Cyrus, now a prisoner, forward.

"Hold his hand," Zane commanded.

The other two clones came forward and held Cyrus as the third clone held his hand steady.

Zane looked at Bradley. "Place your ring on top of the green one."

Bradley did this. Zane then placed his ring on top of Bradley's. Bradley's ring turned green and that of the prisoner glowed clear. Zane, now with his new memories, knew his purple ring could swap designations. Because the rings of other clones did not change, this put Cyrus's ring at the bottom of the order rank.

The prisoner's eyes widened in horror. "No! This is unjust. I have served you well all of these years!"

Zane nodded and, as the three Bradleys pulled Cyrus from the room, he yelled. "Wait! Wait, my lord! *Bradley?* There is no such clone with that name."

"I've never seen a clone so desperate," Alex said. "Please take him away."

In a matter of minutes, Cyrus was gone, and the five friends were alone together again.

Marla was the first to speak. "Is the ordeal over? Really over?"

"We were successful," Grant said in a state of near disbelief. He bowed to Zane. "A job well done, my lord." He bowed to Alex. "And my queen."

Zane laughed. "All thanks to you three. The 'job well done' goes to you."

Bradley held up his hand and admired the ring. "And we are all now legitimate. We don't have to hide anymore."

Marla patted Bradley on his shoulder. "Congratulations, Bradley. Plus, we pulled off the coup and eliminated the rebel faction. Now the path has been cleared to accomplish the main mission."

"All that is true," Bradley said. "But . . . " He looked at Zane. "Those three Bradley clones were the ones sent to Earth to kill you—most likely by Cyrus."

Zane nodded. "I know. But they were pawns in all of this. Just carrying out orders. They will likely not continue with that pursuit. I'll find another mission for them."

Grant got a concerned look. "But if these three were in league with Cyrus, what's to say they won't just let him go?"

"Well, let's find out," Zane said. "You still have your tablet, don't you?"

Grant nodded as he pulled out the device. "Our belongings were returned to us yesterday." He smiled. "Thanks to you, I assume."

Zane stood and walked forward. "So, bring up the feed to the glass room."

Grant's eyes widened. "Ah, good idea." He did so and they all gathered around to see the video of Cyrus and the three clones. As the video feed displayed, Grant turned up the audio so they could hear the conversation.

Cyrus was speaking: "Hector, you can't do this to me."

"You failed, Cyrus. Someone must take the blame, and it won't be us. Lord Gilgamesh doesn't suspect us—only you."

"With you out of the way," one of the others said, "we're free and clear."

"But what about our plans for a coup and world domination?"

"Your plans, you mean," Hector said. "We were part of your plot for the compensation. Which, by the way, you never delivered on."

Cyrus held out his hand. "But I will. I promise. I'll even triple what I agreed to."

Hector grinned. "Don't think so. We're now back on lord Gilgamesh's good side and, with you out of the way, we can have our share—and yours." He smiled. "Bye, Cyrus. Marduk appreciates your sacrifice."

Hector pressed the statue in the same spot Alex had at the end of the earlier ceremony. Again a white light shot from the statue's eyes, surrounded Cyrus, and he disappeared.

One of the three looked at the other two. "So, what do we do now?"

Hector put a hand on each of their shoulders. "We forget all about what Cyrus was doing and we comply with Gilgamesh. No one has to know anything about this."

They each nodded, picked up the clothes and ring that were left behind, and left the glass room.

CHAPTER 31

IT'S GREAT TO BE KING

Many things were going through Zane's mind as he sat on his balcony overlooking the part of the city he had not yet visited. This side of the city looked similar to the opposite one, but instead of a lake, as he had seen previously, this side of the city boasted a golf course. Zane shook his head. At first glance around this place, one would think they had arrived at a resort paradise, but Zane knew darker forces were clearly at work. Just going over the memories he now possessed helped him understand that evil was at the heart of everything. There were many memories he purposefully repressed; they were too disturbing.

There were memories of being back in Babylon where he had impregnated various temple priestesses and then had their newborns sacrificed while still alive to Marduk to show his devotion . . . then, here on this very golf course those he had talked with so casually to get a feel of their loyalty and then having their lives snuffed out just because he considered them a potential threat—no tangible proof, but he acted on his feelings anyway . . . then there were the feelings of lust, greed, and power: all now within his grasp—no need for inhibitions any longer as all his actions were basically without consequences.

He stood and went to the balcony's edge. To think that just a short time ago he was an archaeology professor. Now he was the ruler of Adversaria! He chuckled and gazed over the city—this was now his realm. Never in his wildest dreams would he have thought he would be experiencing this.

A knock at the door caused him to turn. Zane waved the man onto the balcony; he could tell it was Bradley with a cart of food.

"Good morning, Bradley. Really, you don't have to do this. I can get someone else to do the servant duties."

Bradley shook his head. "It's not a bother. I'm getting in good with the chef. She lets me sample many things."

Zane chuckled. "Servitude has its privileges, huh?"

Bradley smiled as he transferred dishes from the cart to the patio-style table where Zane sat. Bradley looked at Zane. "If I start to get fat, you can have me do other duties."

Zane laughed. "Fair enough." He sat down and studied what Bradley was serving. His eyes widened. "Bradley, I'm the one who's going to get fat. I can't eat all this."

Bradley looked around. "I assumed Alex would be joining you."

Zane shrugged. "I haven't seen her this morning. Not really like her. She's typically up before I am."

While their rooms were separate, the balcony went across both living area exits so they could join each other when they wanted or be alone if desired. The design likely helped each royal couple keep up appearances as no one had to see one of them leave for their own room in a huff. Hopefully, Zane thought, that would not be his experience with Alex.

As Bradley set the table, Alex stepped onto the balcony with a yawn. "Oh, hi, you two." She came over as she looked at her watch. "Did I really sleep that long?"

Bradley smiled. "You're just in time. Breakfast is being served." He took the cart and headed back inside Zane's room.

Alex called to him. "Bradley, please come eat with us." She looked at Zane, who nodded his agreement.

"But I'm now your servant. Eating with you would be unseemly."

"For crying out loud, Bradley," Zane said. "I made you our advisor. Advisors need to eat." He pushed another chair away from the table with his foot. "So come eat."

Bradley returned to the balcony and pulled up his chair.

"Plus," Alex said, "we do need advising."

"For sure," Zane said as he took a bite of something like a cinnamon roll and then a sip of Adversaria's version of coffee. "I need to know how to get to the power facility without my being there seeming suspicious."

Bradley put food on his plate. "I think you can do whatever you want now."

Alex tore open a roll and buttered one side. "I don't know. We can't come across as dictators and raise suspicions."

"Well, many of the others came across as such."

Alex sighed. "I know, Bradley, but also look what happened to them. Their reigns were usually cut short."

"Did the other royal couples ever visit the power facility?" Zane asked.

Bradley shook his head. "Not to my knowledge. I don't think they even cared about such things. They only wanted power." He stopped and smiled when he realized what he had said. "Political power, that is. Nothing else concerned them."

There was silence between them as they ate while in thought.

"What if we got Marla and Grant assigned to the power facility?" Alex asked as she looked from Bradley to Zane. "It may take us a little longer to achieve our mission, but they could better understand the workings of whatever it is that powers this place."

Zane nodded. "That makes sense." He turned to Bradley. "Do you think this Farzad guy could use assistants?"

Bradley stopped chewing and chuckled. "Probably, but he's very arrogant, obnoxious, and opinionated. So he likely would never admit he needs help with anything."

Zane forced a smile. "Great. Sounds just like a guy Marla and Grant would love to work with. Can you have them both come to our receiving room?"

Bradley reciprocated the forced smile. "Would love to." He took a final bite of toast, stood, and headed to find them.

Zane raised his eyebrows and looked at Alex. "How bad could he be?"

Alex gave a shrug. "How long could you stand constant doses of Dr. Latham?"

Zane grimaced.

"Exactly," Alex said. "Now multiply that by one hundred."

"Well, hopefully they won't be working with him for long." He stood and held out a hand. "Let's go break the news to our friends."

Alex stood and walked with him. "And hope they remain friends."

Grant and Marla were already at the receiving room when Zane and Alex arrived.

Zane smiled. "Come in."

"Bradley said you have a job for us?" Grant asked, looking from Zane to Alex.

Zane invited them to have a seat at a table near the door. He wanted to treat them like the friends they were, so he avoided sitting in the throne-style chairs. "I want the two of you to work with Dr. Farzad and find the best way to sabotage his equipment," Zane said.

Grant and Marla looked at each other and then back to Zane. "But we know very little about the power system here," Grant said.

"Really?" Alex looked surprised. "But if you understand teleportation, how to interrupt and intercept matter streams, and even how to override a teleportation process, surely you can understand the power system." She shrugged. "I just mean, you may not understand it . . . yet. But you *could*, right?"

Grant shrugged. "I suppose." He looked at Marla.

"Probably," Marla said. "But how would we even get access?"

Zane smiled. "I'm making the two of you Farzad's new assistants."

Grant cocked his head. "I've met him. He's a little . . . ."

"Harsh," Marla said, nodding. She looked at Zane. "Blunt and arrogant." She squinted. "Sort of a downer at parties, if you know what I mean."

"Maybe he's better in a working environment," Alex said.

Marla looked at Grant and then at Alex. "Probably not." She shrugged. "But hey, we'll give it a shot. After all, getting to our goal is more important than trying to avoid harsh remarks."

Grant sighed. "So, when do we start?"

"How about now?" Zane stood and turned to Alex. "You coming?"

She shook her head. "While you do that, I'm going to give Hector and his two clones a job that will keep them out of our hair."

"Oh?" Zane's eyebrows shot up. "And what would that be?"

Alex's mouth curled at the corner. "I don't know yet. I'll let you know when you get back."

Zane laughed. "Can't wait to hear your brilliant plan."

Grant and Marla followed Zane to the nearest teleporter. Now that he no longer had to worry about his use of the device being recorded, using the teleporter was the fastest and easiest route of transportation to any part of the city and any surrounding area. The power facility lay at the far end of the city near the forcefield.

As they entered the lobby, a replica of the power supply was on display, almost like a living sculpture. The display, visible in a glass case several meters long and positioned at eye level, was mesmerizing to watch as the device shot colorful arcs of . . . something . . . from one end of the case to the other. If this was just a replica, Zane thought, he couldn't imagine how ominous the real device would look.

As the three of them walked through the building, with Zane slightly ahead of them, various individuals would turn, wide-eyed, and bow or genuflect as they walked by. In their wake, many whispered in hushed conversations.

"You're creating quite the stir," Grant said with a slight chuckle.

Zane headed up a flight of stairs that apparently led to a large office. The name on the glass wall said, "Dr. Farzad, Director of Exotic Power Generation, Adversarian Power Facility."

It seemed Dr. Farzad thought quite highly of himself. And no wonder, Zane guessed, if no one had ever truly approached him before. Zane looked around this part of the building. Farzad had created a dominion nearly all his own.

A woman at a turquoise glass desk looked up, immediately stood, and quickly bowed. "I'll get Dr. Farzad right away."

Zane nodded, but Farzad was out of his office and next to her desk before she took her first step. Evidently someone had tipped him off as to their arrival.

Farzad waved his hand at the woman. "Don't bother, Jasmine. You're slow as usual." He turned to Zane and gave a deep bow. "Our new lord Gilgamesh. What do I owe the pleasure?"

"I would like to view your facility," Zane said.

Farzad froze for a second—the only movement was in his eyes, which blinked a few times. "I'm sorry. You want to what?"

Zane cocked his head. "I request a tour of your facility. Do you have a problem with that?"

"Everything is working perfectly fine." Farzad seemed defensive. "What is the reason for the request?"

Zane stood slightly taller in his stature. "Do I need a reason to view something in Adversaria?"

"Well, no. But this is highly irregular."

"It may be, but I want a better understanding of our power needs in *my* kingdom."

Farzad started to say something, but Zane interjected with his next thought. "And I wish these two to accompany us," he said, motioning to Marla and Grant.

A scowl came across Farzad's face. "What can they even understand?"

Zane forced a smile. "Let's find out, shall we?"

Farzad acted befuddled, as though he didn't know what to do. He quickly turned to Jasmine. "Hold my calls and appointments until I get back."

She nodded but looked a little bewildered. Zane wondered if Farzad was grandstanding, making himself appear, and sound, more important than he really was. Still, his actions didn't matter. Zane knew he had the upper hand.

Farzad took a few steps and turned. "Follow me."

Zane looked at Grant and Marla and smiled.

CHAPTER 32

POWER FACILITY

Farzad's tour took them to an elevator which descended twenty floors below ground. As the elevator descended, Farzad said, "I'm taking you to the power source room, as I assume that is what you really want to see."

Zane nodded.

"Yet I'm not sure why you want to see the power room," Farzad continued. "None of you will understand how it works anyway." Zane thought Farzad should be quite glad none of the other rulers came to see him as they would have likely taken his head off for his condescending tone. Zane stiffened, remained regal, and let Farzad's remarks pass.

When the elevators opened, all eyes, except for those of Farzad, widened. The place was massive. On this end of the gargantuan room were all sorts of holographic consoles with blinking lights and numerous icons glowing different colors.

Farzad gestured with his hand toward them. "These are the controls that let us keep the power fluctuations stable so no one misses a beat in their power needs. Keeping things that way is all quite complicated and requires constant surveillance. I can monitor all of this from my office upstairs."

Zane looked around and saw no one else. "You have no one down here? What if you have a need to do something quickly?"

"I did just say I can monitor from my office. I can do what I need to from there."

Grant and Marla looked over the consoles as Farzad made this remark.

"But what about the exotic particle matter stream you pull from subspace?" Grant asked. "Wouldn't you need to fine-tune that from here?"

"Oh, Mr. Teleporter is going to teach me about exotic particles now, is he?" Farzad said.

Grant turned and looked at him.

"Yes, I know who you are," Farzad went on. "You're brilliant with teleportation matter streams, but don't even try and say that's anything like an exotic matter particle stream."

Grant's face reddened a bit. "I didn't say they were. But even I know an exotic matter particle stream needs a more delicate touch than a teleporter matter stream. And I have to monitor that very closely."

Farzad gave a dismissive hand gesture. "Well, of course *you* would. Since I have perfected this power source, I'm very well able to manage operations from my office."

Marla interjected, "From twenty floors away? Shouldn't you at least have *someone* down here—just in case?"

"Oh, and that would be you, I take it?" Farzad laughed. "As if that would ever happen."

"Well, now that you mention it," Zane said, taking a step between the two to block their gazes from the glaring battle taking place. "I think it will likely happen."

Farzad's gaze shot to Zane. "What? What will likely happen?"

"That you will have someone down here to monitor the power stream." Zane looked around. "Speaking of that, just where is the power stream?"

Farzad displayed a small grin and touched one of the icons on the nearest holographic console. One half of the wall went into the ceiling, and this revealed windows into another vast room.

Zane walked forward. "Impressive!" was all he could say.

Before him were multiple versions of the replica he observed when he first entered the building. Yet these were massive and there were a large number of them. They seemed to stretch forever. As in the replica, there were numerous arcs that went from this side of the room to the far end of the other, which was barely visible, and each arc seemed to display a different color. The view looked spectacular indeed.

"Let me see if I can dumb this down enough for you," Farzad said as he looked at Grant and Marla.

Zane knew Farzad included him in his derogatory remark, but his actions didn't necessarily indicate they did. Safe ground that could be denied if challenged. Zane once more let Farzad's remarks go unchallenged.

"Exotic matter is pulled in from subspace and trapped between two gravitational fields. The energy created is almost limitless," Farzad said. "We must have these devices relatively small so we can contain and control the power."

Zane's eyes widened. "That's what you consider small?"

Farzad nodded. "Yes, relatively speaking, of course."

Zane nodded. "Of course." In truth, he really didn't comprehend this at all, yet he pressed on. "And why so many?"

"Well, we kept adding more as the city grew and as the power needs of the city continued to grow." He shrugged. "The city no longer grows in size, but the power requirements continue to grow exponentially." He looked at Zane and smiled. "Yet I think we now have sufficient power and even reserves to last for a few more millennia at least, if needed."

"Good to hear," Zane said as he turned and looked at Grant and Marla. He smiled when he saw the look on their faces, which said, "Do we have to be here?"

Zane turned back to Farzad. "And what would happen if someone tried to sabotage this place?"

Farzad's eyes widened. "Sabotage? Who would even try such a thing?" He shook his head. "Impossible that someone on Adversaria would even contemplate such an aggressive act."

Zane folded his arms. "I'm not so convinced. My ceremony was almost usurped by a radical faction group." He opened his arms and gestured to the entire room. "Who's to say they wouldn't do something similar to this place? Doing so would turn the balance of power."

"No offense, my lord," Farzad said. "But trying to gain political power and this power source are not really comparable. No matter who is in political control, they would still need this place even if—forgive me—they don't need the one from whom they took political power."

Zane turned and looked at the spectacular display in the vast room before him. "And what's to prevent someone from just walking down there and creating havoc?"

Farzad walked over and stood next to Zane. "For one thing, they would die as soon as they entered."

Zane gave him a stare.

"The whole place is a vacuum and at a temperature as close to absolute zero as humanly possible. Plus, one needs special access to get a suit to wear that is capable of withstanding both conditions." He turned and gestured to the room they were in. "Actually, it is very hard to sabotage anything here. Everything's redundant." He turned and pointed at the room. "There's another room just like this one at the other end of the city." He smiled. "Destroying one does nothing."

Zane's eyes widened. "Pretty impressive."

"Well, of course it is. I designed it."

Zane pointed to Grant and Marla. "So when do you want them to start?"

Farzad just stared at him. "I don't. I don't want them to start. Period."

Zane continued to stare.

Farzad sighed. "Really, my lord. They will just eat up my valuable time—first to train them and then to answer all of their inane questions."

Zane turned and headed toward the elevator. "Perfect. Tomorrow it is then."

Farzad grimaced and nearly stamped his foot but jerked his body silently instead. "My lord. Really?"

Zane stood at the elevator as if waiting for someone to press the button. He gave a forced smile and said, "Really."

Farzad walked over and slammed his palm on the elevator button. He looked back. "If you two will stop ogling all the mesmerizing lights, we're heading back upstairs."

Grant and Marla walked over, both shaking their heads. Zane knew they were not happy with having to work for this man, but they, like he, knew doing so was important. They needed to learn the detailed information as to how this place worked so they could devise a plan to take the operation down.

The elevator ride was deathly quiet as the car ascended. All that could be heard was the hum of the car. Farzad was fuming, apparently silently talking to himself. Grant and Marla kept looking at each other and at Farzad, occasionally rolling their eyes. Zane would smile when he caught one of their gazes. They would give him a telling gaze back which made him smile even more.

When they arrived at Farzad's office, Zane said, "Thank you, Farzad, for the tour. Your work here is exemplary."

He expected a simple thank you in return, but Farzad's comment was anything but simple. "If I am exemplary without any help, why do I need assistants—and I use that term loosely—to be better than exemplary?"

Zane gave a forced smile. "One can never know the height of their achievement by only measuring their ability against past accomplishments."

Farzad bowed and headed for his office; he did not bother to show them out. As he entered his office, Zane heard Farzad mumble to himself, "I'll be sure and post that on my desk."

"Excuse me, my lord," Jasmine said, looking a little sheepish. "I'm sorry. But am I to understand these two will be working here?"

Zane gave her a genuine smile. "Yes. They start tomorrow."

Jasmine gave Grant and Marla a big smile. "Welcome aboard. Could I get your fingerprint over here so I can have all your paperwork and badges ready for you tomorrow morning?"

Grant and Marla nodded and placed their thumbs on the tablet where she indicated.

"See you both tomorrow," she said. "Just stop by here before you go to orientation."

As they left the building, Grant asked, "So what's the real plan, Zane?"

"Find out how to overcome the redundancies and find the weakest link."

Marla cocked her head. "I'm afraid that may take longer than we hoped."

Zane put a hand on each of their shoulders. "Don't let him get to you. Try to get as close to him as possible. Maybe he'll give something away."

Grant nodded. "Worth a shot."

Marla glanced back and then looked at Zane. "My bet is on Jasmine. I think I'll befriend her. She probably knows a lot, and she's likely not Farzad's biggest supporter."

"Good plan," Zane said. "Now to the teleporter." He laughed. "You only have one night of freedom left."

CHAPTER 33

REMINISCING

Restlessness began to overtake Zane, as well as fear.

Two weeks had passed since Grant and Marla started working for Farzad. They reported back to him almost every day, or at least when they discovered something important. Zane and Alex behaved like the royal couple they were supposed to be, and Zane even played golf with certain individuals so he would be seen by important people and influencing others. While he liked the game of golf itself, Zane did not like the mind games that went with playing with others. Being on his toes all the time and having to be careful what he said and how he said it so his words would not be misconstrued was mentally exhausting.

The longer he and Alex had to portray themselves as the royal couple and wait until he could act on his mission to destroy the power supply, the harder it was to prevent others from seeing behind their façade. Acting evil for a short time to convince someone to do something or to keep someone from realizing they were not who they really claimed to be was one thing, but at a certain point they would have to *become* evil if they wanted to convince everyone they were indeed the expected Gilgamesh and Summer-amat. Zane didn't want to cross that line—wasn't sure he *could* cross that line. Yet if Grant and Marla did not find a way to sabotage the exotic matter stream at the power facility soon, he and Alex would be found out—and he wasn't sure what would happen then.

"My lord?"

"What?" Zane came out of his thoughts. "I'm sorry, Bradley. What did you say?"

"Did you want tea or coffee this morning?"

"Tea, I think. Gotten tired of the coffee, if that's what that drink really is."

Bradley grinned. "Well, something close, anyway. There are a lot of counterfeit things here."

"Tell me about it." Zane looked over the edge of the balcony. "At least some things are pleasurable."

Bradley straightened and looked as well. "Indeed. That part I will miss."

"Speaking of missing," Alex said. "Where are Grant and Marla? I haven't seen them for several days now."

"Oh, they will be at the banquet tonight."

"Is that tonight?" She sighed. "Who started such a tradition anyway?" She scrunched her nose. "Seeing so many of myselves in one place is a little creepy, if you ask me."

"Well, at least you don't have to play golf with them." Zane pointed a half-eaten piece of toast at her. "Now that, my dear, is creepy."

"Well," Bradley said, "the tradition was started to see what the different clones could offer the royal couple regarding traits or repairs to any chromosomal damage. Having a banquet with them was to try and keep up the morale as well as to scrutinize and hear of any potential conspiracies that could be developing."

"At least others will be there also," Alex said.

Bradley gave a brief smile. "It has led to early banishment outside the forcefield for some who talked a little too freely when the wine was offered freely as well."

"Oh, that made me remember," Alex said. "I meant to tell you last night but forgot."

Zane cocked his head. "What's that?"

"The forcefield. I had Hector and his clones walk the perimeter to check for any breaches."

Zane laughed. "So that's how you got them out of our hair."

Alex smiled. "Well, their assignment worked for a couple of weeks, anyway. I thought my having them do so was just something to keep them busy, but they found something."

Zane gave her his full attention. "I'm listening."

Alex leaned in slightly. "They found a weakness in the forcefield. Someone could actually . . . walk through if they wanted."

Zane's eyes widened. "If they wanted to die." He glanced at Bradley. "It's a vacuum outside the city, right?"

Bradley nodded.

"But that's not all," Alex added. "Hector found an energy reading outside the dome."

"What kind of energy reading?" Zane asked.

Alex shrugged. "I don't know. The readings are outside my understanding."

She handed a disc to Bradley. "Can you get this to Grant and Marla? Maybe they can make something of the readings Hector and his doppelgangers found."

Bradley nodded. "Sure. I'm to see them later today, anyway."

"See if they can report back to us at the banquet tonight," Alex said. "Maybe they can let us know if the disc contains something important to pursue or something to just forget about."

Bradley nodded and stood. "Well, I must go oversee preparations for tonight."

Alex took another sip of her drink and followed him. "Hold up, Bradley. I'll go with you. I'm supposed to provide seating arrangements." She turned and threw Zane a kiss. "See you later." She turned her head slightly and gave a little smirk. "I may even have you sit by me."

Zane laughed. "I appreciate that. Just have fun." He remained at the table while finishing his tea-like drink and enjoying the view. There was nothing on his agenda for the day, so he decided he would simply walk around the city. That was something he had not done since his arrival. He had always gone to certain places for certain reasons, but not just walking for the pleasure of walking.

As Zane walked, he grew amused at how folks at first did not recognize who he was, but when they did, they quickly genuflected or bowed. This brought back the memory of when he was in Babylon and many did the same thing. Some he passed gave a greeting, but most did not. He still found having so many clones here odd, definitely a little unsettling. Yet these clones also provided variety he had not expected, as different clones coupled with unexpected partners. He would see a Gilgamesh clone with some other female clone rather than a Summer-amat clone. He would see a Summer-amat clone with a Bradley clone, with a Grant clone, or even some other male clone. All of these he found rather disconcerting as they made him feel Alex was unfaithful to him, even though he knew this was not the case. Yet, he reasoned, she probably felt the same way. He thought back to his morning breakfast. No, she was definitely with him.

While everything looked beautiful and peaceful, he knew there were evil undercurrents throughout this place. Likely many were already trying to plan a coup or looking for ways to discredit him. This way of living evidently had become part of the game to see who would rise to ultimate power. Maybe that was what the Adversary had planned all along: see who could come up with the best version of Gilgamesh—and then he would take possession and control of that willing person. A thought suddenly hit him: the portal was working again. What if the Adversary requested his presence back on Earth soon? Being possessed by the Adversary was almost unthinkable. The memories alone were bad enough, but if he was summoned . . . He shuddered at the thought. Zane knew he could rest assured that the Adversary was not here in Adversaria, even though he had created this place, as the Earth was the domain to which he was tied. He had taken Earth from Adam millennia ago and was now trying to become Earth's ultimate ruler.

While Zane knew he could not stop the last part, he could ensure the Adversary had to work out his plan with someone of Earth and not with some superhuman he had bred to possess and make others worship. If Zane could destroy Adversaria as soon as possible, then the Adversary would have to change his plans. Zane was beginning to think and believe that was his destiny: make the Adversary work with humans and not a super-bred clone.

Zane walked for many hours and would rest periodically as he contemplated everything that had happened to him since birth: his father dying when he was very young, his mother teaching him not to pity himself, her teaching how God could use him in whatever profession he chose, his career choice and where he worked, his decision to teach in Sandpoint—which led him to meet Alex—and how that led him here to, of all places, Adversaria. He could look back now and see how God had directed him to this place and time. Zane took a deep breath. Life had been a pleasurable journey, relatively speaking, and he believed his life would be again. He just had to fulfill his destiny.

Zane suddenly snapped back to reality and looked at his watch. His eyes widened. How had he been gone that long? He picked up the pace to get back to his room. He would have just enough time to change before tonight's banquet.

After taking a quick shower, he contemplated what to wear as he dried off. Yet when he looked at his bed, he smiled. Bradley had already made that choice for him. While he didn't have to accept what Bradley chose, he had to agree that most of Bradley's decisions were spot-on. This time was no different. He looked at the cot on the other side of his bed. For some reason Bradley still slept on the floor not far from his bed.

Zane donned the tuxedo Bradley laid out for him. The garment was a classic style and proper for almost any occasion. Yet this time the tie, lapels, and cummerbund were a gray color to contrast nicely with the black of the tuxedo. After dressing and looking at himself in his full-length mirror to ensure he was in order, he entered the living area to wait for Alex.

He didn't have to wait long. She arrived on his balcony like an angel had suddenly appeared, and she looked as gorgeous as one. He didn't say those words as she would think his remarks corny, he was sure, but they definitely described how he felt about her.

He stood as she entered his room from the balcony door. "Alex, you are so gorgeous."

He meant every word. Her dress, also black, had gray sheer material strategically placed to make her dress look provocative, yet it was also rather modest at the same time. Her appearance reminded him of how Summer-amat had dressed in Babylon, but with a very modern twist.

She gave an expectant look. "Not too much?"

Zane smiled as he shook his head. "No, not at all." He raised his eyebrows. "Yet I may have to beat the men back. I don't think anyone there will look as marvelous as you."

Alex laughed. "You're forgetting my clones will be there."

He shook his head. "No. No, I'm not forgetting that at all."

Alex blushed. He liked that about her. She was drop-dead gorgeous and could have anyone, yet she was choosing him. That made him feel humble and blessed at the same time.

The banquet was to be held atop the building, so they headed to the elevator and rode to the roof. As they stepped off, Zane heard music being played by a small orchestra in the corner of the rooftop taking up one side of the infinity pool area. Stringed lights gave the place an elegant but quaint look. One long table at the head of the pool had been constructed for everyone to sit at. One end was curved so both he and Alex could sit next to each other, displaying unity with both seated at the head of the table and having a clear view of everyone. Zane smiled when he saw a topiary had been placed at the other end of the table to prevent anyone from sitting at the other head of the table. *Hmm*, he thought. Was that Bradley's idea, or one from Alex? He smiled as he realized he could not tell.

After mingling for a few minutes—nothing of importance was said, just pleasantries—Bradley announced that dinner was served.

Zane whispered to Alex as he led her to the table. "Not a moment too soon. I was running out of things to say."

"At least everyone acted interested in what you had to say," Alex said.

Zane laughed. "'Acted' is the appropriate word."

Alex shook her head. "No, I don't think so. You can be very impressive and charming, you know."

Now it was Zane's turn to blush.

Grant and Marla sat next to Zane and Alex. All the others filled in according to listed place settings on placards. As the courses were brought and served, everyone appeared to be having a good time. It was a fairly light atmosphere, Zane observed.

When the entrée was served, Zane reached over to get Grant's attention; he quietly spoke in his direction. "Grant, were you able to decipher the energy reading Bradley gave you?"

Grant shook his head then smiled. "No, but Marla did."

Zane turned to Marla. "So . . ." He paused and looked around as if looking for someone.

Grant followed his gaze. "What's wrong?"

Zane looked at Alex. "Did you sense that?"

She nodded. "Odd."

Grant and Marla looked at each other and then from Alex to Zane. Marla looked at Grant and shrugged.

Zane nodded as he spoke. "It's almost like the feeling I had at the restaurant back at Sandpoint and right before your car blew up. Yet, this is different somehow." He nodded toward the rest of the table. "It seems the clones are sensing the same as we are." Each would look around occasionally like they were trying to see something that wasn't there yet try to act nonchalant at the same time.

* * * * *

"Mikael, are you seeing this?" Raphael said as he stared at those seated at the banquet table.

Mikael glanced at him and couldn't help but smile. "I do, indeed. I'm standing right beside you."

Raphael gave him a double take and then chuckled. "Well, yes, but . . ." His tone turned somber. "What Lucifer has done here rivals what he did with the Nephilim."

Mikael nodded as he and Raphael walked around the table observing the various clones dining. "This is pretty diabolical, for sure. What he does is always surprising, but never in a good way."

"Agreed," Raphael said. "I'm not sure if Ruach allowing us to come here was a good idea or not."

"What makes you say that?" Mikael asked.

"Look at their expressions, Mikael. They seem to be able to sense us. Normally, humans cannot do that."

"Apparently these clones Lucifer has developed can. He must have inbred some of his capacity into them."

"If this plan is successful, then his planned superhuman could be a significant opponent. Not as great as him, but significant nonetheless."

"I think this means we have another mission," Mikael said. Seeing Raphael's eyebrows raise, he added, "We need to delay Lucifer from recalling Gilgamesh and allow Zane a little more time here to accomplish his mission."

"Agreed. Let's go back and see how we can accomplish that."

Both angels disappeared.

* * * * *

Alex put her hand on Zane's arm. "The sense is gone."

Zane nodded. He had felt the same. His spidey senses were keen for one minute and then simply vanished.

Zane looked back at Marla. "What did you find?"

Marla took a sip of wine as she glanced at Grant who simply shrugged. "Oh, I was wondering when to bring this up to you," she said. "Very strange."

Grant laughed as he was taking a drink and almost choked, coughing several times.

Marla laughed. "Sorry, I didn't mean to make a pun." She suddenly looked quite concerned. "Are you all right?"

Grant held up his hand and cleared his throat. "Yes, I'm fine. Just wasn't expecting that."

Alex looked from one of them to the other. "I'm sorry. What . . . pun?"

Marla continued. "Oh, well, the energy signature is that which would be given off by strangelets." Alex had a blank look. Zane had to admit he had no idea what Marla was talking about either. Apparently seeing the blank look on Alex's face, Marla added, "You know, when at least three quarks—composed of up, down, and strange—are grouped together."

Alex looked from Marla to Zane. Zane simply shrugged.

Marla held up her hand. "Anyway, the energy reading is from a rather unique form of matter."

Zane cocked his head. "And is this important?"

Grant gave a very large smile. "I think this may be the key to everything."

CHAPTER 34

OUTSIDE THE DOME

After arriving at the wharf—the meeting spot Grant had asked of Zane—Zane found Grant had already arrived. He waved Zane over to a small boat and helped him step onboard.

Grant smiled. "Ready for an adventure?"

Zane stepped into the boat and gave Grant a curious look. "Well, I thought I was, but didn't realize we'd be traveling by boat." He sat. "What gives?"

Grant handed him his tablet as he got the boat started and headed toward the middle of the lake while making sure to stay as close to the edge of the forcefield as possible. "As you can see, the power source is just outside the forcefield exactly where the instability of the forcefield is located," Grant said as he maneuvered the boat.

Zane nodded. "I see, but how do we go from the boat through the forcefield?"

"Very carefully."

Zane cocked his head and gave Grant a stare. "You don't say."

Grant laughed and pointed at a box on the floor of the boat. "With those."

Zane opened the box and saw two protective suits. He looked back at Grant.

"Those are the suits we would use to go into the room containing the exotic matter stream—if needed." Grant shrugged. "I don't think these have ever been used. No one has ever been required to enter. Yet the room is as close to absolute zero as humanly possible to achieve, and is in a vacuum, so they should do well for us on this excursion."

Zane nodded, but then looked over the side of the boat. "Uh, how deep is the water?"

"Where we're going, the depth will be about eight meters or twenty-five feet. Others come here periodically to fish or sail, so I don't think anyone will think it too odd we're out here."

"Good to know," Zane said. "But that wasn't my main concern. The water ends at the forcefield, right?"

Grant nodded.

"So, our first step through the forcefield will be a twenty-five-foot drop?"

Grant again nodded as he patted a long metal arm next to him. "That's the reason for the boom." He cut the engine and threw out the anchor so the boat wouldn't drift. "Here, let me show you."

Grant took the tablet back from Zane and verified they were in the right spot. He then tied a long rope onto the boom's end and cranked the boom into place out over the side of the boat toward the forcefield. The end of the boom passed through without much resistance.

Zane's eyes widened. "I see. We'll lower ourselves down."

Grant held his hands out and gave a slight turn of his head. "Unless you have twenty-five-foot legs I don't know about."

Zane laughed. "No, I'm no Gumby." He stood. "I like your plan much better."

Grant walked over and patted Zane on his shoulder. "I thought you'd see things my way."

Grant picked up one of the suits and began putting it on. Zane did the same. Afterward, each checked the seals of each other's suit and turned on the light inside the edge of their helmet. This light would allow them to see in the darkness that certainly awaited them just on the other side of the barrier.

Grant picked up the end of the rope and handed it to Zane. "Hold on to this so I don't pull the rope all the way through on my journey."

Zane nodded and waited as Grant eased out of the boat, through the forcefield, and out of view. He waited for a few minutes, unsure of when to follow. He then felt a jerk on the rope. He assumed that was his cue, so he followed the path Grant had taken. As he swung out of the boat holding onto the rope, the boom pulled him through the forcefield and into darkness. The forcefield itself gave off some light for a short distance. As he turned, he could see the boat and the city, but they looked hazy as he looked back at them through the force-field. That made him feel better, as this meant they should be able to find their way back more easily. The farther down he went, the darker things became because he was now under the water's surface causing the glow from the forcefield to be extremely faint. Occasionally he would see a fish swim by, but the creature would quickly dart back in another direction. He wasn't sure if their sudden change in direction was because they could detect him or detect the forcefield. He assumed their change was due to the latter.

As he neared the bottom of the rope, his foot touched something that seemed solid. He loosened his grip on the rope a little, but then felt a crack as his foot went through something—there was again a feeling of nothing solid underneath him. He held more tightly to the rope again and let himself down until he assured himself he had solid footing. Yet he could feel something around his feet and legs.

Once Zane let go of the rope and turned to face Grant, he turned on his flood lamp and recoiled in initial horror. He realized he was knee-deep in skeletons!

"Oh, gross!" Zane said as he looked at Grant, unsure how to even move forward.

"Just don't think about what you're actually doing, Zane." Grant waved him over. "Just walk through them."

Zane did so, but each step produced a vibration that reminded him of a crack or a crunch. Being in a vacuum, there was no sound, but the feeling of the breaking bones still tricked his mind into hearing the cracks and crunches, which continued to bother him greatly.

Once he finally stood where Grant was, he looked at him. "Now what?"

Grant looked from his tablet and pointed in the direction of what looked, faintly, like a large mound of some kind. "The signal is from that direction. I don't think it's too far."

They walked together for about fifteen minutes, mostly in silence. All Zane heard was his own breathing. As they got closer to the signal where Zane's light could reach the source, he stopped and grabbed Grant's arm.

Grant looked up from his tablet at Zane. "What's wrong?"

Zane just pointed. Before them stood a mound of skeletons! The mound was about twice their height!

"Whoa!" Grant said as he looked up. "This must be where the individuals are deposited, and they have rolled down over time to where we are now."

"Unbelievable!" Zane thought about how many people had been sent here over the millennia. He shook his head. "This is just diabolical."

Grant nodded but stayed quiet for a moment. Finally, he pointed again. "Unfortunately, the signal comes near the bottom of the pile," he said.

"What?" Zane said, eyes wide. "Don't tell me we have to dig through all that."

Grant looked at his tablet again. "It doesn't seem to be in the center, but closer to the edge. We do have to dig for it, though."

Zane closed his eyes and shook his head. He couldn't believe he was going to be digging through skeletons for an energy source that . . . well, he had no idea what this energy source would look like.

Grant pointed again. "It should be right in front of us, about two meters in."

Zane nodded, took a breath, and began pulling on skeletons. Of course, as he got a certain distance, others fell from above into the space he had already cleared. He then realized he had to be more careful in how he dug. He wished the thing would glow in some way so he would know how to find the energy source.

Zane stopped for a moment and looked at Grant. "Any idea what we're looking for?"

Grant shook his head. "No. It could be anything—any size."

Zane sighed and got back to work. Grant would pass his light every so often, and on one pass, Zane thought he saw a twinkle. He grabbed Grant's arm. "I think I saw something."

"What? What did you see?"

"A glimmer of something." He passed his light across the lower tier of skeletons. He saw the glow again. "There! Did you see that?"

Grant nodded. Both men began to dig faster.

In a matter of minutes, Zane reached and pulled out the source of the glimmer—a pendant of some kind, about the size of his hand and yet triangular. One side had three colored crystals and the other an indentation. He cocked his head. A sense of familiarity overcame him. He had seen this pendant somewhere before. *Where?*

At that moment a body tumbled off the top of the pile and landed directly in front of Zane. The body caught on another skeleton, but the guy's face was eye level with Zane. Zane jumped back quickly, stumbling over the bones at his feet, and fell. He scrambled back to his feet, his heart racing.

Zane heard Grant give a slight laugh.

"Not funny."

Grant held up his gloved hand. "Sorry, Zane. Didn't mean to laugh, but your stumbling was a little comical."

Zane started to retort, but then noticed who the skeleton was staring at him. "Hey, that's Cyrus!"

"Really?" Grant came closer. "Wow, it really is. I guess that confirms this is where all those offered to Marduk wind up."

A thought came to Zane. Cyrus was not a skeleton yet, but if they were in a vacuum, how did the bodies become skeletons in the first place?"

Zane reached for Grant's arm. "Grant, I think we need to get out of here."

Grant laughed. "You're just now getting creeped out?"

Zane shook his head. "No. Well, maybe yes. But, uh, how did these bodies go from that . . . " He pointed to Cyrus's corpse. "To that." He pointed to the skeletons below Cyrus's body. He paused and then added, "In a vacuum?"

Suddenly, a creature burst through Cyrus's abdomen. Both Zane and Grant jumped back. They steadied each other to keep the other from falling.

"What in the world?" Zane asked.

The creature seemed to not move; it looked like a grayish blob of some kind. Zane couldn't recognize any anatomical features: no head, limbs, eyes, or other observable distinguishing features. Since the creature seemed to be dormant for some reason, Zane got the nerve to step closer.

"What are you doing?" Grant asked.

"Just want to see what this is." Zane picked up an arm bone—an ulna, he recalled it as. He wasn't sure why that thought came to him as the type of bone was very unimportant at this point. He poked the creature, but the blob didn't move. He tapped the creature on its back, and it seemed to be very hard. Well, that would make sense, he thought. To be in a vacuum, a creature would need to protect its soft tissue from the vacuum here in some way, just as his suit was doing for him. Zane managed to turn the creature over, although with difficulty, as it seemed to be stuck to Cyrus's skin. Once the creature flipped, Zane jumped again. The underside also looked gray and hard, but there was a round . . . *something* looking like gnashing teeth going back and forth.

Because the creature couldn't right itself, the creature started vibrating. The vibrations caused bodies higher in the pile to cascade down, suddenly producing dozens of these creatures coming out of the fallen bodies. Their number rapidly turned into hundreds. Zane's eyes widened as he took several steps backward. Next thing he knew, the whole pile tilted and crashed around him causing the creatures to be everywhere.

He felt Grant's pull on his arm. "Let's get out of here!"

Zane nodded. He was more than happy to oblige. Yet running proved most difficult as they trudged through the bones and skeletons which lay in their path. Once in a while, Zane would feel one of the creatures run over his foot. He kicked his leg and kept trudging. If one of the creatures were to bite into his suit, he would become one of these skeletons in short order. As he looked over at Grant, he saw utter panic on his friend's face. He knew why. They were in mortal danger.

Once they reached the rope, Zane motioned for Grant to go first. There was no time to argue, so Grant grabbed the rope and began pulling himself up. Zane didn't wait for Grant to get too high before he started climbing. Yet, as he climbed, he felt one of the creatures on his boot. He quickly tried to kick the blob off with his other foot. His thrashing, he knew, likely was impeding Grant's ascent.

"What's the matter?" he heard Grant yell in his direction.

"One of these stupid creatures is on my boot."

It took several attempts, but he finally managed to get the creature off, but not without a small tear in his suit. Although not large, he could tell his suit was losing oxygen and pressure. He began to climb as rapidly as possible.

Yet before he could reach Grant, he heard his suit announce, "Oxygen level critical. Replace immediately."

Zane ignored the announcement and kept climbing. What alternative did he have? His climb began to go increasingly slower as the exertion caused him to breathe more heavily, and this in turn caused him to use more oxygen.

He heard Grant encouraging him from above. "Come on, Zane. You're almost here!"

"I'm . . . I'm . . . trying. Not much . . . strength . . . left."

"Grab hold of my leg."

Zane looked up. He was almost there. Yet he knew his destination was a couple of reaches too far. He wasn't going to reach Grant.

"You can do it, Zane! My leg. Grab my leg!"

Zane reached up and took hold of Grant's leg. He didn't understand, but he was too tired to think, so he just followed instructions.

Grant lifted his leg. "Now grab my hand."

It took several attempts, but he soon felt Grant's tight grasp on his hand.

Grant pulled him up to the boom. "Now, put your arms over the boom. You don't have to do anything but just let your body hang."

Zane did so, but he wasn't sure he would have the strength to continue clutching the boom. He was afraid he would pass out and his arms would give way. "Not . . . much air . . . left."

"I know. We're almost there." Grant pulled the rope up and cut off two lengthy pieces. As quickly as possible, he tied each of Zane's arms to his legs so Zane couldn't fall off the boom. He then used the rope to swing from the boom through the forcefield and onto the boat.

Zane felt the boom moving, going from the darkness he was in to the brightness of the other side. The next thing he knew, he was in the boat with Grant lifting his helmet off. He took in large gulps of air and then collapsed on the floor of the boat breathing hard. It seemed to take forever to once again feel he was sufficiently oxygenated and regaining strength.

Grant patted his shoulder. "You just lie there and breathe. I'll get us back to shore."

After a few minutes, Zane had his strength back, for the most part, so he sat up and removed his suit. Grant handed him his as well, and Zane had both suits packed away before they got to shore.

Zane sat and pulled out their find. He realized he had seen this before. A vision surfaced in his mind. He was standing in a room with Gilgamesh and Summer-amat, and suddenly a gleam of light hit his eye off one of the crystals from the pendant around Gilgamesh's neck. That was it! This was Gilgamesh's pendant!

CHAPTER 35

THE PLAN COMES TOGETHER

As Zane sat waiting for Grant and Marla to join them, he laid the pendants on the table.

Alex picked up the larger one. "Oh, it's a little hefty." She turned the pendant over in her hands. "So, this is what Gilgamesh was wearing when you first met him?"

Zane nodded. "But why did he have this pendant? Did he know what it was?"

"Maybe," Alex said. "But I'm sure Marduk did."

Zane shook his index finger. "That's probably it." He sat back. "But why would he want something that would destroy what he had built?"

Alex curled the corner of her mouth. "Hmm. That's a good question."

They heard a knock. Bradley opened the door and welcomed Grant and Marla inside. Invitations to the royal living quarters were rare but not totally uncommon. Bradley had told them in the past such an invitation usually meant the royal couple was attempting to extract information. He smiled when he heard that, as these types of rumors helped their façade even more.

Zane motioned for the other three to join them at the table. Bradley brought some food and drinks to the table and sat with them.

Bradley raised his glass. "Here's to space slugs."

Alex scrunched her nose. "Gross! I'm not toasting to that."

Bradley laughed. "Well, if they had not turned almost everyone to skeletons, Zane and Grant likely would not have found the pendant." He tilted his head slightly. "Or, not nearly as easily, anyway."

"But how do they even survive—reproduce—out there?" Marla asked. "I mean, even if the adult version has the hard shell that you saw, their offspring would likely have to grow their hard casing after being born."

Grant grimaced. "I think that was what the bodies were for. Embryos placed inside the bodies to keep them protected from the vacuum of space until they develop their shell. Plus, a viable food source for them to grow and mature."

Alex waved her hands. "Uh, can we change the subject? I was getting hungry before you all arrived. Now I'm just nauseous."

Zane reached over and squeezed her hand. "Sorry." He looked at the others. "Pendants. That's what we need to discuss. What are they, why did Gilgamesh have one, and how did it wind up outside the forcefield?"

Grant nodded toward Marla. "We went over the energy signature again and still believe the pendant we found contains strangelets." He shrugged and pointed at the center of the table. "I'm not sure how they're contained in there, but somehow they're stable—for now at least."

Alex looked from Grant to Marla and back. "You mentioned that at the banquet. But why are they important?"

"They're known to exist but usually decay back into normal matter." Grant shifted in his seat and brought his hands up to help explain his statement. "You see, all atoms have protons and neutrons in their nuclei, and these are composed of quarks—typically of up and down quarks."

Marla jumped in. "But you can get strange matter if one of them is a strange quark. Strange quarks have higher energy and typically decay to a lower-energy-state quark—like an up or down quark."

"Unless," Grant said, "you can put sufficient energy into it to keep it stable."

Zane sat there waiting for the punch line, but Grant didn't say any more, as if what he had said was the complete story. "Well, don't leave us hanging," Zane finally said. "I know you're leading up to something."

"I think he's talking about annihilation," Bradley said. "The annihilation of Adversaria."

Grant nodded. "That's exactly right."

Evidently Marla saw Zane's continued state of confusion, so she added, "The power station has sufficient energy to keep the strangelet from decaying so the strangelet will set off a cascade of turning matter into strange matter. Because the exotic matter energy stream generates so much power, it can initiate the cascade, and as the cascade continues, more and more energy is released, and this further fuels the cascade. This will continue until all of Adversaria becomes strange matter and ceases to exist."

"And the planet . . . what? Explodes?" Alex asked.

Marla tilted her head back and forth slightly. "Well, yes and no."

"Explain," Alex said.

"The strangelet cascade draws energy from subspace and, at some point, that energy has to be returned. So you get an explosion that immediately resorts into an implosion."

"Like a 'poof'?" Zane asked, smiling.

Marla looked at him with a strange expression on her face. "Kind of, but with a dramatic flair."

Alex laughed and looked at Zane. "You become poof-man after all."

Zane smiled, then said, "Not if we can't figure out how this pendant works."

Grant picked up the pendant and turned it over. "It does have a triangular indentation." He then looked at the other pendant and placed it near the first one.

Marla reached out and grabbed his hand. "I wouldn't put that one in the indentation."

Grant looked at her and then raised his eyebrows. "You think this one is a key?"

Marla nodded. "Very possibly. So we can't risk checking that hypothesis until we're ready to accept the consequences."

Grant pulled the two apart and set them back on the table.

Zane looked at Marla. "By 'key,' you mean . . . "

Marla nodded. "It will release the strangelets."

Zane sat back. "Well, in some ways, problem solved." He looked at Bradley. "But why would the original Gilgamesh have it, and how did it get beyond the forcefield?"

Bradley sat in thought for several seconds. "Maybe Marduk wanted a contingency plan in case things got out of his control. Likely, if he couldn't be in control, he would want no one to be."

Zane nodded slowly. "That actually makes sense."

Bradley continued. "Maybe, over time, the clones didn't realize what the pendant was for."

Zane cocked his head as that didn't sound right. "But it would seem the beam from Marduk's eyes is different from that of the portal. We can go through with clothes intact." He pointed at the table. "It even kept the pendant Ekmenetet gave me." He shook his head. "No, I think it being out there was deliberate."

Alex looked at Zane. "Maybe the faction that was trying to take over? Maybe they wanted it out of the way so no one could stop them—likely thinking this was the only way."

"Exactly," Marla interjected, looking at Grant. "No one would have predicted a brilliant plan like yours."

She smiled at Grant, and he smiled back.

Zane nodded. "Quite possibly." He paused in thought for several seconds. He could think of no better explanation. "Anyway, the reason likely doesn't matter in the end." He picked up the pendant. "We have it." He looked at Grant. "And apparently, we know how to use it."

"Ekmenetet was smart," Bradley said.

Everyone turned his way.

"What makes you say that, Bradley?" Zane asked.

"He gave you the key to the solution of your mission here."

"You think this was his plan all along?"

Bradley nodded. "He always said you were the key to success. Maybe he was speaking of the elements he had given you. And he always said it was fortunate Marduk was not present when he presented you to Gilgamesh."

Zane's eyes widened. "Because Marduk would know about the key but Gilgamesh did not."

Bradley nodded. "Likely Marduk had the plan but kept it to himself and would enact his plan as he desired—and not as someone else desired."

"But how did he know?" Alex asked. "I mean, if Gilgamesh and Summer-mat did not know, how would a servant know?"

Bradley smiled. "Servants are invisible. People speak secret things when invisible people are present." He looked at them. "Somehow he knew and ensured both pieces arrived here in Adversaria."

Alex nodded and looked at Zane. "That's plausible."

"Very possible," Zane said. "Ekmenetet was very resourceful."

Bradley picked up the pendants and examined them closely. He looked from one to the other and suddenly put the smaller into the indentation of the larger.

Everyone gasped.

Zane yelled, *"No!"*

Nothing happened.

Zane stood. "Bradley, what on earth were you thinking! You could have gotten us all killed!"

Bradley shook his head. "No, these need a way to make them bind to each other." He pulled the two pendants apart and put the smaller into the larger a couple of more times and then calmly looked at Zane. "Did Ekmenetet give you any-thing else to wear?"

Zane took a deep breath while willing his heart rate to slow. He stood in thought. It seemed that had been a lifetime ago. Remembering, he touched his chest. "He put the pendant around my neck." He then touched his arm, remembering what Ekmenetet had put there. "An armband of some kind—a serpent!"

"And where is that?"

Zane turned in thought and went to his bedroom. On the dresser was a large box. He opened it and brought out the bracelet for the others to see.

Bradley held out his hand and Zane gave him the bracelet.

Marla was the first to speak. "It's beautiful. Its eyes almost glow."

Bradley smiled as he looked closer. "That's because they're diamonds." He removed one of the eyes and held the small diamond up in one hand and one of the pendants in his other. "If you look on the back of each pendant, you'll see a small hole behind one of the crystals. I think this is where the diamonds go."

"What are they for?" Alex asked.

"Activators."

Alex shook her head. "I don't understand."

"Somehow, the diamonds will activate the crystals in each pendant." He glanced at each of them. "If I'm right, one of the diamonds will make the key become attracted to the other pendant, and the other pendant will be able to release the strangelets when the key is used."

They each leaned in to watch as Bradley put one of the diamonds in the key. He then handed the pendant to Marla. "Once activated, I don't want them to get near each other."

Marla swallowed hard but nodded.

Bradley then put the diamond in the larger pendant and handed it to Grant. "Be sure and keep this one away from the key until you plan to use it."

Grant's eyes widened. "It's vibrating. Very slightly—but noticeable."

He let the others hold it, and each nodded their agreement. This made Zane somewhat nervous as he held the pendant in his palm, and this made their mission seem more real—and dangerous.

"I felt a change in the key at the same time Bradley put the diamond in the larger pendant," Marla said. "Something like an attraction even when this far away."

"I suggest," Bradley said, "you each keep the piece you have so there is no chance of them coming together. If we were to put them back down on the table, I'm pretty sure they would come together on their own."

Everyone looked with a stunned expression. Grant and Marla each wrapped their pendant in a cloth before putting them away.

Grant looked at Zane. "So, we're doing this?"

Zane nodded.

CHAPTER 36

GOODBYE
ADVERSARIA

Questions were plentiful, but answers were few. Zane sat and sipped his tea as he looked out toward the horizon from his balcony and thought back over all that had happened. In one way, he would miss this place. Well, at least its beauty and the good friends he had made. Yet, he was also anxious for all of this to be over.

It was one week after when Grant and Marla had come by and the weapon had been activated. At least he thought of the pendant as a weapon. Grant kept trying to tell him why it wasn't a true weapon. But the nuance made little difference to Zane. The final result would be the end of Adversaria.

Who knew? It could be the end to them all. He and Alex couldn't keep their charade up much longer without being discovered. Plus, this was their only chance of getting home. It was either home or oblivion—there was nothing in between.

Alex stepped from her bedroom onto the balcony and sat at the table with him. "Are you ready for today?"

"I think so," Zane said. "I'm ready for my king-for-a-day thing to be over."

She nodded, stood, and held out her hand. "Let's go, then."

As they left their living quarters, she said, "Let's go by air." She smiled. "It may be the last time in our lifetime we get to experience something like it."

Zane nodded and led them to the elevators, which ascended, and they stepped onto the building's roof. They sat in the seat of the sky car, a forcefield came over them, and the craft took off toward the opposite side of the city from the location of Farzad's office.

"I do think this is a better plan that Grant and Marla came up with," Alex said.

Zane nodded. "Yes, the power facility on this side of the city is less busy, so there will be fewer people to run into who may be curious about our arrival."

Even in their nervousness, both enjoyed the view from the sky car. Zane had to admit the panorama was truly spectacular. If on Earth, this place would be one of the wonders of the world, for sure. A Scripture came to his mind that described when the Messiah called the Jewish leaders of his day "whitewashed sepulchers"—beautiful on the outside, but full of dead men's bones. Very apropos to this place, Zane thought. The analogy was almost correct. He had literally seen dead clones' bones in this place.

Once they arrived at the power plant's auxiliary entrance, they saw Grant and Marla walking up the steps. Bradley was already there waiting for the four of them. *Efficient to the core,* Zane thought. If they did survive this, Zane hoped and prayed with all his might Bradley would survive it as well.

Alex gave Marla a hug and then hugged everyone else. "I want to say my goodbyes now. I'm not sure if I'll have a chance later."

All were misty-eyed by the time the hugs and back pats were done.

Marla took a deep staccato breath. "Well, I hadn't expected such an emotional event so early."

"All is in order?" Zane asked.

Marla nodded. "I transferred all controls over to this side of the power station just before coming. We should be all set."

Zane looked at Grant. "And you have the pendant?"

"I do," Grant said. "And Marla has the key."

"Okay, let's go," Zane said as he waved them toward the entrance.

Since this was the auxiliary entrance, there was no one to prevent their entering except for their needing an entrance key. They made their way in without any resistance.

As they traveled down the twenty floors, Grant said, "There is a window where things can be passed to anyone who would have to go into the power room. We can use that to get the device into the room once activated. The strangelets should then do their thing automatically."

All nodded as they waited for the elevator doors to open.

When they entered the control room, they stopped in their tracks. Jasmine was sitting at the console.

"Jasmine!" Marla exclaimed. "What are you doing here?"

Jasmine stood, a phaser now pointed at them. "I think the better question is, what are *you* doing here?"

Marla motioned with her hands for Jasmine to calm down. "Just put the phaser down, Jasmine. There's a perfectly logical explanation as to why we are here."

Jasmine gave a small laugh. "Yeah, I bet." A hurtful look came across her face. "And here I was thinking what good fortune had come my way. Finally, another female in this male dominant place. Someone I could relate to, confide in, who could be a good friend." Her face became stern and her eyes teary. "But no. You're not a friend, you're no confidant." She put both hands on her phaser, steadying her grip. "You're a liar, a fraud. Someone who just uses someone else for their own agenda."

"No, Jasmine. You have it all wrong." Marla took a step toward her, but Jasmine's stance stiffened.

"This is on stun. You know this has two settings. Don't give me reason to use the second."

Marla stopped moving forward. "I am your friend, Jasmine. My friendship is genuine. Just let me explain."

"Explain what?" Everyone turned with a jerk. The words were from Farzad, who now stood looking at all of them.

"Jasmine, I got your message," Farzad said, looking confused. "What in blue blazes is going on here? And why do you have a phaser?"

"These people are traitors."

Farzad looked from Jasmine to the others. "What? How do you know?"

Jasmine sighed. "I just do. Look at where they are. Why would they be here on this side of the power station?"

Farzad stopped and seemed to be in thought. Zane took that opportunity and quickly lunged for Farzad, grabbing him. Jasmine pointed the phaser at Zane but stopped since Zane had Farzad as a shield directly in front of himself. At that moment, two security guards entered. Zane turned, and this caused the guards to pause as they saw Farzad held against his will. Jasmine pointed the phaser at Zane and fired, but Bradley

THE HOLY GRAIL OF BABYLON

jumped in its path before the stun ray reached Zane. Bradley crumbled to the floor.

Jasmine's eyes widened; she now looked uncertain what to do. Grant took the opportunity to grab the phaser from her and then turned to fell the two security guards, doing so all in one swift motion.

Alex ran to Bradley. "Bradley! Bradley!" She patted his cheeks, but there was no response.

Marla came over and helped Alex to her feet. "He'll be fine. Just out for some time. He'll come around."

Zane and Grant made Farzad and Jasmine sit and tied them tightly to chairs in the room. They also secured the guards' feet and hands together, although they were still unconscious.

"What are you going to do?" Farzad asked. "I activated the forcefield around the power room, so you can't get to it."

Zane looked at Grant. "Will the window well still work?"

"It should."

"What are you talking about?" Farzad asked. "You can't do this."

Grant came over, ripped a piece of cloth from Farzad's shirt, and made a gag, stuffing it in Farzad's mouth. He looked at Zane and shrugged. "Sorry. He was getting on my nerves."

They gathered near where Bradley lay. Grant took out the pendant he had and Marla took out hers. They looked at each other—then paused.

"Is it activated once we put the key in the pendant, or does the key have to turn or something?" Marla asked.

Before Zane could voice his thought he saw movement out of the corner of his eye. In that split-second, he knew Farzad had somehow gotten himself free from the chair. Before he could do anything, Farzad whipped his chair across the floor and into Grant, causing the pendant to fall out of his grasp and onto the floor. Farzad then tackled Zane, causing him to plow into Marla, who fell to the floor, dropping the pendant key.

All they could do was watch the two artifacts, which vibrated while drawing closer to each other . . . quickly picking up speed while doing so. Alex, the only one not knocked down, dove for the pendant to keep it and the key from coming together, but her attempt was too late. Once close to each other, the pendant and key snapped together in the blink of an eye.

All cringed while waiting for the inevitable to happen. But nothing did. Zane opened his eyes and saw the pendant and key together, vibrating lightly on the floor.

While Grant and Marla dealt with Farzad and Jasmine, tying them up again, Zane retrieved the pendant and key. The vibration felt strong—like something desperately wanting to be released.

He saw Bradley start to stir.

Alex stooped down to help him sit up. "Are you okay?"

Bradley put his hand to his head and nodded. "Yeah, I think so." His words, however, came in painful whispers.

"You're a good friend, Bradley," Zane said.

"And you're a painful one," Bradley said, giving a small chuckle.

Zane extended his hand and helped Bradley to his feet. His eyes immediately grew wide. "You put them together?!"

Zane smiled. "Not exactly. Long story. Come on over."

They all gathered at the window to the room housing the exotic power stream. Grant pointed out the window well where things could be passed into the room without losing vacuum.

Grant looked at Bradley. "How will I know if the device is activated?"

Bradley gave a small shrug. "I think you will just know."

Grant's eyebrows went up, but he didn't say anything. He turned the key, and this caused the diamond to align with the colored crystals. The light refracted through the facets of the diamond and caused the colored crystals to glow.

"I think that's it," Bradley said.

Grant nodded. "I can feel the vibrations increasing." He quickly put the artifact in the window well and turned it to face inward.

They each took a step backward, unsure of what to expect.

In a few moments the arcs that were going down the long room began to bend erratically. Arcs now shot wildly in all directions. Some hit the glass wall in front of them, creating a huge flash. They all jumped back, nearly simultaneously.

"Whoa," Grant said. "I think we need to get out of here."

Bradley looked at him. "It won't matter where we are. We aren't escaping."

Zane put his hand on Bradley's shoulder. "That is true, my friend, but I'd rather see us disappear from above rather than from down here, below."

He pushed the elevator button and the doors opened.

"Are you going to chance the elevator?" Bradley asked.

Zane smiled. "Fastest way. As you say, if we don't make it . . . well, it doesn't really matter, does it?"

Bradley shrugged. "Good point."

They all climbed in and the elevator began its ascent. Occasionally, the elevator pitched one way or the other, yet the car managed to keep rising. By the time they reached the top, everything was shaking and shifting.

As they looked at the city, everything was quaking. Zane could see the glass tiers of the ziggurat cracking and crumbling causing shards of glass to plummet to the ground. Screaming could be heard everywhere. The end was only a matter of time now.

They all joined hands and made eye contact with one another.

"It has been a pleasure to know you all," Zane said.

They each nodded but said nothing more. A huge explosion occurred, and this threw at least one-third of the city into the air. However, only a few moments later, after the debris exploded into the air, the debris imploded on itself. This created another explosion, which did the same. Each explosion and resulting implosion made its way closer and closer toward them. Zane knew their end was now only a matter of seconds away . . .

They would either be part of the annihilation of Adversaria—or they would be hurled back to where they had originated.

Zane hoped with all his heart their fate was the latter.

Their grips on each other's hands tightened. All stood without moving to let the inevitable happen. Zane felt a rumble beneath his feet, heard the explosion, felt himself fly into the air—and then felt himself losing consciousness.

His last thought: *mission accomplished.*

CHAPTER 37

DÉJÀ VU

Zane suddenly found himself in a chair . . . sitting at a desk . . . in his office . . . someone talking to him.

"The question is: why does the paper have a 67 at the top of it?"

A feeling of déjà vu swept over Zane. He looked up at the man leaning over his desk, looking rather irritated, his cheeks red. "Andrew?"

The man jerked to an upright stance. "Don't get smart with me or try to change the subject. Answer my question."

Zane, still in a fog, looked from Andrew Latham to the paper on his desk. A large red 67 was circled at its top. *I've had this conversation*, Zane thought. He looked at the paper again. *This is Evan's paper on the Holy Grail.* Realization suddenly flooded over him. *I'm back! I'm really back!*

Concern suddenly came across Andrew's face. "Zane, are . . . are you okay? Anything wrong?"

"What?" He sat back. "Uh, no." He waved his hand slightly and then put it to his forehead. "No, everything's fine. I was just thinking."

Andrew cocked his head, evidently trying to decide if Zane was well or not.

Zane looked up at Andrew and smiled. "You're right, Andrew."

Andrew's head jerked back. "I . . . am?"

Zane nodded as he turned the paper around. He pulled out his red grading pen, changed the 67 to an 87, and turned the paper around once more.

Andrew's eyes widened. "Really?"

"It's like you said, Andrew. Evan did do the assignment." He picked up the pen and twirled it, holding the pen with fingers of both hands. "Although he didn't complete the assignment as required, he did complete the assignment with its intent."

Andrew just stared and blinked a couple of times.

Zane smiled and tapped the paper with his index finger. "The intent of the paper was to get students to think and argue their point. He did argue his point, just not the point he was supposed to be arguing." Zane shrugged. "But since this is the first assignment, I'll give him points for intent rather than purpose."

Andrew had a stunned look. "Well . . . wow . . . uh, thank you. That's generous."

Zane continued to smile. "Just tell him next time to complete the assignment as requested." He raised his eyebrows. "I may not be as generous next time."

Andrew held out his hand and shook Zane's. "Thank you again, Zane. I'll be sure and tell him he needs to submit to the question at hand."

Zane threw his hands slightly wide. "That's all I ask."

Andrew smiled, nodded, and left the room, looking lost as he did so. He turned after exiting, smiled, then headed down the hall.

Zane sat back and let out a long breath. He was home and had lost no time at all. Actually, he had gained some of it back. He wondered about Marla, Grant, and Bradley. *Did they make it?* With all his heart, he hoped so. They deserved a happy life in the here and now. And Alex. *Did she make it?* If he did, he reasoned, then surely she did. Maybe he should go check.

As he turned, Alex stepped into his room. "Getting soft, I hear."

Zane stood and walked over to her. "I've learned to pick my battles." He smiled. "Back in one piece, I see." He leaned in and gave her a kiss. She didn't budge but reciprocated. *Good sign,* he thought.

"You remember everything?" Alex asked.

Zane paused and did a mental check. "Yeah, I do. Mostly. You?"

She cocked her head. "Mostly? Everything does feel somewhat like a dream."

Zane chuckled. "More like a nightmare." He turned somber. "I remember everything that happened, but all of the creepy memories from the previous clones seem to be gone. I mean, I remember having them, but not what they were."

Alex stopped and cocked her head. "You know, I had not realized that, but, yes, the same for me. It's like we've been brought back from the darkness so we can remember to be thankful."

"That's a great way to look at it. I have to say, I'm very grateful for that gift God has given us. Being perfectly human again is a blessing."

Alex nodded. She exhibited a smirky grin. "So, I was part of your nightmare, huh?"

Zane waved his finger. "Now don't go getting me into trouble I wasn't even in." He smiled and kissed her on the cheek. "You being there was what got me through the nightmare."

Alex cocked her head and smiled. "Good recovery." She suddenly straightened in stature. "Oh, I came over to tell you something. I just got off the phone with my uncle."

"Oh?"

"Yes. He just found the portal."

Zane's eyes widened. "Don't tell me we're going to live through this all over again."

She patted his chest and chuckled. "No. I don't think so, at least. Anyway, he's going to encase the portal in clear resin so it can be admired—but stay unusable."

"Good thinking."

"I thought so." She flashed a wide smile. "And he's going to donate the portal to Dr. Latham and the school." She looked at her watch. "Actually, they should be talking about now."

"Wow," Zane said. "You two wasted no time."

"My phone rang as soon as I returned. My uncle was at the dig site and let me know he had just found it."

"And he just willingly decided to donate it?"

She gave a coy smile as she fiddled with one of his shirt buttons. "He likes me."

"Yes. And . . . ?"

"And I may have suggested the idea to him."

"And . . . ?"

"And my uncle will get a percentage of whatever the school gets for lending the artifact to various museums and galleries."

Zane laughed. "I thought it might be something like that. Still sounds like a win-win."

"I thought so." She patted his chest. "So, is our sushi date still on?"

He smiled and held out his arm. "For sure. We can go in my car, and I can drop you by later to get yours."

"Oh, so I can drool over your yellow Corvette?"

Zane grimaced. "Oh, I wouldn't drool if I were you. With the top down it could get into your eye."

She slapped his arm and laughed. He loved to hear that laugh of hers. It was contagious; he always laughed when she did.

Just as they stepped from the office, Andrew came running down the hall toward them. "Dr. Hadad! Dr. Hadad!"

They turned. Andrew was all smiles and gushing. "Thank you. Thank you!" he said to Alex. "This will be such a big boon for the school. Such an important find. We can do tours, speaking engagements, and be in the press. This will definitely put us on the map." He slapped Zane's upper arm. "And good for you too. Right, Zane?"

Zane chuckled. "I suppose. And you're talking about . . . ?"

Andrew's eyes widened. "The Sumerian Grail, of course. Keep up. I thought this was your alley."

"Well . . . "

Andrew turned before he could complete a sentence, then turned back. "Oh, Dr. Hadad, your requisition for an assistant is approved."

"But I thought . . . "

Andrew held up his hand. "That was before I knew we had money coming in. Approved. Definitely approved."

Alex smiled. "Well thank you."

Andrew shook his head. "No, thank you." He turned to Zane. "And I'll put in a requisition for an assistant for you as well."

"But . . . "

Andrew held up his hand again as he turned. "No thanks needed. Have a good night." He was nearly floating as he headed back down the hallway.

"But I don't want an assistant," Zane said in an almost defeatist tone as he opened the door for Alex.

She looped her arm back through his. "Well, you might change your tune when you're away traveling and speaking."

Zane bobbed his head back and forth. "Maybe. But I still don't like it."

Alex squeezed his arm as they walked to his car. "You're impossible. Just accept what's been given."

"But who would I get?"

"Well, you can't know until you interview."

"That's such a pain."

Alex rolled her eyes. "The right person will come along. You'll see."

He opened the car door and she stepped in. Zane rolled the top down, then jumped in the driver's seat.

He looked over at Alex. "Ready to drool?"

She laughed. "Only if you sit behind me."

"Oh, is that how this is going to go?"

She raised her eyebrows. "Apparently."

He leaned over and gave her a kiss. "Okay. Game on."

She sat back and smiled. "Sushi, driver."

"Yes ma'am!" Zane revved the engine and they were off.

CHAPTER 38

ALL'S WELL THAT ENDS WELL

The valet smiled as Zane pulled up in his Corvette. He opened the door and helped Alex out as Zane came around and patted the guy on his shoulder.

"Take good care of her."

The valet looked from Alex to the car and back.

Zane laughed. "You take good care of this one . . . " He patted the car. "And I'll take care of this one." He wrapped his arm around Alex's shoulders.

The valet gave a broader smile and a quick salute. He hurried around to the driver's side.

The maître d' seated them immediately at a table with a lakeside view. Zane certainly hoped this evening would end with a better outcome than last time. When the waiter came with menus, Zane ordered the same items as they had the time before. He wasn't sure exactly why he did that, but the meal tasted good, and Alex seemed agreeable with the suggestion. The waiter bowed slightly and turned to leave.

Zane did a quick sweep with his gaze around the room and then focused on Alex.

She smiled. "Looking for the man who was here last time?"

Zane nodded. "I'm just not sure what to expect. I'm hoping things will not be the same, but it's hard to trust in that one hundred percent." He smiled. "But so far, it seems to be different from last time."

"Except for our order."

Zane laughed. "Yes, except for our order." He took her hand. She seemed okay with that, so that gave him the courage to interlace his fingers with hers. "Still going to the Middle East this winter?"

She cocked her head. "I don't know. We likely have other options now. Rather than we going to them, they may come to us."

Zane's eyebrows went up. "Oh, now that you'll be a celebrity?"

She laughed. "Oh, I think that category encompasses both of us." She suddenly looked downcast. "We may actually have to travel together."

Zane at first was taken back, but then he smiled when she broke into laughter. "A sacrifice I'm willing to suffer," he replied.

Suddenly Alex's eyes went wide, and she gasped.

"What's wrong?" He looked in the direction she was looking, and a gasp escaped from Zane as well.

Approaching them were two Bradleys and Officer Marcy Kinnick.

"Officer Bradley! Good to see you."

Bradley gave a nod. "Dr. Archer, good to see you as well."

Marcy looked from one to the other. "I didn't know the two of you knew each other."

Zane suddenly realized that, in the other timeline, their acquaintance was made after this particular time.

"Oh," Bradley said, "we were introduced by a wandering elk." He turned from Marcy to Zane. "I do hope your car is fine now."

Zane nodded. "Why don't you all join us? That is, if you wish." He glanced at Alex, who nodded with a smile.

"Yes," Alex said. "Please do."

Zane helped Bradley move another table next to theirs. Zane then sat next to Alex. Marcy and Officer Bradley sat opposite them and the other Bradley at the end next to Zane. The waiter arrived, likely wondering what was going on. To make it simple, they all ordered the same as Zane had ordered. The waiter smiled with a slight bow and left.

Bradley grinned. "Now for proper introductions." He turned to Marcy. "This is Marcy Kinnick."

Both Alex and Zane nodded. The situation was a little strange: they already knew her, but she had no recollection of them, so they played along as though this was their first meeting.

He turned to Bradley. "And this is my nephew Bradley."

Again, they acted as though this was their first time meeting so Marcy would not be suspicious.

Marcy giggled. "Isn't it uncanny how much they look alike?"

Alex nodded. "It is. And they even have the same name."

Marcy shook her head. "Well, not exactly. Bradley is Madison's last name. Bradley is his nephew's first name."

Alex's and Zane's eyebrows shot up.

"Really?" Zane said as he looked at Bradley. "Your first name is Madison?"

Bradley started to respond, but Marcy jumped in. "Well, he'll probably not forgive me for telling you that. He hates the name Madison, so he tells everyone his name is Bradley and they assume his name is Bradley Bradley." She giggled again. "How funny is that?"

Bradley cocked his head. "Not very, really." He smiled again. "Anyway, Marcy here is a fan of yours, Dr. Hadad."

Marcy looked a little embarrassed. "Well, of your work at least. I just loved your last article in *Archaeologist Digest.*"

Alex's eyes widened. "Oh, thank you. I guess I'm a little surprised. And your profession is?"

Zane knew Alex already knew Marcy was a police officer, but she was trying her best to not act surprised.

"Oh, I'm a police officer. I work with Bradley."

"And she's good at it, too," Bradley said. "But ancient writings are a hobby of hers."

Alex gave an admiring look. "Well, I'm pleased to meet a common enthusiast of all things ancient."

"I told her you may have an opening at the school in your department."

Marcy gave a shocked look to Bradley. "Now, I told you not to do that."

"Well," Alex said. "I do have an assistant position opening up. It's part time, at least initially." She shrugged. "No promises, but you can definitely apply."

Marcy's face lit up. "Oh, really? That's great." She waved her hands. "Yes, totally understand the applying part." She beamed.

Zane smiled to himself. He recalled all the positive things Alex had said about her before their excursion to all things past and future. He knew Marcy likely had the job already, even though she didn't know it.

When the wine arrived, the waiter poured each of them a glass and left the remainder in an ice bucket. Zane lifted his glass. "A toast to new friends."

"Hear, hear," each of them said, clinking their glasses together and taking a sip.

"I do hope your toast comes true," Marcy said. "Good friends are hard to come by."

"Very true, my dear." Bradley reached over and kissed her on her cheek. She returned an adoring smile.

Zane gave a quick eyebrow raise and returned a broader smile.

"Excuse me," Alex said. "I'll return in a few minutes." She looked at Marcy. "Wish to join me to freshen up?"

Marcy smiled and nodded.

Once they left, Zane looked at the "nephew" Bradley and grabbed his arm. "Bradley, is that really you?"

He gave a large smile and nodded. "Yes, Zane. It's me."

Zane slapped his arm. "That's wonderful, Bradley. Just wonderful."

Officer Bradley nodded. "Yes, he showed up this afternoon. Just showed up."

Zane smiled. "Bradley, I'm so happy you're here with us. Any idea what happened to Grant and Marla?"

Bradley shook his head. "Unfortunately, no. But since you returned to your time, I assume they returned to theirs."

"Well, I certainly hope they have a good life . . . and are still together. They were great friends."

Bradley nodded his agreement. "Yes they were." He smiled. "As are you."

Zane patted his arm again. "I feel the same way. So, what do you plan to do?"

Bradley shook his head. "I have no idea. I wasn't even sure if I would be here, so I've not thought that far ahead."

Zane took another sip of wine. "Well, I have an idea, if you're game."

Bradley raised an eyebrow. "I'm curious at least."

"I also have an assistant position that has just come open. Would you like it?"

Bradley looked shocked. "You want me to apply?"

Zane shook his head. "No. It's yours if you want it. I hate to interview. I know you and what you're capable of."

Bradley nodded, then smiled. "Yes. I'd like that. I'd like that very much."

Zane held up his glass. "To continued friendships."

The three of them toasted.

"And where is a good place to stay?" Bradley asked.

Zane gave a dismissive wave. "Hey, stay with me."

"What? Really?"

Zane shrugged. "Bradley, we've been together for what seems like forever. Why break the tradition now?" He laughed and gave a quick pat to his upper arm. "You can at least get acclimated and then decide where you want to live." He smiled. "No rush."

Zane looked from one Bradley to the other. "So, what are the ramifications of what we have done?"

"I'm sure Marduk is very unhappy," Bradley, the former Ekmenetet, said. "He now has to find and work with someone here on Earth."

"Unfortunately," Zane said, "I'm not sure he will have a hard time finding willing participants."

The women returned just as the entrées arrived. As they started their meals, Marcy turned to her fellow officer and said something in ancient Akkadian.

Officer Bradley answered her instinctively, also in ancient Akkadian. He then stopped and stared at Marcy, seemingly unsure of what to do or say. His gaze turned to Zane. All Zane could think to do was give a shrug to signal he had no idea what just happened.

"So, it's true then?" Marcy's eyes glanced over Bradley's face as if looking for a ray of acknowledgement. "Alexandria gave me the question to ask. I just needed some assurance that what she told me was true."

Bradley's gaze then landed on Alex, who smiled and gave him a nod.

He turned back to Marcy and smiled. "Yes. I'm not sure of all that Alex has told you. But yes, it is true."

Marcy put her hand to her mouth and her eyes grew wet.

Bradley took her other hand. "I'm sorry, Marcy, if I've upset you. I just didn't know how to tell you."

She shook her head. "No. No, I'm fine." She gave a weak smile. "It explains some of the tension I felt between us. I knew you had feelings for me, but I always felt you were holding something back. Now I know why."

"So . . . you believe it?"

"Well . . . " She smiled. "It is a lot to take in. But I trust Alexandria." She glanced at Alex, who gave a broad smile back. She turned back to Bradley. "And I trust you most of all."

Bradley reached over and gave her a kiss on her cheek. "I'm glad, Marcy. So very glad."

"Plus," Marcy said with a gleam in her eye, "it fulfills my mother's prophecy."

Bradley cocked his head. "Prophecy?"

Marcy nodded. "Yes, she said I would fall in love with a much older man." She smiled. "She and I just never realized how much older he would be."

Everyone laughed. Bradley kissed her hand and replied, "Yes, but incredibly young in heart. Thanks to you."

After that, all tension eased. The talk was light and natural the rest of the meal.

Alex pointed at the two Bradleys with her chopsticks. "We need a convention to distinguish between the two of you." She pressed her lips together. "Hmm. Let me see." She pointed at Officer Bradley. "We met you first, so we should call you Bradley." She looked at the Bradley clone. "We actually met you sixth, so you could be Bradley the *sixth*, or maybe just Bradley Six."

Both Bradleys nodded.

Zane cocked his head. "Well, that will still require explaining to others."

Alex bobbed her head slightly. "Yes, I guess it would. But we can just say Bradley Six is the sixth born into his family's generation."

Everyone seemed to agree with her, so the choice seemed settled. Bradley Six seemed to like the idea of being born in a family. That was good, Zane thought. After all, they all felt like Bradley Six *was* family.

They had a great time together with much laughter; each shared with Marcy and one another the adventures they had experienced. Marcy was especially attuned to Bradley's stories. Zane could tell these two were getting serious about each other. He was very glad for Bradley. This had turned out to be a wonderful homecoming for all of them.

After a great meal and conversation, it was time to go their separate ways.

Alex gave Marcy a hug. "Be sure and come by sometime tomorrow and I'll get you an application." Alex shook her head. "Who am I trying to kid? The position is yours, Marcy, if you want it. I already know how talented you are and all your organizational skills. I'd be a fool to give the position to anyone else."

Marcy opened her mouth in surprise and then gave Alex another hug. "Thank you. Thank you. You won't be disappointed."

Alex laughed. "Of that I have no doubt."

"I'll stop by when my shift is over, and we can work out details."

Alex nodded and turned to give both Bradleys a hug.

Bradley looked at Zane. "I'll drop Bradley Six off at your apartment."

"Thanks. I'll be there just as soon as I get Alex back to her car."

They went their separate ways. As Zane opened the car door for Alex, she said, "It's nice of you to provide a place for Bradley Six to live, at least temporarily."

Zane shrugged as he started the car and began driving. "Seemed the least I could do after all he's done for us."

"Are you going to help him find a job somewhere?"

Zane gave her a bright smile. "Already done."

"Oh? How's that?"

"Bradley Six will be my assistant."

"Really?" She gave Zane a smirk and repeated, in the same whiny voice Zane had used earlier, "Oh, I don't want an apprentice."

Zane laughed. "All right. All right. Obviously, I didn't know Bradley would be available."

Alex sat back and sighed. "I feel blessed we are back to our original lives, but they are now a lot richer with some of the friends we made along the way."

Zane nodded. "I feel the same."

Once he parked next to Alex's car, Zane opened her car door for her. He gave her a kiss, she smiled, got in, and drove away.

As Zane arrived back at his apartment, he found Bradley Six sitting on the steps. "Come on up, Bradley."

Once inside his apartment, he showed Bradley Six the extra bedroom, bathroom, and where all the towels and extra linens were stored.

"Just feel free to use the kitchen or anything else here." He put his hand on Bradley Six's shoulder. "This is your home now, Bradley. It's the least I can do after all you did for us. Okay?"

Bradley nodded. "Thanks, Zane. This is quite nice."

They said their goodnights and Zane headed to his bedroom, took a shower, and went to bed. Being back in his own bed felt wonderful, and he was asleep in minutes.

Later that night, Zane awoke. He felt someone was in his room. He opened his eyes. Everything looked to be in shadows. He slowly rolled over as his heart rate increased; he told himself to be ready for anything. Yet he saw nothing. Maybe his senses were playing a trick on him. He then looked down upon seeing movement on the floor. He jerked and sat up quickly, ready to defend himself . . .

Yet the form was merely someone sleeping on the floor. As he looked more closely, he recognized it was Bradley Six.

Zane lay back down and smiled.

Just like old times.

CHAPTER 39

FUTURE BLESSING AND CONCERN

Mikael and Raphael stood looking at the two men sleeping.

"I think we can count this a victory," Raphael said.

Mikael nodded and looked at Raphael with a smile. "I concur."

Bradley Six stirred, turned over, and then fell back into slumber.

"Did you notice that, Mikael?"

Mikael looked at Raphael with a confused look.

"He didn't sense us. Why do you think that is? All the clones on Adversaria sensed us when we appeared there. Although they couldn't see us, they sensed us. Bradley, here, did not."

Mikael smiled. "Well, that can only mean one thing."

Raphael paused, but then his eyes grew wide. "You really think so?"

Mikael nodded. "I know no other explanation. Our Creator has performed a miracle and has brought him out of Adversaria as completely human."

Raphael glanced at Bradley and smiled. "Such a great outcome from all of this. Our Master is really something, isn't he?"

Mikael patted Raphael's arm giving a chuckle. "For sure, Raphael. For sure, indeed." He then turned somber. "But he also gives us a warning."

Raphael's eyes widened. "Oh? What is that?"

We have seen the havoc Lucifer has accomplished with limited technology and what he is capable of with advanced technology. While the time in which Bradley and Zane now live is not as advanced as Adversaria, they have much more technology at their disposal than when Lucifer worked with Gilgamesh. Likely, Lucifer will take advantage of this advanced technology at his disposal."

Raphael developed a worried look. "What do you think he will do?"

Mikael shook his head. "I don't know, but what we can be sure of is that it will not be good."

Raphael nodded, but then smiled. "There is another thing we can know for sure."

Mikael cocked his head in a questioning gesture.

"Our Master has ultimate control and will empower us for whatever Lucifer may devise."

Mikael chuckled. "True, Raphael. So true."

They each took one last look at the two sleeping men and then disappeared.

I hope you've enjoyed *The Holy Grail of Babylon*. Letting others know of your enjoyment of this book is a way to help them share your experience. Please consider posting an honest review. You can post a review at Amazon, Barnes & Noble, Goodreads, or other places you choose. Reviews can also be posted at more than one site! This author, and other readers, appreciate your engagement. Also, check out my next book, *The Defining Curse*, coming soon!

Also, check out my website: www.RandyDockens.com.

—Randy Dockens

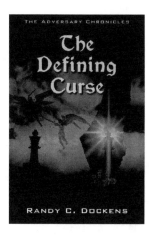

(BEFORE FINAL EDITING)

SAMPLE CHAPTER FROM
THE DEFINING CURSE
PART OF THE ADVERSARY CHRONICLES SERIES

The Defining Curse

CHAPTER ONE

The Curse Revealed

Mikael found a seat at his favorite spot. He leaned back, placing his hands behind him on the large boulder on which he sat as he gazed across the bubbling brook at a flying creature coming toward him. The creature then diverted its flight to land on the limb of a tree on the other side of the brook. The tree was in full bloom and covered in hundreds of tiny, yet beautiful, white flowers. *What was it Adam named such a creature? Oh, yes. Bird.* Mikael realized he had never before seen a flying creature of such magnificent beauty. Its feathers were a flaming red in color and this hue morphed into orange and then a brilliant yellow as its feathers formed its long flowing tail. It stood out like a beacon against the pure white of the flowers now surrounding the majestic creature.

The bird at first seemed to ignore him as it looked from one side to the other in quick, staccato head jerks. The creature then seemed to look directly at Mikael, gave a trill, and produced a sound so melodic Mikael stopped breathing for a few seconds.

"Master," Mikael whispered in awe. "You really know how to astound."

Mikael then whistled in a puny attempt to call back to the bird. He had to laugh as the bird just cocked its head back and forth a few times as if in confusion.

"Oh," Mikael said. "My music is not good enough for you. Is that it?"

The bird flitted its head back and forth as if answering his question.

Mikael laughed again. "Well. I see I'm not up to your standards."

The creature gave its melodic trill again and flew up and over Mikael in a high arc.

Mikael smiled. Everything here in Eden was wonderful, beautiful, peaceful. He shook his head. His Creator could really create.

That was one of the reasons he loved coming to this dimension. There was always something new to behold. It seemed the Creator was constantly creating something unique and wonderful. But he knew this beauty was not just for him and his fellow angels to enjoy when they had time to come here. One day, those in the righteous part of Sheol would be brought here. He wasn't yet sure how that would happen. But his Master had said it would happen, so Mikael knew it would. The timing was up to him.

He looked around again and smiled. He had been to Sheol when it was first created. While beautiful, it did not compare to Eden. This paradise was so much more wonderful. There, the feeling was foreboding even while beautiful. Here, there was such peace and beauty, almost beyond comprehension.

Mikael looked back into the sky and watched the path of the bird as it headed for a grove of trees on the other side of the grassy meadow behind him. It was then Mikael noticed his fellow angel-warrior Raphael appear in the distance, turn in a three-sixty, focus on him, and then stride toward him in an almost militaristic, determined cadence. As Raphael neared, Mikael sat up straighter.

"Hello, Raphael. Anything wrong?"

Raphael displayed a serious, determined look. "Mikael, come at once. He's done it again."

"He? As in?"

"Lucifer," Raphael said with a tone of: *Who else?*

Mikael stood; he turned quite serious. "What did he do this time?"

"He's got the prophet Jeremiah so riled, Gabriel says he's about to put a curse on King Jehoiachin."

Mikael's eyes widened. "What kind of curse?"

With a slight shake of his head, Raphael replied, "Gabriel didn't say. But it can't be good."

"Well, curses usually aren't."

"Of course," Raphael said. "I just mean . . . "

Mikael put his hand on Raphael's shoulder with a small smile. "I know what you mean. So, what's the plan?"

Raphael gave a shrug. "Not sure there is one. Gabriel is going down to observe. I thought you might want to join him."

"Definitely."

"You know," Raphael said as he looked down and then back at Mikael. "I don't understand why our Lord allows him to do all of these things."

"Our role is not to question, Raphael, but to obey."

"Yes, yes, I know," Raphael said. "But look at all he's done so far. First he rebelled in our dimension when he had a position that any other angel would have gladly traded positions with him for. He then deceived Serpent and Chavvah, manipulated both Serpent and Adam to actually *rebel* against our Creator, almost annihilated the human race before our Lord saved Noach and his family by destroying the wickedness Lucifer had brought to the earth, and almost created another coup at Babylon with Nimrod and his wife attempting to create a superhuman with the power to control the earth.

"Now he's trying to get Jeremiah to reverse the promise our Master made to King David. I mean, he just doesn't stop. Why?"

Mikael put his arm around Raphael's shoulders and gave him a light pat. "Remember what the Master said in the beginning. It's all about choice. There is no love without choice. There is no freedom without choice. But there are consequences—some immediate, but others delayed." He gave a smile. "Don't worry, Raphael. Our Creator will make it all right in the end." He squeezed Raphael's shoulder. "He promised it, so it has to come true."

Raphael nodded. "I know you're right, Mikael. But it's hard to see everyone suffer so much. And all for the vain ego of one." He stiffened his stance. "But you're right. Our job is to serve, not solve the problem. That is the job of our Creator. We do our part, and he will definitely do his."

Mikael smiled. "That's the spirit. Now let's go meet Gabriel." They each teleported to the angel dimension and searched to find Gabriel. After a short time they found him conversing with several other angels.

Gabriel held up his hand in greeting. "Mikael. Good. You're here." He nodded at the three angels with him. "I was just telling them of my plans."

Mikael looked at the three and gave them a slight nod of recognition. He focused once more on Gabriel. "Do we need to bring a contingent of angels?"

"I don't think so," Gabriel said. "I thought the three of us could go and evaluate." He then nodded toward one of the angels with him. "I've told Quentillious here of the possibility of that need just in case."

Quentillious bowed to Mikael. "With your permission, though, certainly. You are, after all, the Captain of the Lord's Host."

Mikael gave a slight nod. "Thank you, Quentillious. Yes, prepare a contingent, just in case." He looked from Gabriel and then back to him. "Hopefully, that is as far as we will need to go in this instance. But we should be prepared for battle if the need arises."

Quentillious nodded. "Very good, my captain." He and the others turned to act on these orders, leaving just the three of them remaining.

Mikael looked at Gabriel. "Raphael told me about Jeremiah. What has him so worked up?"

"As you know," Gabriel began, "Jeremiah has had to put up with so much abuse from the royal household ever since the death of King Josiah. He has been an extremely faithful servant of our Lord despite being placed in prison many times for speaking the truth of Yahweh."

Mikael nodded. "Yes, I'm sure that has to weigh heavy on him as it's like speaking to a brick wall. Yet several of the kings, including Jehoiachin's father, were almost as bad, weren't they?"

"Indeed, they were," Raphael interjected. "Several of them suffered greatly for their refusal to follow our Master's directions that he provided in the Law of Moses."

Gabriel nodded. "That's very true. Their actions have also had great consequences to their subjects as well. Not only physically, but spiritually. I think the latter is what is weighing heavily on Jeremiah's heart."

"And we're going there to change his mind?" Mikael asked.

Gabriel shook his head. "Not exactly. I think Ruach, the Lord's Spirit, is the one leading Jeremiah in this direction."

"What?" Mikael grew wide-eyed. "Why would he do that?"

Gabriel gave a smile. "His ways are above ours."

Raphael looked from one to the other. "Wait. Gabriel, I thought you said Lucifer was behind this."

Gabriel nodded.

Raphael then squinted. "And Ruach is *also* behind this?"

Gabriel nodded again.

Mikael held up his hand. "Hold on. Lucifer *and* Ruach are together on this? That doesn't make sense." He shook his head. "That doesn't make sense at all."

"Oh," Gabriel said, "Lucifer is never on the side of Ruach." He smiled. "But Ruach can still use the plans of Lucifer to his own advantage without Lucifer even knowing it."

Mikael rubbed the back of his neck. "Yes, that's likely true." He looked at Raphael and then back to Gabriel. "So, what are we supposed to do?"

"Observe," Gabriel said.

Mikael started to make a reply, but Gabriel held up his hand. "But be ready for more action if the need arises."

"Okay," Mikael replied. He didn't know what else to say. From experience he knew Ruach was never completely straightforward, but always had a plan, and it always worked out as designed. Mikael's job was to serve, and that was what he was willing to do.

Raphael developed a confused look. "I don't get it."

Mikael smiled and patted Raphael's shoulder. "Remember our conversation just before teleporting here."

Raphael sighed, then nodded. "We are his servants."

Gabriel smiled. "And we obey."

"All right then," Mikael said. "Let's go observe."

All three disappeared from their dimension so they could enter the time dimension.

ERABON PROPHECY TRILOGY

Come read this exciting trilogy where an astronaut, working on an interstellar gate, is accidently thrown so deep into the universe that there is no way for him to get home.

He does, however, find life on a nearby planet, one in which the citizens look very different from him. Although tense at first, he finds these aliens think he is the forerunner to the return of their deity and charge him with reuniting the clans living on six different planets.

What is stranger still is that while everything seems so foreign from anything he has ever experienced . . . there is an element that also feels so familiar.

Available now!

THE STELE PENTALOGY

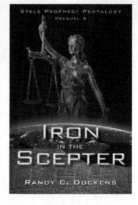

Do you know *your future*?

Come see the possibilities in a world God creates and how an apocalypse leads to promised wonders beyond imagination.

Read how some experience mercy, some hope, and some embrace their destiny—while others try to reshape theirs. And how some, unfortunately, see perfection and the divine as only ordinary and expected.

Available now!

THE CODED MESSAGE TRILOGY

Come read this fast-paced trilogy, where an astrophysicist accidently stumbles upon a world secret that plunges him and his friends into an adventure of discovery and intrigue . . .

What Luke Loughton and his friends discover could possibly be the answer to a question you've been wondering all along.

Available now!

Why Is a Gentile World Tied to a Jewish Timeline?

The Question Everyone Should Ask

Yes, the Bible is a unique book.

Looking for a book with mystery, intrigue, and subterfuge? Maybe one with action, adventure, and peril suits you more. Perhaps science fiction is more your fancy. The Bible gives you all that and more! Come read of a hero who is humble yet exudes strength, power, and confidence—one who is intriguing yet always there for the underdog.

Read how the Bible puts all of this together in a unique, cohesive plan that intertwines throughout history—a plan for a Gentile world that is somehow tied to a Jewish timeline.

Travel a road of discovery you never knew existed. Do you like adventures? Want to join one? Then come along. Discover the answer to the question everyone should ask.

Available now!